SECOND SKIN

SECOND SKIN
Michael Wiley

Severn House Large Print
London & New York

This first large print edition published 2016
in Great Britain and the USA by
SEVERN HOUSE PUBLISHERS LTD of
19 Cedar Road, Sutton, Surrey, England, SM2 5DA.
First world regular print edition published 2015 by
Severn House Publishers Ltd., London and New York.

British Library Cataloguing in Publication Data
A CIP catalogue record for this title is available from the British Library.

ISBN-13: 9780727894298

Severn House Publishers support the Forest Stewardship Council™
[FSC™], the leading international forest certification organisation. All
our titles that are printed on FSC certified paper carry the FSC logo.

MIX
Paper from
responsible sources
FSC® C013056

Typeset by Palimpsest Book Production Ltd.,
Falkirk, Stirlingshire, Scotland.
Printed and bound in Great Britain by
T J International, Padstow, Cornwall.

Acknowledgments

My thanks to the many people who helped make this book happen, especially:

To Dr Mike Lehman, former Navy Lieutenant Commander, for experiences and pathologies, familiar and strange. To Homicide Detectives K.L. Haines and John Hinton, for shades of darkness. To Staley Pattishall, for the grim work in another fight long ago. To Howard Edde, Nancy Kane Ohanian, and Robert Zieger, for pulp and paper, and to Wilbur Cross, Faith Mitchell, and Joseph Opala, for insights into the Gullah. To Julia Burns and Sam Kimball, for readings and talks. To Philip Spitzer and Lukas Ortiz, for the good fight. To Julie, Isaac, Maya, and Elias, for loving and laughing. To George, Sally, Deb, and Peter, for loving and forbearing. To that *noir*est of poets, Emily Dickinson, for '"Hope" is the thing,' 'My Life had stood,' 'Apparently with no Surprise,' 'After great pain,' 'I cannot live with You,' 'I heard a Fly buzz,' 'Not with a Club,' and 'I'm "wife."' And to Walt Whitman, for 'When Lilacs Last in the Dooryard Bloom'd' and 'The Wound-Dresser,' and Lord Byron, for 'Fare Thee Well.'

NOTE ON THE DANIEL TURNER THRILLERS

In each of the Daniel Turner Thrillers, Homicide Detective Daniel Turner plays an important secondary role. He is the common element in others' lives and deaths, getting caught in the spirals of crime that he investigates. These are North Florida city and swamp thrillers – set far from the well-traveled crime fiction of Miami Beach, Disney World, and the Everglades – and the people who star in them are city and swamp characters.

In writing about them, I dig into the psychologies and motives of heroes and antiheroes, persecutors and victims, criminals and seekers of justice (legal or vigilante), the beautiful and the ugly. Daniel Turner is a character in *their* stories. He is their brother, their childhood friend, their enemy, and their protector, and they love him or hate him – or sometimes think barely at all about him – as we do the people in our lives who hurt us and save us.

Emerging from others' shadows, Turner is the man who, at the end, wears a badge showing his right to use deadly force and to order the world. When the dust settles, *if* it settles, he embodies the law – shaky, just or unjust, sometimes arbitrary but generally necessary.

When we were children, our nurse, to keep us quiet, often poured molasses in our hands and then gave us a wad of feathers.
                                        Lillian Smith

'Hope' is the thing with feathers.
                                        Emily Dickinson

PART ONE

One

Lillian

No one ever calls desire a deadly sin but they should – more than lust or greed or appetite or envy. William Blake says it's better to murder an infant than nurse unacted desires. Satisfy desire or kill it, or it will kill you. I've always known that. That's what first threw me into Johnny's arms. And that's what I taught Sheneel Greene. But then her chair was empty – empty as an empty cradle, an empty bed, an empty heart.

Her chair stood in the front row, third from the right. She sat between a tall Cuban boy named Angelo and an Asian kid whose name I could never remember though I saw him every Monday, Wednesday, and Friday afternoon for more than a month; couldn't remember because when my eyes scanned the room, they stopped on Sheneel Greene and stayed too long, until she smiled or looked away.

She had pale skin, like a salt block, so translucent the blue of her veins seemed to rise through it. Her white hair dropped past her shoulders. She had slate-gray eyes like the eyes of some fair-skinned blacks. Mostly she wore jeans and a red T-shirt with the word *Ngafa* on the front. Midway through a class on Emily Dickinson, I asked what *Ngafa* meant.

3

'Bad spirit,' she said.

'In what language?'

She smiled and looked away.

So I read to the whole class from Dickinson, but mostly to her:

> *My Life had stood – a Loaded Gun –*
> *In Corners – till a Day*
> *The owner passed – identified –*
> *And carried Me away.*

I said, 'Dickinson was tiny, like a wren, but she called herself a loaded gun. You can hear her desire. A loaded gun aches for a finger to shoot it.'

Angelo grinned. In our town, almost everyone owned a gun – for hunting, sport, protection, aggression, all four – and mixing a rifle with sex could make a poetry lover even of a kid whose grammar consisted mostly of grunts.

Sheneel Greene's eyes lit up too. The words seemed to thrill her as a lover's hands on her body might. After class, she said, 'I *love* Emily Dickinson,' intoning *love* the way only a nineteen-year-old can, with a mix of crumbling innocence and half-secured experience.

I taught *to* her, and she seemed to hook into the books we read with a tender-fleshed intensity. Every good teacher knows that there's an erotic to teaching, not *so* different from the kind that drives a girl down between her teacher's knees in his office after class or carries a boy to his teacher's bed where she touches his hairless chest. It's a dance in which teacher and student

4

anticipate each other's moves and they move with a grace that feels almost physical, though it need not be.

I danced with Sheneel Greene. Every Monday, Wednesday, and Friday afternoon for a month.

Then she was gone, her chair empty. One class meeting, two, a week, ten days. I felt the class slipping from me.

None of Sheneel's classmates knew her phone number. I asked them with the false airiness of a woman who suspects a friend is avoiding her, or a new lover whose calls have gone unanswered. 'She lives in Fernandina,' said the Asian boy whose name I couldn't remember.

'Samuel Huang. Sam,' he said, annoyed, when I gave him an uncertain look.

The department secretary pulled the phone number and address on her computer. Samuel Huang was right: Sheneel lived in Fernandina, a beachfront town on a barrier island thirty miles to the north, where people moved when they tired of the city, though fumes from the paper mills overpowered the ocean air both day and night, and the noise of shipping trucks sounded over the bell-like music of halyards and metal hardware on the shrimp trawlers.

I closed my office door and dialed. Sheneel's number rang four times and voicemail picked up. Her voice still surprised me. It was deep and rough for a pale, little girl, though it lilted Southern as only the voices of multigenerational Southerners' voices did. 'Leave a message,' she said.

5

I did, with false airiness. She had missed five classes, I said. We'd finished Dickinson and started Whitman. Read 'Song of Myself.' Feel free to call me. 'Please,' I added, though it was a *non sequitur* except in the economy of desire.

Her chair remained empty all the following week.

Students often dropped out of classes. They got jobs, got pregnant, got high or drunk, got into fights with their families or friends, and going to school no longer mattered. I should have forgotten Sheneel Greene, focused on the kids who remained.

Then Eileen Rothenstein called from Student Counseling and asked, 'Has Sheneel Greene come to class this week?'

'She's been gone for three.'

'Has she emailed or called?'

'What's happened?'

'Her friends haven't seen her, and her brother has reported her missing. I can't say much, but we're worried. Let me know if you hear from her.'

'Why would she contact *me*?'

She hesitated. 'She talks about you during our sessions. I think she feels close to you.'

What sessions? Why did she talk about me? I wouldn't go there. 'Have you talked to her parents?' I asked.

'Sheneel and her parents had a falling out. She has her brother and her friends. And people like you.'

'I'll let you know if she calls.'

'She's a good kid,' Eileen Rothenstein said, 'but she's also a danger to herself.'

6

'Oh.'

'You understand, I'm crossing professional lines in saying this much.'

'What kind of danger?'

'You'll let me know right away if you hear from her?'

When we hung up, I sat for a long time. A picture of Emily Dickinson stared at me from the cover of a book on my desk. Her face was as pearl-white as Sheneel Greene's. But her eyes were dark and spread too far apart, her hair also dark and parted crookedly, her black dress topped by a black ribbon at her throat. Only the gentle inward curve of her neck indicated that she might have sweated with desire.

The afternoon sun shined through the window into the office. During the summer, heat radiated from the glass, but now in late February, though the weather outside was turning warm, the glass seemed a solid barrier. What did Dickinson say? *The blonde assassin passes on, The sun proceeds unmoved.* Dickinson had violence in her heart. She was as tiny as a wren – and she wrote wren-like poems, poems of few words and bird-like immediacy – but wrens eat meat and they tear other living creatures mid-flight from the sky.

Sheneel was a danger to herself. What did that mean?

I should have let Student Counseling deal with this. I should have returned to my class and taught the students who showed up.

But I carried my thoughts about Sheneel Greene home to Johnny. I talked with him about her with forced airiness. I told him all I knew. I said that

7

he should look for her. I did it for myself, though I pretended it would be good for him, since he too had torn at himself ever since he'd been back, and maybe searching for a self-destructive girl would turn out well for both her and him.

Two

Johnny

Felicity came through the glass door of my office, dragging a wicked trail of truck exhaust and the bitter smell of roadside weeds that always hung over Philips Highway.

'Cigarette?' she said.

She was a tall, black woman, heavy-boned. Her skin, tight over her cheekbones, glistened with sweat. She generally wandered the mile stretch of highway between Emerson and University with a brass-topped cane, though I once saw her with a wooden walking staff topped by a head whittled and painted to look like a grizzly bear.

'Cigarette?' she said again.

'I've told you I don't smoke,' I said.

'The hell you don't.' She turned to leave.

The stories said she'd worked this stretch for forty years and more, from before the government built the Interstate, when traffic backed up a quarter-mile at the stoplights and a girl could walk the line ignoring all but the men in Cadillacs.

8

Now, in the two months since I'd set up my agency in the rental, I'd never seen a car stop or slow for her. A guy named Farouk Bashandi, who'd opened a restaurant called Sahara Sandwiches Shop a hundred yards south from me, said he'd once seen her get into a beat-up Chevrolet van, but that was it. Few men fantasized about a sixty-year-old hooker with a gimp leg unless sex had come to smell to them like death and dying.

I asked, 'How's business?'

'I'm too old for the butcher,' she said. 'You can lead me around on a chain but I can't carry a load, so what good am I?' She smiled, and she still had all of her teeth. 'Business is middling.'

'You can sit here awhile,' I said. 'Breathe the air conditioning. Stay out of the dust.'

She stared at me, and her eyes glinted with something – gratitude, shame, craziness?

'No,' she said. 'It's time for me to go back where I came from.'

'Where's that?' I asked.

She smiled again but with a nasty edge. 'I crawl outta de swamp.'

She was making fun of me, but I said, 'Like the rest of us.'

'Ain't that the truth.' The mockery was gone. Or was it? 'How's business with you?'

'Middling,' I said.

'Far as I see, sugar, I'm the only one that's walked through your door since you unlocked it and hung up your sign.'

'Takes a while to build up clients.'

'Sure it does,' she said, and looked at me slyly.

'Isn't your job to find things? That's what skip tracing is?'

I nodded. 'More or less.'

'Then find me a cigarette.'

'Sorry.'

'You give me a cigarette, you can take me any way you want.'

'I don't want you, and I don't smoke.'

'The hell you don't. Look at yourself in the mirror. Your head's on fire.'

'You're more than a little crazy,' I said.

She laughed at that. 'Bye-bye, sugar, till next time,' and went out through the glass door.

Afternoon sunlight bent through the gap between the door and the frame, and I stared at it until the door swung closed. Light like that could blind a man, but I'd learned that if you closed your eyes for even a second – if you let your mind wander to the skin of the woman you loved, or you whistled a song you'd heard that morning in your bunk – a bomb might explode under your feet, or a quarter-inch piece of metal, shot from a shadowy window a block away, might rip into your jaw. I'd seen the damage. I'd tagged it and zipped it into bags. I'd smelled the meat and ammonia of dead men in gray-metal rooms, two decks down, as the ship around me lowered side to side so slowly I felt the movement only in the deep part of my belly. But it moved and in its movement revealed that the whole earth at its center is liquid and undependable. They called the job *soft duty* and gave it a name that painted over the bloody rooms in which I performed it: Corpsman, HM3, in the Deceased Personnel

Mortuary Affairs Division. Preparing plastic bags for the 346th Airlift Wing, who would refuel in Germany and then fly straight to a giant warehouse in Dover, Delaware. Joint operations duty. *Soft duty* – a hundred miles offshore from the bombs that exploded under men's feet and the pieces of metal that ripped into their jaws.

'That's good,' Lillian had said when I'd told her about the posting. 'Safe.' When I looked unconvinced, she'd added, 'Hemingway drove an ambulance in World War One and he came home alive.'

I should be fighting, I thought. I said, 'What's Hemingway got to do with it?'

'He saw the same things. An ammunition factory blew up in Milan. He carried out the bodies.'

I said, 'Didn't he kill himself with a shotgun?'

She looked worried. 'That was later. Much.'

Later.

I had a pistol in my desk drawer. Why wait?

My head was on fire, the hooker said. How did she know?

I had all ten toes. Lillian had counted them as we lay in bed my first night home. I had all ten fingers. Lillian had counted them too. I had my feet and my legs, my hands and arms, stronger because I'd worked out with free weights in the ship gym. I had my dick, thank God. The organs in my belly pumped, cycled, and cleaned like beautiful machines. But did I have my head?

I opened the top desk drawer. My SIG 9mm lay on a green oilcloth rag. When I rented the office, I imagined sliding the drawer open as

11

another man sat across from me. The oilcloth would keep the SIG from rattling. The man would suspect nothing as I lifted it and pulled the trigger.

That was a joke. My hands shook even when I was alone – especially then. And *no one* had sat across the desk from me except Felicity the hooker and, a few times, Farouk Bashandi who came to complain about the lack of business at Sahara Sandwiches. He'd fitted out an empty building with grills and picnic tables. A sign by the highway side showed a man eating a pita sandwich while riding a camel. In its day, the building was a Skinner Milk House. Back then, the Skinner family owned the largest dairy in Northeast Florida and they made a fortune by selling milk directly instead of through grocery stores. But shopping habits changed, and the Interstate drained traffic from our stretch of highway, leaving the building to crumble. 'The rent was cheap,' Farouk said. 'Can you believe it?' He'd imagined happy families eating falafel and gyros at the outdoor tables he'd fitted with umbrellas. The stinking air and the boarded windows across the highway on a restaurant called Chopstick Charlie's hadn't worried him.

I lifted the SIG from the drawer. It felt as heavy and cold in my hand as a chunk of bone, more solid than the liquid center of the earth.

I'd never shot it or any other gun off range. In training, I'd put holes through paper targets and blasted plastic manikins, I'd spotted man-shaped shadows through a night vision scope, and I'd learned to compensate for wind and gravity so an enemy would die as hard at a quarter-mile as he would at point-blank range. I'd played simulation games and watched hundreds of hours of videos meant to desensitize us so that, when we faced real blood and violence, we would charge in as if they were all we'd ever wanted. But I'd never picked up a gun really intending to kill a man.

First time for everything. I held the barrel to my chin. If I pushed hard enough, I could shove the barrel through to blood and bone without pulling the trigger.

The phone rang and my heart jumped. My heart had no right to do that. I'd suffered no physical trauma of that kind. I'd just stuffed together the pieces of other men after the blood had drained into the earth and the adrenaline had lifted like steam into the hard dry sky. If anything, my heart should stand still. When the phone rang, I should lie on the floor behind my desk like a dead man.

It rang again. I put the pistol back on the oilcloth and closed the drawer. I breathed in, out, in. 'Hello?'

'That's not how you're supposed to answer.' Lillian. She meant well.

I breathed in. 'Johnny Bellefleur.'

'Better,' she said. 'But with enthusiasm.'

I breathed. 'It's fake in my ears.'

'Make it real.'

Nothing was real. 'I'm trying.'

'No business?'

'The hooker came in. She said I could screw her if I gave her a cigarette.'

'Sorry.'

'Actually, she was pretty good.'

13

'Not funny.'

'I guess not. What's up there?'

'Let's eat dinner out tonight,' she said.

'You all right?' She didn't sound it.

'I'm fine. Everything's good. We'll talk tonight.'

Not at all convincing.

She said, 'I love you.'

I spent the rest of the afternoon at my desk, glancing from my gun drawer to my phone. The phone never rang, but I also didn't open the drawer. I tried taking my mind elsewhere, to circumstances that made me happy: Lillian on the beach, Lillian on our bed, Lillian in the woods – the shadows of green loblolly bay leaves falling on her skin, unbothered by stinging insects, snakes, and wild pigs, this being my fantasy, not theirs.

A truck horn blasted outside and tires screeched. I eyed the rays of sun through the glass door. All happy dreams come to an end. I had trained to account for glint and glare and the warping optical effects of a setting sun. On the range, I could hit a target in the fading light at a hundred yards, two hundred if I got lucky. With a few adjustments, I could point an M72 at a building or another ship and put a hole in the side big enough to crawl through. I could do it all, and I should have *done* it all. That's what my papers said.

But I'd known plenty of fully trained and desensitized men who in actual battle had snapped their wrists up and fired over the heads of the enemy instead of assuming the burden of ending another man's life. Was I made like that too?

14

That would also be a burden – knowing that face-to-face with a killer I would surrender to his killing hands rather than kill. The history of battle, as far back as histories were written, said both were heroic: kill or be killed, either way you were brave. The only cowardice was running away. I hadn't run from battle, but I hadn't run into it. I'd stood at my table on the ship and packed meat, bones, and organs into bags.

The counselors at the VA warned against *intrusive thoughts*. If the music of the past eighteen months played on an endless loop, I would be in trouble, they said. I needed to keep my head from catching fire.

They handed me a stack of prescriptions. Xanax, Ambien, and Celexa. Give the Celexa a month or two to do its magic, but beware of suicidal thoughts – usually not a side effect for men my age. Come back for more meds if none of these worked.

At home, I'd dropped the prescriptions in the kitchen garbage.

Lillian had said I was an idiot.

I'd said, 'This is news?'

'When going over the side of the bridge looks better than crossing to the other end, you need help,' she'd told me.

'Which of your writers said that?'

'*I* said it.'

'Sounds like bullshit.'

'Fine,' she'd said. 'Kill yourself.'

That had made me laugh, and then she'd laughed too. The side of the bridge looked like a spot of shadowy gravity, and I suspected I would always feel its pull, but I had taken her hand and we'd climbed the stairs to our bedroom. There were better and worse gravities to give in to. As we lay in bed afterward, she looked at me, worried, and I smiled at her, but she said, 'You're not waving but drowning.'

'Huh?'

'Stevie Smith. British poet.'

'I wish you wouldn't do that,' I said.

At five-thirty, I turned off my computer and locked the SIG in the drawer. Safe for another day. Unless I hit traffic, I would get home in time to walk the dog before Lillian arrived.

But then Farouk Bashandi came through the door carrying two white paper bags, which he set on my desk before dropping into the chair across from me. He said, 'For you and Lillian.' The bags smelled of garlic and fried meat.

'What is it?'

'Shawarma, hummus, tzatziki, and I put in some grape leaves. You eat it tonight, or you can freeze it, all but the hummus and tzatziki.' He was a short man, balding, heavy at the middle but not yet fat, with a moustache that he had a nervous habit of fingering.

'You're a good man,' I said. 'But you've got to sell this stuff.'

He raised his eyebrows. 'Who will buy it? No customers. The whore comes for cigarettes and food. I make her lunch. She says she has no money for it.' He laughed, but his face also reddened. 'She says she would let me do her on the counter, except she never would do it with

16

an Iraqi. I tell her I'm Egyptian. She tells me I look Iraqi. I kick her out of my restaurant.'

'You're a good man,' I said again. 'The food smells great.'

'Your business is finding people, is that right?' he said.

'Sure,' I said, 'if anyone ever hires me.'

'Do me a favor and find me some customers,' he said. Old joke already.

The building where I'd set up business had once housed a tire dealer and before that a little thrift store, but it mostly had stood empty. Lillian's brother Daniel, who was a cop, talked one of his friends into letting me rent it for the cost of the taxes he paid on the land. I'd Windexed the windows, painted the front, and hung a sign over the door, but my closest neighbors were the boarded-up Chinese restaurant and Farouk's fast-dying falafel shop. 'You're second on my list,' I said. 'As soon as I find some for myself.'

Lillian beat me home, and she and our black lab Percy greeted me together. Lillian had showered and wore a yellow sundress and sandals. She kissed me, but she gave me the same uncertain look that she always gave me since I returned, as if she was checking for visible cracks. I wanted to tell her to stop looking at me like that – I wanted to break through to where we were before I shipped out – but I kept my mouth shut. The distance in her eyes only reflected what she saw in mine, I figured. Besides, she'd talked with the VA counselors too, and they'd told her she was front line and needed to watch me. Still, I pulled her to me, my hand on the bare skin of her back at the top of the sundress, and held her. Percy barked, wanting in on the action, but I held Lillian still.

Three

Stephen Phelps

Sand and blood. Sand behind the knees, between the legs where thigh touches thigh meets groin. Sand in the mouth. Tiny, tooth-breaking rocks, grit and grind. Sand – one grain only – in my eye, where Felicity flung it, and *I'd rather go blind than see you walk away from me* – the pain of a grain of sand in the eye, and I'd rather go blind. A funny form of Felicity.

'Not my fault,' I told her. 'You overcame me. In spite of yourself. In spite of myself.'

'We could have gone somewhere,' she said. 'I would've. I have a bed. They make furniture for these things.'

'Not my fault,' I said. 'I was overcome. I'm not ashamed.' An early lesson: *Never be ashamed. Shame those who would shame you.* I spat out the grains of sand.

I blinked and blinked but the one grain of sand lodged deep in my eye, and she said, 'Take me home. I want to go home.'

Four

Lillian

Toni Morrison called Jacksonville *bad, bad country*. The government said it was the murder capital of Florida. The kids in my classes called it *Bang 'em Town* as if the sound of gunfire was dance music. But to think of it that way, they must have never driven the Wonderwood Expressway in the early evening through the swamp and pine forest, over the Intracoastal Waterway, and into the marsh surrounding the dragon-body winding of Cemetery Creek. They must have never hooked north on to Highway 1A, crossing more wetlands and endless nameless streams, where egrets and blue herons stood knee-deep in the brackish water and giant fish crows perched on the branches of faraway trees. They must have never swung east again past the naval station into the little Mayport shrimping village, where the big, lazy mouth of the St Johns River opened into the Atlantic Ocean.

Johnny and I ate dinner on the waterside deck at Safe Harbor Seafood Market. On the other side of the railing, shrimp boats – with salt-burnt hulls, spars, working booms, and drying nets – hung to the docks from wrist-thick lines. The car ferry angled across the river, grinding its

19

engines against the current. Brown pelicans dove into the water at the end of the docks. The sun grew orange and huge as it set over the far riverbank.

A waitress put a basket of shrimp and oysters on our table, but when I reached for it, Johnny took my hand. He'd done that lately – taking hold of me as if I was slipping away.

'What?' I asked.

'Nothing.' Then he nodded toward the river and the setting sun. 'This is good.'

He told me once, years ago, that he saw a brown pelican dive into the water and never come up. He said for a soldier with a gun there's nothing more blinding or dangerous than a setting sun. I wondered now if the river he saw over the Safe Harbor railing looked anything like the river I saw. 'There's no place more beautiful than this,' I said, and he let go of my hand.

We drank Coronas and, after the shrimp and oysters, ate grouper that the Safe Harbor fleet had just brought ashore, and when the sun dropped below the far riverbank and the sky turned black, Johnny said, 'What did you want to talk about?'

'A student of mine seems to have disappeared. Counseling thinks she might've hurt herself.'

'How old is she?'

'I don't know. Nineteen?'

He drank from his Corona. 'At that age, it's her right.'

'To hurt herself?'

'To disappear. Maybe she doesn't want to be found.'

'What are you talking about?'

'Who is she?'

I told him about Sheneel – her intelligence, her appetite for Dickinson's poems, her disappearance from class, her brother's worries, the rift between her and her parents. I left out that we danced together in class and that she haunted me like desire.

'OK,' he said. 'What are you going to do?'

'I'm hoping you might do it.'

His face fell. 'I don't know what I *can* do.'

'That's your job. Finding people.'

He said, 'I'm thinking about trying something else.'

'You just started this job.'

'I've been doing it two months and no one has called. No one has come in the door. No one.'

'I'm offering you work.'

'This isn't work.'

'Try?'

'No.'

'My brother—'

'He gave me the rental. I appreciate that. I've told him I appreciate it.'

'And he got you the license—'

His face turned hard. 'I know. But I don't owe him—'

'What are you going to do?'

He glanced at the dark river. 'Open a falafel joint?'

A breeze crossed the water and made my arms and back cold. 'Sheneel Greene needs help. I think she must. Try to find her.'

He kept his eyes on the river, as if its dark

comforted him in ways I never would. 'I can't.'

'She needs help,' I said.

'How do you know?'

I didn't. 'I just do.'

He had no answer.

I left him at the table, walked to the exit. He called my name once and fell in behind me. After he paid the bill, we crossed the parking lot in silence – the moon rising in the east, the river water silvering in the moonlight – but before we reached the car, he turned from me and jogged to the rail that separated the lot from the river. He leaned on the rail as if he would climb or dive over.

I ran to him. 'You have no right!'

He nodded at the water. 'Dolphin.'

In the silver light, the fin of a single dolphin rose from the surface a hundred feet or so from the docks. 'Oh,' I said.

He pointed downriver. 'Two more.'

I stood by him and watched the three fins dip under the surface and, twenty seconds later, re-emerge upriver. When the Greek poet Arion was drowning, a dolphin supposedly saved him, and afterward artists made mosaics and rulers stamped coins that showed him riding the dolphin like a horse, sometimes playing a lyre. During the Renaissance, Salvator Rosa painted him riding side-saddle, the sky behind him as silver and dark as the sky over the St Johns River.

Before shipping out, Johnny said he'd watched from the deck of the hospital ship as a pod of dolphins herded a shoal of mullets toward shore

22

and massacred them. Johnny said they turned the water as bloody as a battlefield.

'Let's go home,' I said.

By crossing the river on the car ferry, in less than a half-hour we could be in Fernandina, where Sheneel Greene lived. Instead, we drove back the same way we came.

After we put Percy into the backyard, we stood together in the bright light of the kitchen. When we first met, Johnny had the tight muscles, lanky torso, and deep suntan of the boys I knew in high school who spent their summers surfing or life-guarding at the beach – looked just like them except for his Navy haircut and occasional dark seriousness. I desired him from the beginning.

Now, his hair was growing and curling the way it curled in the pictures he'd shown me from when he was a teenager, but in the hard light his skin looked sweaty and cold. He came to me, but I turned away. 'No,' I said – the word he'd said to me at Safe Harbor.

He went into the backyard with Percy, and I climbed into bed, picturing Sheneel Greene as I closed my eyes.

During the night, Johnny came to me again, and I took him in the warmth and dream wash of the dark bedroom as though the night and our love were the flowing brown water of the river, and sharks and predator fish swam past, invisible, brushing their hard skins against us.

Five

Johnny

In the dark bedroom, I kissed Lillian's sleep-softened lips, and, thank God, instead of turning away, she rolled me gently on to my back and mounted me. For a while, I found peace in a bright spot of the dark room, and then she rolled off, still panting, a sweaty thigh against my sweaty thigh, and soon she slept again. Most nights, at two or three a.m., I wondered about the wisdom of throwing out the Ambien prescription. Vodka sometimes helped me drift between sleep and waking. Other times, I lay awake and willed my heart to beat harder – willed it to burst – but my heart ignored my will, and it was still beating when the sun rose, and I was sleepless and exhausted.

Tonight, I got up, put on shorts and a sweatshirt, returned to the backyard, and lay on a lawn chair. The night air had cooled and the sweat inside the shirt beaded on my skin, but the chill felt better than the skin-crawling warmth of the bed. During my last tour of duty, I often went above deck at night and watched the same stars that I knew shined on Lillian as if I could triangulate our love. In the winter, when I missed her most, I looked for Orion, the brightest constellation in the sky, his hunter's belt as tight over the Arabian Sea as along the Atlantic coast.

Now, I fell asleep as the sun came up and the moon and stars disappeared, and when I awoke again in the mid-morning heat, a bed sheet covered me. Lillian had draped it over me before she left to teach her classes. Many mornings, the sweet chemical smell of the paper mills up the coast hung in the air, but this morning a breeze blew the vegetable scent of oak trees, camphors, and magnolias across the yard. Percy lay in the sun at the foot of the recliner. Three years ago, while driving home from class, Lillian had seen him tied to a post in an overgrown yard. His owner had left no water for him, and by his looks he'd gone short on food for a long time. Lillian approached cautiously, uncertain of his temper, but he never raised his head. So she knocked on the front door and, when no one answered, unchained the dog and carried him to the backseat of her car.

That evening, the vet at the animal hospital said the dog was badly dehydrated and sick besides with who knew what. His kidneys were failing, other organs too, he said, and if we were humane, we would put him down. Lillian insisted on giving him a day and, after a day passed and his condition seemed no worse, another. A week later, the dog stood trembling on his own feet. After a second week, we took him home. At his three-month checkup, the vet found no organ damage, kidney or otherwise. Lillian wanted to call the dog Persistence. I said that was assholish. She said, 'Percival?' and I said, 'Yeah, right.' So we called him Percy.

He followed me as I walked inside. Lillian had

left the kitchen a mess, her breakfast half eaten on the counter. Next to her breakfast plate, she'd folded open the Metro section of the morning *Times-Union* to an article with the headline 'Wetland Body Identified as Missing Student.' The photograph showed a pale girl with white hair, not albino but close. Dread filled my belly as I read:

> The partially decomposed remains of a woman found yesterday afternoon on land abutting a Heckscher Drive clay pit have been identified as Sheneel P. Greene, 19, of Fernandina Beach. The Sheriff's Office is calling the death an apparent suicide. Greene was reported missing by relatives on February 16. She was last seen riding a bicycle on Heckscher Drive in the Little Marsh Island neighborhood near where her body was discovered. Anyone with information on Sheneel Greene's whereabouts in the days leading to February 16 should contact the Jacksonville Sheriff's Office.

Sweat broke inside my shirt.

Partially decomposed remains. A body could decompose in many ways. Rig a roadside bomb and, in a flash of light and sound, you could decompose a body into the stuff shovels are made for. Expose a body for a couple of days on a North Florida wetlands during a warm February and the results would be just as terrible.

She needs help. By the time Lillian said those

26

words last night, Sheneel Greene was past helping.

And what had I said to Lillian? *It's her right to disappear*. I'd been stupid to say it. But did I believe it? Maybe. More so at night than in the morning.

Lillian had covered me with a bed sheet as I'd slept on the lawn chair. Had she done that before or after she'd read the newspaper article? If before, then the gesture had nothing to do with Sheneel Greene's death. If after, then either Lillian had forgiven me or she'd draped the sheet over me the way you drape a sheet over a dead man. One also could decompose while sleeping on a lawn chair.

I called Lillian's cell phone. It rang twice and jumped to voicemail. 'Hey,' I said. 'I saw.' I hung up. What else could I say?

Sheneel Greene's photograph stared at me from the newspaper. I'd seen hundreds of dead men's stares – glassy-eyed, hard-eyed, bloodshot, bloody, milky, recessed deep into skulls from the force of an explosive concussion – and I'd stared back. Sheneel Greene's slate-gray eyes were the eyes of a living girl in the photograph, but that made staring back no easier.

I called Lillian's brother Daniel at the Sheriff's Office. Seven years older than Lillian, he'd been a detective in the homicide unit as long as I'd known him. Lillian revered him, and he'd only done me good, helping me get the rental space on Philips Highway, and picking me up and taking me home one night after I got back, when I went into the woods alone with my SIG. But

I'd heard stories about him, and, when he stood, he bent to the left from a couple of bullets that had splintered his ribs in circumstances that no one ever quite explained, and there had been a trial at which a lawyer proved that a couple of detectives had planted the gun they said was the defendant's.

When Daniel heard my voice on the line, he said, 'Hey, Johnny. How's tricks?'

'You guys deal with suicides, right?'

'Uh huh. And accidentals. You planning an event?'

Seeing it every day either turned a person into a man like me or made a person funny. I said, 'You know anything about Sheneel Greene?'

He hesitated only a moment. 'Sure. I took the call. What do you need?'

'She was one of Lillian's students.'

'I know. Lillian phoned.'

I said, 'She asked me to look into her yesterday.'

'The girl's been dead a couple of days.'

'What did you tell Lillian?'

'Same as I'm telling you,' he said.

'How'd she take it?'

'Hard. How well did she know the girl?'

'Not well, I think. You're sure it's her?'

'Lillian asked that too,' he said. 'She died face down in the dirt. Insects and animals got to the rest of her. Relatives came in and ID'd her.'

'Lillian said she was estranged from her parents.'

'Maybe so,' he said, 'but she's got family all over this area. A half-dozen of them showed up to tell us it was her.'

28

'Who found the body?'

'Does this matter?'

'Lillian asked me to look for her.'

'Yeah,' he said, 'but she's not missing anymore.'

'Who found her?'

'A guy who was looking at property by the clay pit.'

'Does he have a name?'

'He does. A private name unless he decides to make it public.'

'How do you know it was suicide?'

'A history of attempts. And her brother says she'd been depressed.'

'How did she do it?' I asked.

'We don't know yet. Probably pills. I've seen a lot of these, Johnny, and this is an easy one.'

'The newspaper says you're looking for people who saw her in the days leading to her death. Why are you doing that if it's suicide?'

'Loose ends. I'll do telephone interviews, won't bother asking them to come in. As I say, this is an easy one.'

'Nothing's easy,' I said.

'Can I give you some advice?'

The last thing I wanted from him. 'Sure.'

'Get your own head together,' he said. 'Forget about Sheneel Greene. Take care of yourself and then do something nice for Lillian. Hell, take her to Key West or the islands for a weekend – start living your life again.'

'Thanks, Daniel.'

'Don't take it wrong. I'm trying to help.'

'Always.'

'You're a good man, Johnny.'

'Could I come by and see the file?' I asked.

'I mean it. Drop this and pay attention to what matters. There's nothing here but a dead sad girl.'

'Would ten o'clock be OK?'

'Why would you want to?'

'For Lillian. I need to do this much.'

'The file is confidential.' But his words lacked conviction.

'Ten o'clock?' I asked.

'Fine.'

'You're a good man too, Daniel.'

When we hung up, Percy looked at me expectantly. 'And you're a good dog,' I said, 'as dogs go.'

I dialed Lillian's cell again and left a second message, telling her I was going to the Sheriff's Office to look at Sheneel Greene's police file.

A minute later she called back. 'It's too late,' she said.

'It's always been too late,' I said. 'But when did that stop me?'

'You're not making sense,' she said.

'No. I suppose not.'

The sun hung over the city as I drove across the Mathews Bridge into downtown. Long rows of shipping containers lined a riverside industrial lot to the north. Just over the side of the bridge exit to the south, East Beaver Street dead-ended into the riverbank. If you got on the street and drove west, it hooked into old Route 90, and you could keep driving for seventeen hundred miles until you reached New Mexico. Since coming home, I'd felt the lure

30

of that road, as I'd felt the lure of all avenues leading elsewhere.

The Sheriff's Office headquarters on Bay Street looked like a concrete bunker I once saw in an aerial photo of Basra – a low-rise slab with almost no glass but plenty of little terraces, and railings behind which a marksman could sight a target with little chance of getting hit by return fire. If the rumors were true, the architects designed the Sheriff's building, which the city put up in the early 1970s, to withstand the revolution that the mayor was sure would come after the violence of the 1960s.

I found my way to the homicide unit and asked for Daniel.

He was sitting in a double cubicle with his partner, a little dark-haired woman whose nameplate said she was Denise Nuñez. Daniel was a big man with small feet. He was mostly bald but had a close-shaved moustache that probably broke department regulations, though homicide detectives got away with more than street cops and Daniel liked to push the limits. He wore a short-sleeved button-down shirt and a dark blue tie and, as usual, had a knowing grin as though he'd just heard a mean joke. But he was always polite. After introducing his partner to me, he asked if she would excuse us to talk in private, and, when she did, he removed a green binder from a shelf above his computer and set it on the desk. He gave me the knowing grin. 'You've got five minutes. Then you can tell Lillian you did your best.'

The file contained a transcript of the

nine-one-one call reporting the discovery of Sheneel Greene's body and named the man who discovered it as Peter Lisman.

'You got a pen?' I asked Daniel.

He shook his head. 'No notes.'

The next pages included records from the responding officers, an interview with Peter Lisman, and more records from Daniel and Denise Nuñez. Lisman said he'd come to the Little Marsh Island neighborhood to look at a fifteen-acre plot of scrubland and swamp that stood between Heckscher Drive and the clay pit. A hundred and fifty feet from the road, he'd smelled what he thought was a dead deer or wild pig. Another twenty-five feet and he'd seen scraps of clothing and a single bloodied tennis shoe. He said he'd gone no closer but had called the police and retreated to the hot dry pavement of the road. The responding officers had followed Lisman's path through the trees and then followed their noses the rest of the way to Sheneel Greene's remains. They reported finding her face down in the sandy soil. Daniel and his partner arrived around the same time as the Crime Scene Unit technicians. The technicians found no blood spattering, which, since the weather had been dry, would have been present if Sheneel Greene had died from a gunshot or had been stabbed, and found no other body fluids. When the technicians gave Daniel permission, he rolled Sheneel Greene's body on to what remained of her back and found, to everyone's surprise, that her face remained intact.

I looked up from the records to see if Daniel's expression showed traces of the work he did. It showed none, and I wondered whether that made him strong or callous. 'You done?' he asked.

I pulled a manila envelope of photographs from a file pocket. 'Almost.' I needed to look into the dead girl's eyes.

The first three photos showed the scene surrounding Sheneel Greene's body. Orange evidence markers lay next to shreds of cloth from her T-shirt and shorts. Yellow markers lay next to crushed beer cans and a dirty Doritos bag. I pointed at the shreds of cloth. 'Animals?'

'Surprisingly few,' Daniel said. 'Sometimes, after a day or two, we find pieces of clothing a mile away.'

I pointed at the yellow markers. 'What's this stuff?'

'The neighbors say that kids party back there. We found beer cans, cigarettes, a condom.'

'Is that why she picked the place?'

'Could be.'

The next picture was a shot taken after Daniel had turned the body on to its back: a shot of Sheneel Greene's face from the shoulders up. I broke into a cold sweat. The girl was more beautiful in death than she had been in the living picture that appeared in the morning paper. A smear of dirty sand masked her chin and the red of her lips had purpled, but her cheeks looked smooth, her white hair parted neatly at her brow, and her eyes seemed to beckon. A black string was stretched over her forehead like a thin head-band, and in the middle, where Indian women

33

have bindis, the string held a dark square packet the size of a Band-Aid pad against her skin.

I must have paled, because Daniel said, 'I know you've seen a lot of bad stuff, Johnny. But I've seen the worst of the worst. And you know what? The world's still OK. Sure, there's ugliness, but, overall, we've got it pretty good. You should remember that.'

'Right,' I said, and pointed at the pad bound to the girl's forehead. 'What's that?'

'Weird, isn't it?'

'What is it?'

'We've seen it a couple of times on suicides in the past but only on backwater blacks. It's Geechee.'

'It's what?'

'Geechee. Or Gullah. They're a bunch of descendants of slaves who lived on the barrier islands. You still find them in Fernandina and the islands around there. They talk their own language and make their own medicines.'

'And they put Band-Aids on their heads when they kill themselves?'

'It's leaves. They come from Indian shot plants. Flowers. You see them in their gardens. They do it for a bad head. If someone's acting crazy or depressed, or they've got a migraine, they put the leaves on their foreheads. They claim it works.'

'It didn't work for Sheneel Greene.'

'Guess not.'

'How did a white girl get the leaves?'

'Fernandina's a small place. The Gullah still keep pretty much to themselves, but they've mixed a little over the years and you see them around. Anyway, you know how kids are. Rich suburban white boys dress ghetto. Rich suburban white girls put their hair in dreads.'

'Sheneel Greene comes from money?'

He looked impatient. 'The point is—'

'Yeah, I get the point.' I flipped to the final photo. It showed the tattered remains of Sheneel Greene's T-shirt, stripped from her body and spread on a white evidence table. Across the shreds, a single word appeared: *Ngafa*. 'What's that mean?' I asked Daniel.

He shrugged. 'It might be Gullah too.'

I slipped the photos back into the envelope and closed the file.

He eyed me uncertainly. 'Does that take care of it? You see what you needed to see?'

'I suppose so.'

'Good. Then go to your office. Do your work. Or blow off the day and go to the beach. Go fishing. Do something you like to do. But stop treating the world like a piñata now, will you?'

'I'll try,' I said.

'Whacking at it won't do you any good, and it definitely won't do Lillian any good either.'

I thanked him and left him at his desk. As I walked out of the police building, sunlight, glinting off the hood of an SUV parked at the curb, blinded me.

I blinked through it and got into my car. *Stop treating the world like a piñata*. A good thought, but I felt as if I was the one taking the whacks.

The sun had warmed the inside of the car, but I left the windows up and the engine and air conditioning off. I dialed Lillian's number on my cell phone. When she picked up, I said, 'I saw her. Pictures of her. I saw the reports.'

She remained angry. 'So?'

'That's all.' When she said nothing, I asked, 'What does *Ngafa* mean?'

'Bad spirit,' she said.

'How do you know?'

'Sheneel Greene told me.'

'Is it Gullah?'

'I don't know what it is.' Her voice was cold.

'You shouldn't treat me this way.' Sweat from my forehead stung my eyes.

'How do you want me to treat you?'

'I couldn't have done anything for her. It was already too late last night.'

'You don't get it,' she said.

'She was already dead. What more is there to get?'

'You refused to help before you knew.'

'Jesus, Lillian. What difference would it have made?'

'I would think of you differently, that's all.'

'Don't do that,' I said, 'don't *ever*,' and hung up. My eyes were wet – with the sting of perspiration, with tears, I don't know what. I sat in the heat and listened to the sound of my own breathing and the hard pulsing of my heart.

When I got home, I put Percy on a leash and climbed back into the car. 'Road trip,' I said. Now I was talking with a dog.

We drove to the Dames Point Bridge – a huge white span with two central concrete towers supported by strands of heavy white cable. It looked like a giant fallen white angel. We crossed the river to Heckscher Drive and drove east past the Blount Island shipping terminal, where side-by-side tower cranes lifted matching white boxes from a container ship. We crossed an inlet to Little Clapboard Creek and drove on to Little Marsh Island.

On one side, single-story stucco houses with neat lawns, small flower gardens, and well-mulched palm trees fronted the street. On the other side, the land fell hard to what existed before the developers arrived and what would exist again if the neighborhood canceled its lawn services, gardeners, and fertilizer trucks. It was ragged and wet, with oaks, palmettos, wild grape vines, marsh grasses, and a thousand other kinds of scrub plants pulling at each other, tangling, struggling at the roots for the fresh water that pooled in the rotting detritus before evaporating under the sun or leaching into the brackish marsh and creeks. Every hundred yards or so, a path cut through the border scrub into the shadows and clearings. We passed four paths before I saw a Watson Realty sign advertising a fifteen-acre property suitable for a hunting camp, residential development, or light industrial use. The police report had said that Peter Lisman had come to Little Marsh Island to look at a fifteen-acre plot.

I pulled on to the grassy shoulder, parked, and stepped into the brush, Percy beside me. The ground was soft and sandy, marked with the foot-prints of the cops, detectives, and technicians who'd worked Sheneel Greene's death. Insects buzzed in the branches, and marsh birds sang in

37

the distance. As I walked from the road, the air smelled of salt water and rotting vegetation, then of animal death, as if the marsh land was slowly consuming the carcass of a bird or raccoon. Percy tugged at the leash, and I yanked him to my side. 'Respect,' I said, though I was unsure what I meant.

The path bent to the left and opened to a clearing that the police had ringed with crime-scene tape. Inside the tape, next to two long logs that the neighborhood kids who partied in the clearing had dragged together to sit on, a dark-skinned man kneeled on the ground and stared at the sky. His short gray hair was matted to his head. He wore blue pants, a sun-bleached red T-shirt, and sandals. His face tilted up toward the treetops and he swayed slowly side to side. If he was praying, he was doing so without speaking.

I watched him for a full minute, then said, 'Hey,' to let him know I was there.

For several seconds, he remained as he had been. Then he stood and wiped the dirt from his knees and hands. He stared at me, defiance shining in his eyes as if I'd accused him of something.

I tried again. 'Hey.'

But he walked across the clearing, ducked under the crime-scene tape, and disappeared through a stand of palmettos and low bushes.

I ducked under the tape and went to the spot where he had been kneeling. He'd used a piece of broken stick to scratch a small drawing into the sandy soil. It was an almost complete circle with an open-mouthed snake's head at one end

38

– a snake eating its own tail. 'Huh,' I said, and Percy stuck his nose into the drawing, knocking the sand into its shallow grooves. I yanked him away and again said, 'Respect.'

Percy nosed back to the drawing, so I unclipped his leash and shooed him away. As he ran off to explore, I looked around the rest of the clearing. The police had trampled the grass and weeds, making the place look as if someone had made a long encampment, but a hollow in the ground showed where Sheneel Greene had lain as she died. I crouched by it and smelled the air. The odor of animal death was fainter than on the path, and that meant the evidence technicians had bagged the sand under Sheneel Greene's body. I sat in the hollow. The earth felt warm under me, and I understood why Sheneel Greene might choose this place to die. The scrub trees and bushes blocked the road. The sun beat down. The salt air stood still, the breeze blocked by the vegetation. Other than a fly that landed on my arm and then flew off, nothing disturbed the silence.

The hollow was about five feet from the two logs and the old man's drawing. Sheneel Greene might have sat on one of the logs before killing herself. I wondered whether she had kneeled to pray or just to sway slowly under the hard blue sky. Eventually, she would have moved from the logs and lain on the ground.

I stretched my legs into the indentations in the hollow and lowered my shoulders to the dirt. I rolled toward my shoulder the way Sheneel Greene must have lain. I closed my eyes.

39

Stop treating the world like a piñata, Daniel had said.

Easy enough. Sheneel Greene had stopped treating the world like a piñata.

My heart raced. I breathed in deep and breathed out, trying to slow it.

Then Percy charged through the brush into the clearing.

He brought back a prize: a salt-white object the length of a rolled-up newspaper and, with it, the terrible stench of death.

He dropped it beside me. It was a girl's hand and arm, extending almost to the elbow. Its skin was as pale as the skin on Sheneel Greene's dead face in the photos that Daniel kept in his case file, and the fingers were long and thin. An animal must have dragged it into the brush, and now Percy had brought it back. Its sickly whiteness gleamed in the sun. On the ship, I'd seen arms and legs torn from bodies and had tried to match them with the ID tags that I took from the soldiers' boots before bagging them for transport home. Most of them were men's limbs and were grimed with red Afghan dust and clay, not startlingly white and female like this. I stared at it. On the soft skin on the inside of the wrist, there was a tattoo of a snake circling to bite its own tail. The tattoo covered less than an inch, and the skin through the middle of it looked split as if by a razor blade, as if Sheneel Greene had tried to dig the tattoo out of her body or had made a partial attempt to slit her wrists. It matched the drawing that the old man had made in the soil.

Worse, the bone and flesh toward the elbow

40

looked neatly cut. No roadside bomb could take off an arm so cleanly, and no wild animal had teeth so sharp or jaws so strong. Someone had cut off Sheneel Greene's arm with a blade.

Six

Stephen Phelps

Shades of white stationery paper in the *Phelps Paper* catalog:

> *Alabaster, Bone, Calcite, Chalk, Eggshell, Pearl, Snow White*

Whites of the eyes. Ghost white. Wedding dress. Mirror, mirror.

At the mills, we bleached wood pulp until the skin tones of sap and bark turned as fair as Snow White, the trade name we used for the finest paper we produced: nothing on the market whiter than *Phelps Snow White*. But in Alabama once, I saw a freshly split pine with wood even whiter – as white as Sheneel. If we had made paper from it, I would have named it after her. The tract manager took me into a shed where he'd laid out an eight-foot length, sliced down the middle – side-by-side pieces like twin corpses at a viewing. He spat on his hand and rubbed the raw wood. It shined like white ice. I knew too well that diseases and genetic abnormalities could do that to people: albinism, Griscelli syndrome, leukoderma. But a tree?

'What is it?' I asked.

He rested his hand on one of the pieces as if he'd made it himself. 'Slash pine.'

Slash pine is yellow wood. 'Can't be.'

'I swear. It was in a slash grove. But it's the only one like this. If you could isolate it and grow more, you could clean-process it or sell it premium for furniture.'

'What made it like this?'

He shrugged.

'Could be disease,' I said.

'Could be.'

'Insects?'

'No,' he said.

'Genetic?'

'Maybe.' He rubbed his palm on the wet spot. 'Money in it if you figure it out.'

It *was* beautiful but also monstrous – more monstrous in its discoloration than the gnarled, misshapen trees that sometimes grew among the straight pines. Monstrous because it was too perfect, too clean. 'Pulp it with the others,' I said.

'You don't want to test it?'

'Pulp it.'

Sheneel's mother, Laura, shared only Sheneel's eyes. Her skin was darker than my own. Did I love her? Could I have loved her?

When she took me in the kitchen – the first to take me – I thought I could love her. She was angry afterward, like the rest of them. *Not my fault*.

Now Sheneel was dead, her blood soaking

42

into the sand on Little Marsh Island, her white bones yellowing in the sun, her beautiful and monstrous white skin of my skin as shredded as a torn sheet of *Phelps Snow White*. When she was sixteen, I touched the soft fatty skin on the inside of her thigh – tender as a baby's belly. I had always felt compelled to touch strangers' wounds and had gripped my own wrists or grabbed the wood of a chair to keep my fingers off. No wonder that I needed to touch a beautiful monster.

And now she was sleeping. Dead. For a hundred hundred years. Until whose kiss? Not mine.

Not my fault.

Some people are born like that.

Seven

Lillian

After teaching my first class, I went to my office, closed the door, and fought an impulse to climb under my desk. What remains of a woman who swallows herself? If she swallows herself, can the new self swallow herself again? How many self-consumings can occur before nothing remains – not a shoe, not a nipple, not a rib bone?

The cause and effect made no sense. The equal and opposite – no sense. Johnny hadn't caused Sheneel's death, and yet I *felt* that he had – that, in refusing to concern himself with her, he'd torn a hole in the tissue that kept her in this world, and now she had fallen through it. There was no logic in that. I'd told Johnny about Sheneel after she'd died. If the newspaper was right, all that was left of her when I told him were 'partially decomposed remains.' Before last night, she was my secret. I'd held the secret too long. My secret, my fault. Should I blame Johnny for failing to act on a secret that I held to myself? No. But still . . .

I left the window shade down and the light off. No student conferences today. Office hours canceled. I typed Sheneel's name into Google. The first link led to Sheneel's Facebook page. In her status postings, all more than a month old, she quoted Emily Dickinson, which upset me and made me glad at once. Her photos showed her in a red cocktail dress that, with her pale legs, made her look younger than nineteen. Other photos showed her at a party with friends, including the Asian boy from class – Samuel Huang.

At the next link, for a site called Spring.me, a boy named Rick told Sheneel she was *hot* and asked her to meet him, before admitting that he lived in Cleveland. Her profile picture showed her in the red *Ngafa* T-shirt and with wet hair as if she'd just come in from the rain or stepped out of a shower.

A third link led to Florida Mugshots, a site summarizing Florida municipal arrests. The page said that at three a.m. last June seventh, the Fernandina Beach Police Department had charged Sheneel with battery using a 'personal weapon.'

The page listed her gender as female, her race as white, her hair as blond, her eyes as gray, her age as nineteen, her weight as 105 pounds, and her height as five feet four inches. It said she had bonded out of jail for $10,000.

What did Sheneel do? What was a 'personal weapon'?

My Life had stood – a Loaded Gun. Sheneel's eyes had lit up when she'd heard those words. I'd felt that we were dancing. But I wondered now if she really was dancing alone, moved by the private music in a memory of desire and violence.

My cell phone rang and pulled me out of myself. Caller ID said it was Johnny. I silenced the ringer. I would talk with him later. Now, I would sit in the quiet of my office, dark except for the light of the computer monitor.

On Florida Mugshots, a gray box appeared in the spot where the site creators would have put a photo of Sheneel if they'd had one, and in the middle of the gray box, a darker gray silhouette of a generic human face, and in the middle of the silhouette, where facial features belonged, a large white question mark.

I clicked on the question mark and the silhouette appeared enlarged on the screen. *If you don't want to see it, don't look.* When, as a child, I first heard those words, a coyote had destroyed the neighbor's cat. It had dragged the carcass across our backyard. Daniel and I had walked barefoot across the wet grass, and Daniel had picked up a piece of the cat's tail. Even as a boy, he could do that with casual ease, as another child might

45

pick up a broken tree branch. I looked then but shouldn't have. I should have closed my eyes and tucked inside myself.

Under the website silhouette, a disclaimer said, 'The information presented here has been collected from County Sheriff websites. Contact the County Clerk or State Attorney's Office for more information.' But I could do better than that. I dialed Daniel's number at the Sheriff's Office.

Before he could answer, someone knocked on my door. I hung up, closed the browser, and flipped on the light. Samuel Huang stood in the hall – a thin, clear-faced boy, wearing an untucked button-down shirt, khaki shorts, and flip-flops. His eyes looked uncertain.

'Come in,' I said.

He sat in the chair facing mine, his backpack on the floor between his ankles. He glanced at the books on the shelves as if they would tell him what to say.

I knew why he had come. 'Sheneel?'

His face screwed a little and he looked at the floor.

I said, 'It hurts.'

'Yeah,' he said.

I thought, *After great pain, a formal feeling comes* – Dickinson, whose words would do him no good right now. 'You were her friend.'

'Yeah.'

'Do you know why she did it?'

His eyes turned again to the bookshelves. 'Her family was messed up – her dad – she had problems. She tried to kill herself two years ago. Her brother saved her.'

46

'Were you her boyfriend?'

He smiled at that. 'No.'

I had spoken to make sound so we wouldn't have to listen to the emptiness, but he turned his eyes from the shelves and looked at me with a sudden ferocity that made me wonder why, until that moment, he had failed to meet my gaze.

He said, 'You've got a lot of books.'

'I do.'

'Why?'

A strange question. I said, 'They've made me what I am.'

He looked as if I'd confirmed some new thought of his. 'That's sad.'

'Why?'

He offered no answer.

I said, 'I'll make an announcement about Sheneel in class. If you would like, you can say a few words.'

An hour later, I stood in front of Samuel Huang and the rest of the class and said, '*I mourned, and yet shall mourn with ever-returning spring.* Walt Whitman wrote those words after Abraham Lincoln died. Whitman wrote of grief but also of beauty. In the same poem, he spoke to death, saying, *I cover you over with roses and early lilies,* as if he were talking to a lover who was full of sexual energy.' The eyes of the students looked uncomprehending, so I said, 'This morning, we learned of the death of one of your classmates.' I told them what the newspaper had reported and said that therapists at Student Counseling would talk with anyone who made an appointment. I dismissed class after twenty minutes.

When I returned to my office, Tom Corfield was standing outside my door. Tom taught American history, but the history that seemed to interest him most was the short one between us almost ten years ago when Johnny went on his first deployment. It was a good history: those nights relieved a fear unlike any I'd known before or again during Johnny's absences.

Now, he looked worried. 'Got a minute?' he asked.

'Not really.'

He followed me into my office.

He talked about a lecture series he wanted to start. Interdisciplinary. The Confederate South. Nathan Bedford Forrest. Daughters of the Confederacy . . .

My mind slipped and I imagined the remains of Sheneel Greene in a clearing by a clay pit. How much of her remained when she was found? How much of her had there ever been? The newspaper story said that, when last seen, she was riding a bicycle. I imagined her riding on an empty asphalt road, her white hair streaming behind her. I thought about how the body works and does not work.

Tom stopped mid-sentence and looked at me as if he saw something wrong. Maybe he hadn't heard about Sheneel Greene's death. More likely, he'd heard but saw no connection to me.

I tried a smile. 'I'm sorry,' I said. 'I haven't been listening to you.' I meant the words to sting.

He looked through the doorway into the hall,

but, instead of leaving, he swung the door shut. He said, 'What's up?'

'Nothing. Stuff I need to work through.'

'With Johnny?' He'd met Johnny at the end of the first deployment and had seen him once or twice when I'd brought him to faculty parties.

I said, 'I need time alone.'

He shook his head sympathetically. 'You know I'm here.'

'I know.'

He bit his bottom lip.

'Thank you,' I said.

As he reached for my hand, someone knocked on the door.

'Get that?' I said.

He opened the door a crack.

Johnny stood in the hall. He was sweaty, his hands dirty, his eyes wild and dangerous.

'Ahh,' Tom said. 'I was – we were talking about a series. Lectures . . .'

Johnny fixed his eyes on mine but he spoke to Tom. 'Leave.'

'Right. Of course.' Then, to me, 'We'll talk later.'

Johnny came in, closed the door, and dropped on to the chair. His skin was wet and he looked cold. 'Hey,' he said.

'Are you all right?'

He said, 'Sheneel Greene didn't kill herself.'

'What—'

'She didn't kill herself.'

Hope flooded my thoughts but only for a moment. 'She's dead. The newspaper says—'

'Someone killed her. She didn't kill herself.'

'That's—'

'I went out to where they found her – what was left of her. They didn't find everything. I've got her arm.'

'What?'

'Her arm. The joint is clean cut. Someone sliced it. It's clean.'

'What do you mean, *you have her arm*?'

He seemed to think he'd done nothing strange. 'I've got it. The police must have seen what I saw. Your brother must have. I mean, the cut on the arm is clean. The cut on the body must be clean too. There's no way this was suicide.'

I waved at him to stop. 'You have Sheneel Greene's arm? Where do you have it?'

He gave me a pacifying look, as if I was unduly anxious. 'It's all right. I know how to do this. I've got it on ice. It's—'

'Where?'

'What?'

'Where's her arm? Where do you have it?'

For the first time, he looked uncertain. 'In the car. In a cooler.'

I stared at him. 'Are you out of your mind?'

Eight

Johnny

Lillian looked at me as if I was insane.

'I packed it in ice,' I said. 'It's OK – I know how to do this.' When Percy brought me the arm,

50

I'd taken the steps I'd learned to take so as to slow the breakdown of body tissues. In the VA counseling sessions that I'd attended, men who looked capable of snapping two-by-fours with their hands had talked of losing control of their bowels when they heard a knock on the door. Others reached for their guns and, in their mind's eye, saw enemy soldiers crossing their backyards as clearly as they saw the trees and their children's swing sets. They knew the real basis for all fear and they knew how to kill. Their bodies and minds were determined to do what they had to do, even if the main danger lay six thousand miles away.

I'd never encountered the roadside bombs and snipers that caused those men's particular psychopathologies. So, while loud noises startled me, I never hallucinated about coming under enemy fire. My own nightmares took me to below-deck spaces and subterranean rooms where I processed endless progressions of bodies as efficiently as an assembly line worker. Slam a hammer against a wall and I might or might not draw a gun. But show me a severed arm and I would pack it in ice as fast as the other guys would shoot a hole in their backyard fences.

'What were you thinking?' Lillian said. 'You should have left the arm there. You should have called Daniel and let him handle it.'

I said, 'Unless Sheneel Greene killed herself by cutting off her arm, someone else killed her. Why are the police calling her death a suicide?'

'You're worrying me, Johnny.'

'All right,' I said. 'I'll take the arm to Daniel. But why aren't they calling this a murder?'

51

'I don't know.' She looked exhausted. 'Daniel does this work all the time. The police have people who will explain what happened – people who, unlike you, know what they're doing.'

'Someone cut off the arm.'

'I don't know. Take it to Daniel. Tell him what you see. Let him decide.'

'Fine.'

She softened her voice. 'After you give it to him, make an appointment. You need help. You slept outside again—'

'Sure,' I said.

'When I covered you with a sheet, you yelled as if you were on fire.'

'I don't remember.'

'At first I thought you were awake. You weren't. You need to make an appointment.'

'OK.'

'Good,' she said. Then, as I stood to go, she added, 'I love you.'

'Yeah. I love you too.' I started out the door, stopped. 'First, come with me. I want to show you something.'

'What?'

'Something on the arm.'

'I believe you. If you say the arm looks like it was cut off, I trust you.'

'Not that. Something else.'

'I'm not going to look at Sheneel's arm.'

I stared at her.

She shook her head. 'I'm not.'

'Fine. You got a sheet of paper?'

She peeled a clean sheet from the stack in her printer and gave me a pen. I drew a picture of a snake bending in a circle and closing its mouth on its own tail.

She glanced at it but seemed unimpressed. 'An Ouroboros,' she said.

'A what?'

'It's an Ouroboros – a snake biting its tail. The Greeks thought it symbolized the cycles of life – birth, living, death, rebirth. You see them here and there. The Egyptians used them. Coleridge liked them.'

'Sheneel Greene had a tattoo of one on her wrist.'

She shrugged. 'I had a student who tattooed his legs with every cartoon animal you can think of. Mickey Mouse, Winnie the Pooh, Tigger, Donald Duck, Jiminy Cricket. I asked him why, and he said he liked Disney. I had another who tattooed a barcode, like for a grocery store. I wouldn't worry too much about a snake tattoo.'

'When I went to the clearing where Sheneel Greene's body was found, an old man was crouching on the ground. He was scratching one of these snakes into the dirt with a stick.'

Lillian stared at me. 'Are you sure?'

I forced a smile. 'As opposed to I'm making it up?'

'Why would he scratch an Ouroboros?'

'That's my point,' I said.

I drove downtown to the Sheriff's Office. Lillian thought I was crazy, but I wasn't. Or I was, but not in the way she thought I was. On my third night off the ship, I'd felt like tearing the skin off of my face, and I'd told her she wouldn't

53

understand because she hadn't spent the months that I'd spent in that death factory. She'd asked me to tell her – to bring her in, so she could help carry the pain – but the idea of taking anyone, especially her, into that space horrified me. So, I'd told her nothing, and when I'd felt as if my skin no longer was my own and nothing would feel better than to rip it from my body, I'd kept my mouth shut and gone out to the woods alone or had crawled from bed in the night and lain in the backyard until sleep took me in her arms if she was in the mood. And then Lillian had insisted I talk to counselors – if not her, someone else needed to help – and I'd said, yes, of course. Of course she was right. I'd agreed that no man should bear such a burden alone. But I'd also known that some burdens can't or shouldn't be shared.

I parked at a meter a block from the Sheriff's Office and carried the cooler into the building, but stopped outside the security check with its package X-ray. I called Daniel on my cell phone and said, 'I'm in the lobby and I've got a present for you.'

'What are you talking about?'

'Something of Sheneel Greene's. Something you missed.'

Five minutes later, he stepped through security and I opened the cooler for him. 'Holy shit,' he said, though his face remained impassive. If you'd been watching him from across the lobby, you never would have known. 'Where'd you get this?'

I told him about my drive to the Little Marsh

Island site and about Percy dropping the arm beside me like a chew toy.

'You had no business going out there,' he said.

I welcomed his anger. 'You had no business missing the arm,' I said, 'and you had no business calling this a suicide. Suicides don't look like this.'

For a moment, I thought he would hit me. I would have welcomed that too. I felt like hitting back. But he said, 'Come with me.'

He took me back through the Homicide Room to his desk, opened a drawer, and pulled out a manila envelope. He gave it to me and said, 'See for yourself.'

The envelope contained more photographs of Sheneel Greene's body, unlike the ones I'd seen before, showing what was left of her torso and limbs below her shoulders. They were as terrible as anything I'd seen on the ship in the Arabian Sea. Animals, insects, and the heat had gotten to her, eating through her skin and consuming her insides. The elbow and most of the upper arm above the forearm that I'd found were gone, and something had chewed and ravaged the stump that remained. Nothing on her body showed evidence of a clean blade cut. Everything that remained was the stuff of tooth and claw and the predators that come afterward.

'This is what we have to work with,' Daniel said.

As terrible as the photographs were, I felt a certain peace in seeing them. This was the world I'd come to know. 'Why didn't you show me these pictures when I was here before?'

Daniel scratched his head above his ear. 'I was humoring you by letting you see the case file. Those are the pictures we show to the family so they can make an ID. Why would they want to see more? Why would *you*?'

'I've seen as bad,' I said.

'I know. And I've seen what it's done to you. This isn't your business. You don't belong here. You shouldn't have gone to Little Marsh Island. You shouldn't have touched the arm.' He spoke calmly, but I felt the heat.

'So what do you do now?' I asked. 'The cut on the arm is clean. Sheneel Greene didn't do that to herself.'

'Jesus, Johnny. Forensics will look at it. Until we say otherwise, it's suicide.'

'You've got to be kidding.'

He closed his eyes, as if he was mustering patience. 'Fine,' he said, and picked up the green binder that he'd shown me a few hours earlier. He paged to the end, removed a plastic insert from the rings, and handed it to me. It held a photocopy of a handwritten letter signed by Sheneel Greene. 'She left a note,' Daniel said. 'Her brother found it this morning.'

I read it. Sheneel apologized to someone named Alex – her brother, I guessed – and to someone she called Papa Crowe. She said something confused about missing them when she was gone. She said goodbye.

I laid the note on the desk. 'This makes no sense.'

'The cliché, right? Suicide rarely does.'

'How do you explain the clean cut?'

He shrugged. 'I don't. I've never seen anything like it. But that doesn't necessarily mean what you think it does. Like I said, we'll give it to forensics. They'll figure it out. Maybe it'll turn out an animal can do that. Maybe something else.'

'It's a blade cut.'

'*I* don't know,' he said, 'and *you* don't either.' For him, our talk was over.

I said, 'When I went to Little Marsh Island, there was another man inside the crime tape.'

'So?'

I told him about the black man, the snake that he scratched into the dirt, and the matching snake tattoo on Sheneel Greene's arm.

Daniel shook his head. 'Go home, Johnny,' he said. 'Or go to your office and sit in your chair. I don't care. But leave me alone, OK? Let me do my work.'

Outside, the early afternoon sun glinted from the hoods of cars and the white sidewalks. The bright heat made me light-headed, and I stopped in the shade of a crape myrtle tree. I breathed in deep, breathed out, and breathed in deeper, but the air felt thin and depleted of its necessary oxygen. *Go home, Johnny.* As if that was an option.

I ducked back into the heat and moved down the sidewalk toward my car. I was exhausted, but my head buzzed with nervous energy as powerful and unsettling as an adrenaline burst. Lillian thought I needed help. She wanted me to make an appointment. If I called the VA hotline, they would schedule me as soon as they could. A sign I'd read in the counselors' waiting room said,

Prevention makes strong soldiers. Catch the problem early and you live to fight another day.

I pulled out my cell phone. But instead of the VA, I called directory assistance and asked for the number of an Alex or Alexander Greene in Fernandina Beach.

He picked up on the third ring.

'Is this Sheneel Greene's brother?' I asked.

'Who's calling?' he said.

'That's kind of complicated,' I said. I explained that my wife had taught American Literature to Sheneel. 'I run a little company that tracks missing people, mostly people who've forgotten to pay their bills. Also I do background searches.'

'So what do you want?'

'Could we meet? I'd like to talk with you.'

'Sheneel isn't missing.'

'We can talk wherever you want. Your house. A park.'

'I don't think so.'

I hesitated but said, 'She didn't kill herself.'

'What are you talking about?' There was anger in his voice.

'That's why I want to meet. She—'

'She wrote a note. I read it.'

'Please.'

'I don't know what you want,' he said, and he hung up.

I waited thirty seconds and dialed again.

He answered, 'I'm calling the police.'

'The police will say you're right. They'll say Sheneel killed herself. But I'm telling you you're wrong and they're wrong. Meet with me, listen to what I have to say, and if you don't like it,

58

you can call the police, though you won't need to – I won't bother you again.'

For a quarter of a minute, he said nothing and I said nothing. Then he said, 'Fine.'

I drove up I-95, exited on to the old Buccaneer Trail highway, drove alongside flatbed trucks loaded with slash pine timber, past the little town of Yulee, through a mix of wetlands, woodland, and box-store commerce, and across the causeway to Amelia Island and the town of Fernandina. Amelia was the third in a tightly linked chain of barrier islands that ran up the North Florida and South Georgia coasts – Little Talbot, Big Talbot, Amelia, Cumberland, Jekyll, St Simons, Sapelo – places that long ago housed Spanish and English colonial forts and then slave plantations and, in the past hundred years, the mansions and vacation houses of whites who lived in developments that kept the names of the old plantations and who mostly ignored and, by ignoring, coexisted with the black population of slave descendants who'd settled in pockets on the island interiors away from the expensive seaside real estate.

Fernandina stood at the northern end of Amelia, and the Chamber of Commerce had turned it into a tourist destination, bricking the streets, encouraging businesses and restaurants to hang hand-painted signs with pictures of pirates and parrots, and sending municipal workers on to the white sand beaches early in the morning to rake the trash that had washed up overnight. But trash continued to wash up, and, next door to the seaside mansions, a paper mill fogged the air with thick chemical sweetness that even the ocean breeze couldn't dissipate.

Sheneel Greene had shared a little yellow single-story prefab with her brother on Gum Street on the inside of the island. Ragged grass clung to the sandy soil, and, except for a stunted palm in front of the house and a chain-link fence at the back, the yard was bare. A screened-in front porch mostly obscured the view into the house, and, inside the porch, someone had taped newspaper over the front window. I pulled on to the sandy shoulder and turned off the car. The sky was blue and hot, and the air smelled of cut grass and the paper mill.

A light-skinned black man, who looked in his early twenties, answered my knock. He wore gray knee-length shorts, no shirt or shoes.

'Is Alex Greene here?' I asked.

He narrowed his eyes. 'You're Johnny Bellefleur?' I stared at him, and he read my confusion over his appearance. He said, 'Long story. Come in.'

A window air conditioner blew cool air into the living room. A brown couch with sagging cushions covered by a blanket and headed with a bed pillow, as if someone had been sleeping on it, was pulled against one wall. A skateboard leaned against another. A kitchen extended behind the living room, and a door led to a bedroom and another to a bathroom.

The man pulled the blanket from the couch and said, 'Sit if you want,' and he got a chair for himself from the kitchen.

His eyes looked hard and suspicious, like the

eyes of teenaged kids I'd seen living in the park near the Sheriff's Office downtown. I figured I had only one chance with him. 'This morning, I went out to where they found your sister,' I said. 'I found something the police didn't find. It was pretty bad. Someone did this to Sheneel.'

'Do you know how many times she tried to kill herself?'

I shook my head.

'Three. You know who saved her? I did. The first time she swallowed, like, a hundred pills.' He pointed at the floor by my feet. 'I found her right there. The second time, I came home from work and found her asleep on the couch. I couldn't wake her. They pumped her stomach. I don't know what she took. The third time, she puked it out in the bathroom. I didn't call the hospital.' He stared at me as if challenging me to quarrel or to sympathize with him.

'Someone cut her,' I said. 'Part of her. Her arm. Someone cut it off.'

He flinched, but he said, 'She wrote a note. I found it on her bed.'

'I don't understand that.'

'It's simple. She killed herself. She wrote a note and then she did it.' His voice cracked, but his eyes stayed hard. 'She went to a place where I couldn't save her again.'

I said, 'I'm guessing the killer used a big knife, though it could have been a hatchet. The skin looks sliced. The bone—'

'Don't.' His voice cracked again.

'The bone looks butchered, not broken.'

Then the hard-eyed man was crying. Tears

streaked his face, and his chest heaved, though he remained in the chair as if it held him from an abyss. I let him cry. He cried for a long time. When he finished, he wiped his cheek with the back of his hand and said, 'I don't know what you want.'

'To tell the truth, I don't either.' That wasn't quite true. I wanted to make sense of a death – for Lillian, but more for me – in ways I hadn't been able to do below deck on the hospital ship on the Arabian Sea.

'Why are you here, then?'

I shrugged. 'To try to put the pieces together?'

'What if the pieces don't go together?' he said.

'Then we try to make sense of whatever is there.'

'Look,' he said, 'Sheneel left a note. She killed herself. That's all.'

'If you saw what I saw, you wouldn't believe that.'

He shook his head. 'If you saw what I've seen for the last two years, you would.'

I thought about that. 'Did she write notes the other times?'

'The first two times she did, but not the third.'

'They sounded like this note?'

'Almost exactly.'

I thought some more. 'I don't know,' I said.

'I don't either.'

'Tell me about the string she was wearing around her head.'

'Huh?'

'When she died, she was wearing a black string. I've seen the pictures. She'd tied some leaves to her forehead.'

'Indian shot,' he said.

'Right. The detective I talked to said the leaves are Gullah medicine. What's that about?'

'Our uncle gave them to her. Papa Crowe.'

She'd mentioned him in the note I'd read. 'So, she's feeling suicidal and your uncle tells her to wrap leaves on her head?'

'He also made them into tea. It helped before.'

I saw no reason to argue. 'She had a snake tattoo. What was that?'

'You looked her over close.' He insinuated something dirty.

'A little snake, biting its own tail.'

'Papa Crowe gave that to her too. That was between him and her.'

'Could I meet him?'

He almost smiled. 'I don't think so. Most people don't like him.'

'Take me to see him,' I said.

His smile spread. 'He's got a rifle.'

'I don't mind rifles.'

Alex Greene directed me through the side streets to the main road leading north to the end of the island. We drove past a refinery for the Rayonier Pulp and Cellulose Mill, through a residential neighborhood, along a park, past a bigger refinery, and on to a narrow strip of land with the old Bosquebello Cemetery on one side and the broad Fernandina marsh inlet on the other. He pointed at a half-painted wooden house that backed into the marsh inlet. 'There,' he said.

I pulled on to the shoulder and turned off the car, and we got out.

63

An old man sat on a folding lawn chair on the front porch of the house. As we walked past a ragged little flower garden and across the mix of sand, broken oyster shells, and weeds that served as the front lawn, I recognized him. When Percy and I had come through the woods on Little Marsh Island, he'd been scratching a picture of a snake on to the soil. He still wore the blue pants and sun-bleached red T-shirt.

He ignored us, staring instead at a branch of an oak tree that shaded one side of the house. A hawk, its wings tucked tight to its body as if against a cold wind, was perched at the end of the branch. Then the old man nodded as if in silent communication with the bird, and it dropped from the branch, opened its wings, circled up over the house, and disappeared over the marsh.

The man turned his eyes to Sheneel Greene's brother. 'Alex boy,' he said, grinning, and then, his grin dropping, looked at me, 'and dog man.'

Alex Greene stopped short of the porch. 'This man wants to talk to you about Sheneel.'

'I know he does,' said the man. 'We old friends since this morning.'

'I'm sorry to bother you,' I said.

'No, you ain't.' But then, 'Come up and sit down, unless you like to stand in the heat.'

I took a chair that matched his, and Alex Greene sat on the porch floor, his back against the wall of the house. Flies buzzed around us but mostly left us alone.

The man asked, 'Why you want to know about Sheneel?'

I gave him the same story I'd given Sheneel's

brother, about Lillian being Sheneel's teacher and about my job doing skip trace.

He said, 'That tell me who you are but not why you want to know about Sheneel.'

I considered my words. 'She seemed to be hurting,' I said.

He shrugged. 'World's full of hurt.'

'A special kind of hurt. A kind I think I understand.'

He looked at me close. 'Fair enough,' he said. 'What you want to know?'

I told him about Percy bringing Sheneel's arm to me on Little Marsh Island, the sharp incision in the skin, the clean-cut bone, and the reluctance of the police to see the death as anything other than a suicide.

If the news unsettled him, he didn't show it. He said, 'Why you want it to be something else?'

'I don't. It just is.'

'Then what you need me for?'

'Tell me why you scratched the picture of the snake in the ground on Little Marsh Island.'

'It the same as the tattoo I give to Sheneel.'

'I know that. Why?'

'Something a man like you won't understand.'

'Try me.'

He looked at my eyes as if he was plumbing under them. I wanted to turn away, but I stared back. If he liked the dark behind my stare, he could have it. 'What the hell,' he said. He leaned forward in his chair, and the sunlight caught in the perspiration on his forehead. 'That snake is *Aido-Wedo*. He a god, you know. He live out on the line where the ocean meet the sky. That *his* line. It circle the whole world and bite itself in the tail. You understand?'

'Maybe,' I said, though I worried what kind of kook I was talking to.

'Sure, I think you do,' he said, and he kept his eyes on mine. 'Long ago, about two hundred year, this king – he Ebo, from Benin, Africa, you know, and he is proud – he worship Aido-Wedo, and he have a tattoo like the one I give to Sheneel. Well, an English ship come to Africa and take the king and his family to be slaves, and a man up St Simons way say he want to buy them. But this king, he proud and he don't want to be no slave.'

The old man paused. 'I think you see what coming, don't you?'

I didn't.

He said, 'Wait a minute,' and he pushed himself out of the chair, went inside through the screen door, and returned with a black string and a glass vial of dried leaves that looked like crushed oregano. He laid the vial on a wooden table by his chair. He stepped off the porch and into the garden, selected a leaf from one of the flowering plants, and tore it from the stem. He came back and folded the fresh leaf into a little envelope. He tilted the glass vial toward the envelope, licked the top of the leaf, laid the black string across it, and pasted the envelope flap across the string and back on to the leaf. He blew on the seal to dry it and set the thing aside on the table.

He looked at me again. 'Now, where was we?'

I said, 'A family on St Simons Island wanted to buy the king with the snake tattoo.'

'That right. The trader send the king and his family to St Simons and the ship go to a dock in Dunbar Creek. But this king who don't want to be no slave, he look out the mouth of the creek to the horizon line, and he sing. "Ocean bring me here, and ocean bring me home." His wives and children sing it too. "Ocean bring me here, and ocean bring me home." Then the king step off the dock into the deep water, and one after other, chained together like they is, they step into the deep water after him. They drown to the last little girl.'

He looked me in the eyes. 'You understand?'

'No,' I said.

He shook his head. 'Milk ain't dry off your mouth yet, no?' Alex Greene laughed, and the old man said, 'I give Sheneel that tattoo after the first time she try to kill herself, and I tell her, sometimes there's worse things than you die.'

'You said this to Sheneel?'

'Sure.'

I shook my head.

He said, 'You wrong if you pretend you don't believe it. You know it the truth. Man like you, maybe you never know a time like the king know. But he a brave man that step off the dock.'

'I understand. But I don't see how telling that to a girl like Sheneel would help.'

'Maybe Sheneel understand that kind of bravery too.'

'I don't see how.'

'No, you wouldn't.' He turned his eyes back

67

to the oak tree he'd been watching when Sheneel's brother and I arrived. 'Well, look at that.'

The hawk had returned to the branch with a finger mullet in its beak.

I said, 'What if Sheneel didn't kill herself? What if someone else did it?'

The man kept watching the bird. 'We work that out too, if that what it come to.' Sweat beaded on his forehead. His tight gray hair glistened in the heat. Flies buzzed in the air over him. He seemed at peace.

I stood and nodded to Sheneel's brother. 'Let's go, if you want a ride back.'

'Wait a minute,' the old man said. He handed me the black string with the leaf packet. 'You need this, dog man. Wear it around your head till it turn black with sweat and mold, and you feel better then.'

'Indian shot?'

'That right.'

'What makes it work?'

'Not so much what in it. More about what it take out of you.'

I had nothing to say to that, so I offered my hand to shake.

'No, sir. I never shake the hand of a man like you. I learned that lesson long ago.'

'What kind of man am I?'

He fixed his gaze back on the oak branch, where the hawk had finished its meal. 'You got death in your eyes.'

Sheneel's brother and I were quiet as I drove back to his house. He leaned against the passenger door as if he wanted distance between us. The sun gleamed through the windshield and the air conditioner couldn't knock down the heat. On the roadside, wild grape vines and kudzu clung to the trunks of oaks, hollies, and sparkleberry trees as if they wanted to pull them down into the dirty sand. The houses we passed were tiny and looked shut into themselves, their owners wishing to stay far from the living world.

Just after we passed the Rayonier refinery, I jerked the wheel to the side and steered on to the shoulder. Sheneel's brother looked at me, startled.

I said, 'When did Sheneel write the note?'

'What do you mean?'

'You said, the first two times she tried to kill herself she wrote notes. Did the police take them?'

He nodded.

'How about the third time?'

'I told you, she didn't write a note.'

'That makes no sense. Why would she write a note the first two times and again this time but not the third?'

'I don't know.'

'Sure you do. She wrote a note the third time and you took it and kept it. You didn't call the hospital, so the police wouldn't have it. Then, when she died, you went home and "found" the note from last time – because there was no note this time. She didn't kill herself, so there wouldn't be one.'

'You're crazy,' he said.

'I've heard that enough times to believe it, but that doesn't change what happened here.'

'Why would I do that?'

'I can think of only two reasons. One, you killed her or helped kill her and want to cover for yourself. Or, two, you're scared of whoever did it.'

'I would never hurt her.'

'Which leaves that you're scared.'

He seemed to fight to regain the hardness he'd shown when I first arrived at his house. 'No one scares me.'

'Me, personally, I'm scared most of the time,' I said. 'A lot of people scare me.'

He looked bewildered. 'Take me home.'

We drove the rest of the way without talking. When he got out, he slammed the car door, walked to the house, went in, and slammed the front door too.

As I drove back toward the highway, I called Lillian. I reached her as she was walking from her campus office to her car. She said, 'What are you doing?'

'I'm hungry,' I said.

'Let's get dinner out again,' she said. Then, 'Did you talk with anyone at VA counseling?'

I said, 'I just walked out of a session.'

'They tell you anything helpful?'

I thought about keeping up the lie. Instead, I said, 'They told me that a clean wound like the one on Sheneel Greene's arm must have been made by a blade. A big knife. A hatchet. Maybe a cleaver.'

70

Nine

Lillian

Johnny fell asleep before I did for the first time since he'd been back. I put down my book and watched him – a marvel of tangled hair and deep breath. Sweat sparkled on the skin above his lips, and I wanted to touch it away with my finger or kiss him and taste his salt, but I turned off the lamp and, in the blue dark, moved close to his warmth and strength. I thought of how the body works and does not work, like falling from a tree, like chutes of gravity.

I dreamed, as I often did, of music. Nothing that I could see: only sound, a song I'd heard on the radio as I'd driven home from teaching. The words swayed, as liquid in my mind as an ocean pool. Other words supplanted them, new words that sparked as bright as sun on water, and they poured into a buoyant, comforting wash of sound.

Then Johnny screamed like a man whose skin has caught fire – the whole skin, feet to ears: a last scream, before pain grows so great that the throat no longer can make sound. Still ripping from sleep, I turned on the lamp. Johnny was sitting against the headboard, knees to chest, his hair and his T-shirt darkened with sweat, his eyes wide with fear.

'What did you dream?' I asked.

71

He shook his head.

'Tell me. Talking will help kill it.'

'No.' His body shuddered.

'Try?'

'No.' He stared into the air or into himself – somewhere, but not at me.

I got out of bed and brought him a towel and a dry T-shirt. I stripped the sweat-soaked shirt from his body and caressed him with the towel as if he was a child. I pulled the damp sheet from the bed and brought a blanket from the closet. He wrapped it around himself and I turned off the lamp. For an hour or more, we lay awake in the dark, saying nothing, Johnny breathing raggedly, then deep and long, and, finally, even and steady as if the nightmare that had shocked us awake never happened. I kissed his shoulder. He was asleep.

But his terror had put me on edge. After lying in bed for another half-hour, I got up, went through the kitchen to the sunroom, and turned on my laptop. Percy followed me and curled up on the cool tile near my feet. Outside the window, a quarter-moon was lowering through the branches of an oak tree. An animal moved at the edge of the yard – a neighbor's cat, maybe a raccoon. I played a game of computer solitaire and then another, but I knew why I had come. Johnny had all but kicked me out of bed and sent me to do it.

I made a Google search for *Gullah* and *snake*. The search tallied 588,000 hits, the first sites dealing with Gullah cooking, a Gullah tradition of telling animal fables, and Gullah root doctors who use natural and African medicines to treat snakebites. A Yale University site devoted to the Sierra Leonean background of Gullah retold trickster stories involving a Brer Snake. 'You knew I was a snake before you put me in there,' said Brer Snake to a possum who had been dumb enough to put him in its marsupial pocket. The website never mentioned the Ouroboros symbol that Sheneel Greene had tattooed on to her arm, but it said, 'The Gullah believe in dangerous spirits capable of enslaving a person by controlling his will. They sometimes paper the walls of their houses with newsprint or put a folded bit of newspaper inside a shoe, believing that the spirit must first read every word before taking action.' While eating dinner, Johnny had told me about the little yellow house where Sheneel lived and its newspapered front window.

A site on Gullah cuisine recommended stirring snake livers and fish eyeballs into dirty rice.

Another link led to an electronic edition of a book called *Gullah Culture in America*. It told the Aido-Wedo snake story. It also described *root* medicine – mashed okra flowers for snakebites, rags soaked in hot cotton-root tea for a sore back, sweetgrass bindings for broken bones. The Gullah seemed to trust their own ways more than western medicine. According to one story, a Gullah boy told his family he had snakes in his head, and a white doctor said he suffered from ringworm. The antifungal cream he prescribed did nothing but make the boy's hair greasy, and every night the boy would scream about the snakes, until one morning his mother saw a snake outside the window. She killed it with a stove shovel, and that same day the boy said the snakes were gone and they never came back. According to another story, if you saw a black snake coiling around a root, that was a *fever root*. If you crushed it and applied it to the chest in a poultice, it would draw out even the worst fever.

A noise came from the kitchen – footsteps, the refrigerator opening – and I knew Johnny had gotten up. Percy lifted his head from the floor, set it down again, and slept. 'Hey,' I called into the kitchen.

But Johnny said nothing. I typed the words *Fernandina* and *Greene* into Google and got almost 600 hits. A lot of *Greenes* lived in the town – a lawyer, two realtors, the owner of a corrugated paper products company, a man involved in lighthouse preservation, others. When I scrolled down, I found a site that promised *Greene Family History*. It consisted of short auto-biographical stories written by family members as a gift to celebrate someone's eighty-fifth birthday, but it included nothing by Sheneel or her brother Alex. Someone who identified herself as Deborah Greene-Phelps wrote about her grand-mother Viola and her grandmother's younger sister, Louise.

Viola and Louise Greene moved to Fernandina in 1935 when their father, Nathaniel, the owner of a New England insurance company, decided that his daughters, aged seventeen and fifteen, were too much temptation for the young men they knew in New Jersey. Other members of the extended Greene family had lived on Amelia

Island for several generations. Nathaniel's Fernandina house, a rambling Victorian where the family had vacationed in the winter months, became the permanent residence for his wife and daughters, and he rode the Atlantic Coast Line train from Morristown once a month for a long weekend before returning to work.

According to Deborah Greene-Phelps, Viola and Louise found as many chances to tempt and be tempted in their new house as they had found at the home they'd left.

On one of the long weekends, their father invited a dark-skinned man named Abraham Lincoln Lewis into the house and, after talking with him alone in his study, invited him to join the family for dinner. This was the old South, and such invitations were rarely made, but Nathaniel Greene remained a recalcitrant Northerner, and he delighted in scandalizing the neighbors. A.L. Lewis owned the Afro-American Life Insurance Company and, even richer than Viola and Louise's father, had started developing a piece of shoreline, which he'd named American Beach, to the south of Fernandina. Negroes whose families had moved north and climbed into the middle class could travel by rail, boat, or automobile to a place they could call their own.

Nathaniel Greene's daughters listened as Lewis described the hilarity that would occur each weekend night in the summer months and all week long in the winter travel season eight miles down the shore from their quiet household, though their father's stern glances let them know that he expected them to stay far away. An enlightened invitation to dinner was one thing, his fair-skinned daughters crossing the color line another.

The Greene family kept a black gardener named Axelrod, who also brought them buckets of oysters and who hummed when he worked, whether he was gardening or shucking. When the humming turned to singing, he sang in a language none of the Greene family understood. One morning, Viola heard Axelrod tell a meat deliveryman that Earl Hines's Grand Terrace Orchestra would play at the Rendezvous Nightclub in American Beach that coming Friday night with a young singer named Billy Eckstein whose voice could melt a girl's legs in her stockings.

Viola whispered the news to Louise at lunch, and, on Friday evening, saying that they would stroll on the beach, they walked two miles down the shoreline on Fletcher Drive, then rode the rest of the way to American Beach in a cotton farmer's Chevrolet that nearly ran over them in the dark before the farmer insisted they climb in with him.

The lights, the music and laughter, and the smell of the ocean, whiskey, and tobacco gave the girls everything they'd been missing since leaving New Jersey, and though they'd promised each other that they would start toward home at ten p.m., midnight passed with a bottle of champagne on their table. At two a.m., they were dancing with men who might've been lynched for eyeing a white woman in any other part of

Florida. During one drunken number, Axelrod stepped on to the stage and sang alongside Billy Eckstein whose voice, the sisters agreed, really could melt a girl's legs in her stockings. When Axelrod stepped off the stage, he cut in on the man who was dancing with Louise, and the daughter of the insurance man and the family gardener stayed on the floor, fast dance and slow, until Viola tugged on her sister's dress. The morning sun would rise on their empty beds if they didn't get home soon.

They crept through the back door, exhausted and happy, shoes in their hands, a little after four o'clock in the morning, but they found their father in the parlor with three neighborhood men, all holding shotguns. He'd convinced the men that if the girls hadn't been murdered, they surely had been raped as they'd walked on the beach, and by the time the fact came out that they'd been drinking champagne of their own accord at American Beach, Nathaniel Greene felt so humiliated he was ready to board a train back to New Jersey, never to return.

A sound in the kitchen startled me and got Percy to his feet. Johnny had dropped something metal in the sink. I called to him, 'Are you all right?'

He grunted a sound that I took to mean he was fine, and I kept reading.

Viola stayed home after that wild night. She played the piano in the afternoons and sat at a card table with her mother and her mother's friends in the evenings, and though her physical beauty grew so that she became a favorite of the Fernandina bachelors, something seemed to wither inside her.

But Louise continued to sneak out, climbing down from her second-story window and riding to the Rendezvous in the front seat of Axelrod's pickup truck. The girls' parents never seemed to suspect, but Viola could smell the whiskey and tobacco smoke emanating from her sister's skin when Louise slipped into bed in the late hours of the night.

Two weeks after Christmas, Louise confided to Viola that she was pregnant.

Johnny came into the sunroom, wearing the T-shirt that I'd helped him into but naked from the waist down. My stomach dropped. His hands were bloody up to the wrists, and he carried a steak knife, the blade smeared and speckled with blood. He had pasted his tangle of hair to his scalp with water or maybe a bloody hand. His eyes were wild with panic.

I hardly got the words from my mouth. 'What are you—'

He seemed amazed by the obvious. 'I cut myself.'

'Why?'

He looked at his hands as if they were foreigners. 'I didn't mean to – an accident—'

'You cut *both* hands by accident?'

'I don't know.'

'What were you doing?'

'I don't know.'

I went to him.

He held the knife toward me and looked at me from the corners of his eyes. 'No.'

Percy barked and I stepped toward Johnny. 'Are you going to cut me?'

He stood still, and I realized that the idea had crossed his mind.

'Do what you're going to do,' I said.

He backed from the room.

I caught my breath and followed him into the kitchen. He was sitting at the table under the bright kitchen light. The bloody knife was on the counter by the sink.

I got two dishtowels from a cabinet and wrapped his bleeding hands. Tears had dampened his cheeks, but in the seconds between leaving the sunroom and my following him, he had stopped crying and his eyes were hard.

I put Percy in the backyard, led Johnny to our bedroom, found shorts and his sandals, and helped him into them. I took him outside and to the car. As we drove to the ER, he stared out the passenger window into the dark. We said nothing. I knew what to say but was afraid to say it – he had hurt himself, and he'd seemed ready to hurt me. He'd gone too far.

Johnny sat dumbly in a chair at Baptist Hospital Admissions as I explained what had happened. The intake nurse showed no surprise or evident interest, filling the forms on her computer with sleepy boredom. When we finished, she called for two male nurses who accompanied Johnny through swinging doors.

The intake nurse said, 'You understand that if your husband refuses to commit himself voluntarily, we'll need the police to sign for an involuntary admission.'

'I understand,' I said.

'You want me to call?'

'I don't think he meant to hurt himself.'

Looking more inconvenienced than angry, she picked up the phone.

'Wait.' I pulled out my cell phone. 'My brother's a cop. It'll be easier on Johnny.'

An hour and a half later, after Daniel had signed and dated the forms, a thin-haired doctor in green scrubs came to the waiting room and called my name. In a dimly lighted office, he said, 'Your husband claims this was a mistake, though he can't explain how it happened. As I'm sure you know, mistakes like this don't happen. But he seems calm, and his thinking seems clear now. We can hold him for up to seventy-two hours, but after that the law says we need to cut him loose. He needs help. You understand that, don't you?'

'How bad are the cuts?'

'I don't think he meant to kill himself, just inflict some damage. Most of the wounds are shallow and none are on the wrists. We put twelve stitches in his left hand and bandaged his right.'

'Can I see him?'

His face hardened. 'We've sedated him. There's really nothing to see.'

'I want to see him anyway.'

He shook his head. 'I'm sorry. For the first twenty-four to seventy-two hours, patients are isolated. We'll take good care of him.'

'He'll be furious with me for this.'

'He may be. But I've been doing this for twenty-five years. You've done the right thing.'

A fern in a glazed pot stood on the carpet in the corner of the office. A white orchid stood on a black pebble display on a file cabinet. The antiseptic smell of the waiting room and the hospital corridors seemed far away. I said, 'I need to get out of here.'

Outside the hospital, the morning sun stung my eyes. A seagull shot through the sky toward the river as if something terrible and invisible was chasing it.

I didn't want to go home. I didn't want to see the drying blood on the sunroom floor. I didn't want to see the steak knife on the kitchen counter. If the hospital needed to reach me, they had my cell number. Percy would be fine for a few hours in the backyard.

I got on the highway heading north over the Fuller Warren Bridge. When traffic unbottled on the other side, I drove toward Fernandina, stopped for coffee and breakfast, and, at ten a.m., walked into the Amelia Island Museum of History. The man who charged admission and ran the gift shop directed me to a volunteer docent named Phyllis Chin, a graying Chinese woman in pearls and a black-and-white paisley blouse. She offered to show me through the museum library and archives but said she knew the records as well as anyone.

'What do you know about the Greene family?' I asked.

Her face lit up. 'Controversial.'

81

She told me about them. As I already knew, Nathaniel Greene and his family vacationed and then lived in Fernandina since the early years of the twentieth century, but so did Nathaniel's two brothers, and before them their parents and grandparents. They had expanded their hold on the sandy soil and town governance ever since Nathaniel's grandfather, at age eighteen, served on one of the Union gunboats that chased the last of the Confederate troops from the fort at the north end of Amelia Island.

Nearly eighty years after that soldier sank his feet into the local soil, Viola Greene, having renounced the wild behavior that took her to hear Billy Eckstein sing at the Rendezvous, married Jonathan Phelps of the Phelps Paper Corporation family, merging money with money and a generally respected name with ruthless power. The Phelpses had grabbed hundreds of square miles of timberland throughout the Southeast, wresting tracts from families that had squatted on and sometimes owned outright the land for three or more generations. According to the local joke in Fernandina, when the fumes from the pulp mills got so bad that people had to close the doors and windows even in the worst summer heat, the Phelpses were printing money.

Meantime, Louise fell as far as Viola climbed. She left Nathaniel Greene's house – or he kicked her out – and she moved in with Axelrod, whose last name, from the time his grandfathers were slaves, was Jenkins, though he mostly went by the name Crowe. Nathaniel had run Axelrod off of his property upon first suspecting a relationship between him and his younger daughter. Then, during World War II, the ex-gardener made money pounding sheet metal at the Merrill-Stevens Shipyard and, after the war, raking for oysters on one of the barrier islands where he and Louise lived in a cottage and had nine or ten children, some said as many as twelve.

I asked the docent, 'Did Sheneel and Alex Greene come from Nathaniel's family line or one of his brothers'?'

She went to a computer and opened a database. After a few minutes, she said, 'Sheneel is a direct descendant of Viola Greene-Phelps – Viola's great-granddaughter, Nathaniel's great-great-granddaughter.' She searched again. 'Alex is Sheneel's half-brother. They share a mother, Laura Greene, Viola's granddaughter – I don't know how she got back to being a Greene instead of a Phelps.' She read further and laughed. 'This is why I love this stuff. The Greene family is very messy. Alex also has blood from Louise Greene's side. His mother, Laura Greene, is a descendant of Viola, but his father a descendant of one of Axelrod's brothers.' The docent seemed pleased. 'Come on, I'll show you.'

She crossed the library to a cabinet of map drawers, found a chart of the southern coast of Georgia – from the Florida state line to Savannah – and spread it on a desk. Running her finger to the north from the state border, she said, 'A hundred years ago, this area, from the shore inland to the towns of Woodbine and White Oak, was mostly forest, and Axelrod's extended family, all black, lived there, or that's what the stories say. Supposedly, they owned it, but – again supposedly – they had no deeds to it. The Phelps family wanted the timber, and, around the time that Viola married Jonathan Phelps, the company went in with saws and trucks.' The docent smiled. 'It was basically robbery.'

'How did Louise and Viola get along after that?' I asked.

'They both lived into their eighties, and the stories say they never talked again. But they had other reasons to be mad at each other, and these things usually are more complicated than they look from outside. Alex Greene, with blood from both the black Greenes and the white Phelpses, is evidence that other parts of their families got over their anger.' Again she smiled, as if inviting me to share the pleasure she felt in the disorder of human relations.

At eleven-thirty, I drove across town to the little yellow house where Johnny had said he'd talked with Sheneel's brother. A red motor scooter leaned against a dying palm tree in the front yard. Inside the front porch, as Johnny had said, newspapers covered the front windows, blocking the sunlight or warding off evil. I got out of the car to see more clearly. No birds sang. No traffic passed. In the distance, smoke rose from a mill smokestack. I walked across the sandy lawn and knocked on the porch door. When no one answered, I stepped into the porch and knocked on the door to the house.

No answer.

But as I started to leave, a man's voice spoke from the other side of the door. 'What?'

I said, 'My name's Lillian Turner. I was one of Sheneel's teachers. You talked to my husband yesterday.'

Nothing.

'Would you open the door?'

Again, nothing.

I said, 'My husband is in the hospital.'

The lock clicked, and Alex Greene opened the door. 'Why?'

The house behind him was dark. He wore black shorts and a baggy white T-shirt with a single word scrawled on it in black marker – *Ngafa*.

'I don't know why. He hurt himself. He meant to.'

His face was blank. 'I'm sorry.'

'Do I get to come in?'

The house inside was hot and smelled of his sweat. He cleared a blanket from a couch and let me sit. I said, 'Sheneel was a good person. She was . . .' *Like a wren*, I thought. 'I miss her.'

'I know,' he said.

'I need to understand.'

He let that hang in the air. My presence in the house and my selfish needs were unfair to him and hurtful. I should have apologized for coming and left him alone. Instead, I nodded at his T-shirt and said, 'Ngafa?'

'You came here to talk about my shirt?'

'That's Sheneel's word. It means *bad spirit*?'

'No,' he said. 'It means *hidden devil*.'

'Sheneel told me—'

'Doesn't matter what she told you.'

'It's Gullah?'

'Gullah, Geechee, Mende. Yeah.' He was holding in his anger. 'Why are you here?'

'I need to know,' I said.

'What's to know?'

I said, 'The police arrested her last summer.'

He looked surprised but smiled. 'She was partying and got a little crazy.'

'In what way crazy?'

Still smiling. 'She had a blade.'

'Did she cut herself?'

'Someone else. It wasn't bad. Band-Aids.'

'Who?'

'Why do you care?'

'I just do.'

'A friend who had it coming.'

'And this friend called the police?'

He shook his head. 'I did.'

'Why? If the friend had it coming.'

He stared hard. 'Because she would have killed him if I hadn't called.'

'I see,' I said, though I didn't. The living room was barely furnished. 'I read the report. It said she bonded out of jail the next morning for ten thousand dollars. Where'd she get the money?'

'We have family here. They helped.'

'But not Sheneel's mom and dad.'

'Our mom is in New Mexico. For the last two years.'

'What about her dad?'

His smile disappeared. 'He doesn't matter.'

'Does he live around here?'

He just stared.

'What happened to the charges?'

'The police dropped them. Our friend decided not to testify.'

'That was friendly.'

'Not very.' He gave me a wooden look. My questions had seemed to penetrate only his outer skin. I had no business being here and asking about Sheneel's personal life. If I was unable to stay away, that was my problem, not his.

I stood. 'I'm sorry for your loss,' I said – empty words. My sorrow would do him no more good than my inconsiderate questions.

He watched me walk to the door, but before I could step outside, he spoke. 'You're pretty. Like Sheneel said.'

Sweat broke on my arms. 'I want to give you something,' I said. 'Do you have a pen and paper?'

He went to the kitchen and came back with a marker and notepad. I wrote:

> *You saturated Sight,*
> *And I had no more Eyes*
> *For sordid excellence.*

I tore the sheet from the pad, folded it once, and gave it to him. 'It's from a poem that I never taught to Sheneel but should have.'

I drove home. I fed Percy. I scrubbed the sunroom floor and the kitchen counter. I cleaned blood from the steak knife, thinking I would put it back in the knife drawer, but instead wrapped it in newspaper and carried it outside to the garbage. I called the hospital to check on Johnny, but the nurse would tell me nothing. I repositioned the lawn chair in the backyard and tried to read a stack of student essays, but I couldn't concentrate. When the phone rang, I ran to it, though I expected no news from anyone.

Daniel was on the line. 'How's Johnny?' he asked.

'I don't know. They isolate patients at first.'

'When you see him, tell him I'm pulling for him.'

'Thanks, Daniel.'

'You're my little sister. You'd expect something else?'

Ten

Stephen Phelps

Bastard on the line, Christina said. No, she wouldn't. 'Alex Greene on the line,' she said, as if he deserved the respect – and *that's* why I paid her: to sit politely outside my office with her knees pressed together under her neat little desk.

'Put the bastard through,' I said.

Voice shaking, he told me about the visit. First the husband, now the wife. I knew what to do with a wife. Kitchen counter, bed, or hood of her car. I could take care of that. But the husband? A war vet? Probably armed and, if Alex Greene knew what he was talking about, definitely crazy. Hard to persuade such a man.

'What did you tell her?' I asked Alex.

'Nothing. I had nothing to say.'

'That's right.'

'I don't like this.'

'Who asked you to?'

'I don't like—'

'Your voice is shaking, Alex.'

'What am I supposed to do now?'

'You're a good kid,' I said. 'Don't mess it up.'

'I'm not a kid.' As if I'd called him *boy*.

'Don't mess it up.'

He breathed heavily. He could become a problem. He said, 'She gave me a poem for Sheneel.'

'Cheaper than flowers.'

'A love poem. I think she was in love with her.'

'Did she say so?'

'The poem did. I could see it in her.'

'You're smart, Alex. Smarter than her. Smarter than her husband. Stay calm. Stay cool.'

'And if I don't?'

'You will.' I said it neither reassuringly nor threateningly and let him make of it what he would.

Eleven

Johnny

I waited in my room in the Behavioral Health ward as Lillian filled my prescriptions from the hospital pharmacy. The doctors wouldn't discharge

89

me until I rattled the pill bottles under their noses. Without medication, I would be a danger to myself and others, they said. 'Fine,' I said. 'Fill 'er up,' and they stared at me with worried eyes.

I'd told them I had no wish to kill myself.

I'd told them I had no wish to harm others.

On the tests they'd given me, I'd done the psychological equivalent of walking the dotted line, heel-to-toe, and touching my finger to my nose, and they had no reason to hold me beyond a twenty-four-hour evaluation.

When the first doctor asked me what happened with the knife and my hands, I said, 'The world's rotten. We kill each other. Even if we don't, we'll all die anyway. The world is bloody and nothing turns out well.'

We were sitting in his office, him at a desk, me on an overstuffed chair big enough to swallow a man. The doctor chewed the end of his pen. 'What about all the good things people do? What about people who love each other? What about your wife?'

'They'll die too.'

'You must be a hell of a lot of fun at a party.'

I laughed, and the doctor said laughing was healthy.

I did better with the second doctor. 'I took an Ambien before bed,' I said. 'I got up – half awake, half asleep, whatever you call it when you're drugged and you're only partly aware of what you're doing – and I must have been hungry, because I went to the fridge – or I think I did. I don't know what happened with the knife. Maybe I thought I was making a sandwich.'

The doctor nodded, scribbled notes on his pad, and said, 'What about all you said to Dr Patel?'

'It's true,' I said. 'We die. Sooner or later. And I've seen a lot of bad stuff. But it's no reason to cut myself.'

That evening, they fed us at six, lights went out at nine, and during the night my roommate, a big man with tiny ears, howled until two nurses came with a syringe. There was music in the sounds the man made, the music of the world before we started fooling ourselves into believing in happy endings – paradise, heaven, glory, whatever religious or secular peace we imagine for ourselves at the end. I wanted to howl too, but I clutched my belly and held the roaring in.

In the morning, a third doctor said the hospital would release me if I filled my prescriptions and scheduled a follow-up appointment. 'Show me where to sign,' I said.

When they let Lillian into the room, the bag of meds in one of her hands and a folder of release papers in the other, she hung close to the door.

'Hey,' I said.

'Hey. Are you mad at me?'

'For what?'

'Putting you here.'

'I would have done the same if it had been you. Not that it would've been.'

'I was scared,' she said.

'I know.'

'How are you feeling?'

I tried cheery. 'Ready to go.'

The nurses insisted on wheeling me to the exit in a wheelchair, and Lillian brought around the car. Overnight, the weather had cooled, and thin clouds lined the horizon. I breathed deep.

As we drove from the hospital, I unwrapped the gauze from my right hand. Lillian glanced at me. 'What are you doing?'

I stuffed the blood-caked cotton into the pocket on the side of the door. 'I'll leave the bandage on my left hand, but this one is overkill.' I took a Kleenex from the glove compartment and wiped the brown ointment from the cut. The skin had pinked and swelled, but I'd gone through only a few layers and the bleeding had stopped.

Lillian turned toward the highway and, as if to avoid talking about what worried her most, told me about a call from her brother, a visit she'd made to Fernandina, records she'd looked at in the museum, and a talk she'd had with Alex Greene. But she sounded uninterested in her own stories, and finally she asked the same question she'd asked when I'd come into the sunroom in the middle of the night and that the doctors had asked after her. 'Why did you do this to yourself?'

'Do you really want to know?'

She kept the car in the slow lane. 'I think so.'

'I woke up,' I said, 'and I felt as if I was crawling inside my skin. My body felt like a strange casing, something an insect or a snake would grow and then shed, and if I didn't escape

92

it, it would poison and suffocate me. It was terrible. I needed out.'

Then we rode in silence. The traffic had thickened as we'd come into the city and approached the bridge, but outbound we ran free.

She put her hand on my knee and drove, but when we left the highway and stopped at a red light, I rooted through the pharmacy bag to see what was inside. There were three vials. I pulled out the Xanax, unscrewed the lid, rolled down the window, and poured the pills on to the pavement. Lillian grabbed the bag with the other vials and stuffed it between the driver's seat and her door. 'What the hell are you doing?'

'I hate this stuff.'

'You need to take it. It'll keep you sane.'

'Not me.'

'I'm going to take you back to the hospital.'

'I wouldn't forgive you for that.'

'Christ, Johnny. You can't do this.'

I shook my head. 'It's the only way I can do it.'

She dropped me off at home. She'd canceled her first class so that she could pick me up, and she was running late for the second. I let Percy in from the yard, and he sniffed at me as if I carried a new scent of danger. So I showered and changed, ate breakfast, put him back in the yard, and went out to my car.

When I pulled into the parking lot outside my office, a woman was sleeping against the glass door. She wore a short red skirt, a black sweatshirt, and yellow high heels. Felicity, the old prostitute. Since I'd last seen her, she'd dyed her hair a shade between pink and henna, a dirty color that made her black face look gray in the morning light.

I went to her and prodded a bare thigh with my shoe.

She grunted.

I prodded again. 'Get up. You're blocking my door.'

She opened her eyes, seemed to bring me into focus, and gave me what might have passed for a sexy smile a generation ago. 'Give me a cigarette,' she said.

'I don't smoke,' I said.

'The hell you don't.'

'Come on, get up. I'll buy you breakfast.'

'I want a smoke.'

'You've got to eat.'

'Don't see why.' But she pushed herself to her feet.

I walked her down to the Sahara Sandwiches Shop and asked Farouk to make her an egg and sausage wrap. When Farouk set the plate on the counter and filled her cup with hot coffee, I paid the bill and left them there, though she called after me as I went out the door, 'Next time, I want a cigarette.'

I unlocked the door to my rental and let myself in. Whenever I returned to the office after being away for a couple of days, the air inside smelled as skunky as new rubber, though the tire store that once occupied the building had moved out long before I moved in. I went to my desk. The answering machine said I'd received two calls the previous afternoon, both from the same number, but the caller had left no messages. I turned on my computer and, while it was booting up, phoned the number. After two rings, a recorded message answered. A girl's voice said she wasn't there, but if I would leave a message she would call back. I hung up, typed the number into the reverse number database, and hit search. The record that popped on to the screen said the phone was owned by Sprint Spectrum and registered to a Sheneel Greene of Fernandina Beach, Florida.

'What the hell?' I said to the computer.

Then I figured Alex Greene must have the phone. If the police had it, why would they call me? If the person who killed and dismembered Sheneel had it, why call me?

But why would Alex Greene call me on his dead sister's phone? I had nothing better to do than to go ask him. Besides, fresh off a suicide watch, I knew that sitting alone all day at my desk might tip me in directions I needed to avoid.

Still, before I left, it couldn't hurt to peek.

I slid open the top drawer, and my stomach dropped. Except for a green oilcloth rag, it was empty. I grabbed the phone and dialed.

I caught Lillian between classes. 'My gun,' I said when she picked up.

Her voice was calm. 'I took it.'

Hot anger filled me. 'Don't do this,' I said.

Lillian asked, 'What do you need it for?'

'My job.'

'What job?' She said it gently. 'You don't have a job. What have you done?'

I hung up, shoved back from the desk, and left my office.

The road north to Fernandina, with the white concrete reflecting the sunlight, burned in my burning eyes. My right hand gripped the steering wheel. My left hand, swollen and bandaged, throbbed in my lap. The bank of clouds that had hung at the horizon when I'd left the hospital had crept toward the sun, but I would have bet my life, whatever it was worth, on the sun annihilating the clouds before they could bring shade. So I held tight, accelerated, and a half-hour later stopped in front of the yellow house on Gum Street.

As I stepped into the front porch, Alex Greene opened the front door. 'What?' he said. His eyes were hard, angry.

'You don't work?'

'Not right now. They don't lock you up in the hospital?'

'Who said I was in the hospital?'

He nodded at my bandaged hand and said, 'Your wife told me.'

'She shouldn't have done that.'

'She shouldn't have come here. You either.' He stood in the open doorway, filling as much of it as he could with his skinny body, as though worried that I would push past him into the living room.

I said, 'Why did you call me yesterday?'

'What are you talking about?'

'On Sheneel's phone. Twice. Once around three. Again a little before five.'

96

'I didn't call, and I don't have Sheneel's phone.'
I looked at him close. 'Who does?'

'I don't know. I haven't seen it.'

'Why would someone use it to call me?'

He looked at me as if he was trying to figure me out. 'You know, your wife gave me a love poem for Sheneel.'

I shrugged. 'My wife likes poetry.'

'It said something like *I have no eyes for anyone else*. I gave it to the police.'

'I'm sure the police will like it, those that like poetry.' He smirked, so I asked, 'Who told you to pretend your sister killed herself?'

'What?'

'Who told you to use the old suicide note? It's got to be someone who already knew you had it, someone you trusted enough to tell.'

I'd surprised him. He said, 'No one told me anything. I *found* it on her bed, like I told you before.'

'Right. Why do you cover your windows with newspapers? What are you keeping out?'

Again, he looked surprised, though I couldn't have been the first to ask him about the papers. 'I'm keeping out people like you,' he said. 'You've got craziness all over you. I don't want it in the house.' He stepped back and slammed the door.

I moved close and spoke through the wood. 'It'll take something thicker than paper and words to keep out the craziness. Sheneel knew that. I know it. You do too.'

I drove back toward the highway. As I'd expected, the clouds were gone from the sky, and the sunlight glinted off the back of an empty Phelps Paper Company log truck that I followed out Buccaneer Trail. The truck belched black diesel smoke as the driver shifted gears – something thicker than paper and words. According to Lillian, Sheneel and Alex Greene were members of the Phelps family, though their little, half-furnished house suggested they had no access to the paper company bank accounts. Now, if Alex Greene was telling the truth, Lillian had given Sheneel the words to a love poem. What the hell was that? But even if Lillian had given her a whole book, Sheneel had no words anymore. She was silent and would remain forever silent. Her own words on the suicide note were nonsense, describing a different reality from the one that her cut flesh described.

What about the snake hieroglyph inked on to the skin of her arm? It kept talking even though Sheneel's killer had cut it from the rest of her body. But it spoke in a language I didn't understand.

The log truck shifted gears again and belched more smoke. Splinters of slash pine clung to the metal fittings on the truck bed. Behind us in Fernandina, the Phelps Paper mill fed sweet-filtered fumes into the sky, and they settled to the ground like dew in the morning or hung in the air all day.

I dropped back from the truck, pulled into a Shell station, and bought a tourist map of Fernandina Beach and Amelia Island. I spread the map on the hood of the car, and, as I traced its streets and businesses, I called Lillian and left a message on her answering machine. 'I have three questions,' I said. 'First, why are you giving love poems to Sheneel Greene? Second, why did you tell Alex Greene I was in the hospital? You're starting to worry me, Lillian.'

Instead of continuing, I hung up, but as I got into the car, she called back. 'That was two questions,' she said. 'What was the third?'

'This morning you started telling me about a connection between Sheneel Greene and the Phelps Paper Company. What was that about?'

She told me again about Viola Greene marrying Jonathan Phelps in the 1930s, the Phelps land grab in South Georgia, and Sheneel's mother being part of the Phelps family – the granddaughter of Viola and Jonathan – though she'd changed her name back to Greene.

'Thanks,' I said. 'You want to answer the other questions?'

'No,' she said. 'Not right now.'

'Be careful,' I said.

'What do you mean?'

'I mean there are a lot of different kinds of edges to fall over. Some are more visible than others. But you get hurt just as bad with the invisible ones.'

'I don't know what you're talking about.'

I drove back into Fernandina and followed the map to the north side of downtown. The Phelps Paper Company headquarters stood on a heavily fenced tract of shoreline, the kind of property usually staked out for million-dollar vacation houses. Two factory buildings, painted bright white, stood between a collection of white silos and elevated conveyor belts that were supported by white derrick frames. A single smokestack piped white smoke into the blue sky. A line of railroad tracks cut into the southern end of the compound, a string of empty hopper cars standing idle in the sun.

I pulled my car up to the booth at the gate and talked with a Hispanic woman wearing a blue blazer over a yellow blouse. Yes, she said, the Phelpses had offices at the site – both Edward Phelps, who owned the company, and his son Stephen, who handled Southeastern regional timber acquisitions. No, I couldn't talk with either of them without an appointment.

'Would you call their offices and tell them this is a family matter?'

'You're family?'

'I have concerns they'll want to know about.'

'*Concerns*, huh?'

'That's right,' I said.

'I'm not going to make a fool of myself telling them a stranger out here has *concerns*.'

'You hear about the death of this girl, Sheneel Greene?'

'Sure, it's the talk of the town.'

'That's the concern,' I said.

'What do the Phelpses have to do with her?'

'Would you make the call?'

She gave me a long look. 'Which one do you want to talk to?'

'Try the son.'

She slid a glass window shut on the booth so I couldn't hear what she was saying. After a couple of minutes of talking, getting put on hold, and talking again, she hung up a phone and slid the window open. 'You must be bringing either very good news or very bad,' she said.

'He'll talk to me?'

She handed me a pass to put on the dashboard. 'Take this road a quarter-mile, turn at the second right, and park as close as you can to the glass doors on the two-story building. A man named Bob Peterson will meet you there.'

A minute later, Peterson, dressed in khakis and a blue blazer, waved me into a handicap parking spot. The inside of the building was cool and clean, and the air smelled like fresh-cut pine instead of the pulp and chemical stew outside. We walked past a reception desk, through a maze of hallways, to Stephen Phelps's office.

Phelps, a tall man, with the lankiness of a college basketball player, stood at a desk. In his mid-thirties, he had long hands, a face that looked as if it once had acne, and curly black hair. 'Thanks, Bobby,' he said to the guard. 'I've got it from here.'

As the door closed, he extended one of his long hands, and said, 'I'm Stephen.'

Instead of shaking, I flashed my hand with the Band-Aids, and said, 'Johnny Bellefleur.'

'I know who you are, Mr Bellefleur,' he said. 'You're the man who's been poking around Alex Greene's house.'

'How did you know that?'

'Small town. Everyone talks. If I'm not mistaken, you also served three tours in the Navy, last time on a hospital ship called *The Mercy*.'

A framed eight-by-ten on his desk showed him with a woman and two children – a young boy and a younger girl – all dressed in white pants and white button-up shirts. The woman and the children had blond hair and very white teeth.

I said, 'My background isn't the kind of thing people talk about in a small town.'

He gestured toward the door as if Bob Peterson still stood there. 'It's the kind of thing my security guy finds out when I ask him to.'

'You've taken a lot of interest in me. I didn't even know your name until about ten minutes ago.'

'I take interest in anything involving my family.'

'And that's what Alex and Sheneel Greene are? Family?'

'*Relations* would be a better way of putting it. Their mother, Laura, is my cousin on my father's side, but we've got a big extended family here. Three years ago, at a reunion, we counted sixty-five members living on Amelia Island and more than a hundred in the region. What's your interest in Sheneel?'

'My wife taught English to her.'

'I know that too. What I have a hard time understanding is why the two of you are getting involved in something you're not part of. This is a family tragedy. It's not for you.'

'What have the police told you about Sheneel's death?'

He forced a smile. 'I've had Bobby checking with them each day. I know as much as anyone.

The best guess is she intentionally overdosed, though the toxicology report won't come back for a week or two.'

'Someone killed her,' I said. 'She didn't do it herself.'

The skin on his neck flushed. 'That's nonsense.'

'Someone cut her up.'

'What do you mean, *cut her up*?'

'What's not clear? Someone used a blade on her. It went through the skin, the muscle, and the bone. The police have evidence of it. Have Bobby check in again.'

He seemed to melt back into his chair. 'Damn.'

'Exactly.'

'Christ.' His eyes were far away.

I asked, 'Who would have done this to her?'

He blinked and refocused. 'I still don't understand why you're getting involved in this. What does it have to do with you?'

'That's complicated.'

'I don't mind.'

'When I was in the Navy, I saw things.'

'*Things?*'

I took a deep breath. 'The job I did – I saw men a couple of days after they died. As much as a week. I could piece together their stories from their wounds – gunshot, shrapnel, IED, petroleum and chemical burns – but after a while the faces and legs and arms seemed to join into one . . . I don't know what to call it. That was the problem. It was made of individual human lives, but it was no longer human, and it had no name. It's complicated.'

'But you weren't in combat?'

I felt an accusation in those words, and I said nothing.

He nodded, seeming to process what I'd told him. 'So this is what – a way of redeeming yourself?'

'There's no redeeming this. I just want some answers.'

He seemed to think about that. 'You know, there might not be answers either.'

'Yeah, I suspect there might not be.'

'I wish I could help you. I didn't know Sheneel well. When she was sixteen, she and Alex came to the reunion. Since then, I've only heard the gossip and rumors.'

'What rumors?'

'Sheneel's troubles mostly. The suicide attempts, getting arrested last summer. Rumors had her and Alex taking and selling just about every drug you can name.' He steadied his gaze on me. 'Whatever happened to Sheneel, she was who she was. If you think that finding the answers you're looking for will save you from whatever you need to get free of, there's nothing I can do to stop you from looking for them, as long as you treat my family right. But that won't change who or what Sheneel was. She was troubled. Her mother is troubled. Her brother too. So, let me know if you have more questions,' he said, 'and I'll answer them if I can. But do you mind if I tell *you* something?'

'What?'

'*You* look bad – *real* bad. Don't let this thing make it worse.'

I said, 'I'm sure that's good advice.'

104

He nodded at the bandages on my left hand. 'You get in a fight?'

'A dumb accident.'

He made a sympathetic face.

I turned to go, then stopped. 'Why did your cousin Laura change her name back to Greene from Phelps?'

His face became pained. 'Long story. Let's just say, she's been messed up for a long time.'

When I stepped out of the office, Bob Peterson was waiting. He escorted me through the hallways and to my car, then pointed toward the security booth and said, 'Straight down the road and through the gate.' As I climbed in, he added, 'I hope you found what you were looking for.'

What *was* I looking for? *Answers*, I'd told Stephen Phelps, *not redemption*. I wanted to know who had killed Sheneel Greene.

But that was only part of the truth. For eighteen months, I'd stood, swaying at a stainless steel table that was bolted to an iron floor far below the ocean surface, and processed bodies that were beyond saving. But they had done something when they were alive. They had driven into firefights. They had slept shoulder to shoulder in their cots in tents and barracks. They had put their hands on the bloody but still-living limbs of the men they had fought alongside. They had felt, on their wounded and bloody skin, the sting of other men's tears as their breathing slowed.

I had not.

I was a factory man in a meatpacking plant.

Did I want redemption? I wanted more than

that. I wanted to keep the blurring faces of all the dead men I'd seen from spinning in front of my mind's eye like the cars on a carnival ride. I wanted to pull those men from the ride or fling myself into the mechanism that powered it and jam its gears.

What was to keep Sheneel Greene's face from joining the others on that ride? What was to keep me from packing her and disposing of her as I'd packed and disposed of the bodies that had passed through the hold of the ship on the Arabian Sea?

I thought I knew *that* answer. Stephen Phelps had said that she wasn't for me. But maybe I could be for her. Maybe I could sponge away the dirty circumstances of her death, and, as she lay in her casket, she would be clean.

No, I realized, she would never be clean. *She was troubled*, Phelps had said. The dirt might run through skin and muscle and into the bone. If that was true, I would be unable to cut it away, even with a blade.

When I passed the guard booth, I turned and drove toward Alex Greene's house. I would confront him with the drug rumors about him and Sheneel and see what happened. It was none of my business, but I would stick my fingers into the dirt and measure its depth. If it swallowed my fingers and hand – if it swallowed my whole arm – I would reach in deeper, because I hadn't done so with the dead men whose nameless spinning faces had merged into a monster.

I parked at the curb by the yellow house and crossed the ragged lawn. The newspapers were gone from the front windows. I stepped into the screen porch. The front door stood open a crack, wide enough to jam a shoe in. A new set of wind chimes made of white seashells – silent in the still, hot air – hung from the porch ceiling.

I knocked on the door.

No one answered.

I knocked again and pushed the door with my forefinger until it swung wider. I called into the house, 'Alex!'

Nothing.

I pushed the door open and stepped inside. 'Alex?'

I went to the couch. The blanket and pillow lay on the cushions. The room smelled of sweat and a terrible salt and metallic odor that I knew from six thousand miles away. The skin on my back tightened, and for a moment, in the hot air of the house, I felt the vented breeze that sometimes piped into the hold on the ship, and I felt the slow sway of the floor. I spun, half expecting to find someone else in the room, but I was alone. I went to the kitchen door. A white Formica table, chipped on one corner, was pushed against a wall. A refrigerator hummed in a corner. A mix of plastic and china dishes stood on a counter by the sink. Over the sink, a screenless casement window was cranked open.

That left the bedroom. I went to it, thinking, *I've been gone only an hour*, asking, *What possibly could happen in an hour?* And answering, *Everything. In a flash, in a fragment of a moment – on a roadside or in a car or in the lonely bedroom of a little yellow house.* I looked through the bedroom door. My head spun. Next to a queen-sized box spring and mattress, Alex Greene lay on a green oval rug, his head bloody. He wore no shirt and his chest and belly glistened with sweat. His right arm looked as if it had been torqued until it had broken sideways and backward. His shorts were yanked half-down on one side, exposing a skinny hip.

I opened my mouth to swear, but no sound came out.

I went to him, telling myself, *You can do this. You've done this before. You've seen worse.*

A fly landed on one of his eyes, and I waved it away. Then I saw the tattoo on his exposed hip. It was no bigger than a dime, the faded ink almost invisible in the dim light – a snake wrapping against itself, swallowing its own tail. I bent low, wanting to touch it, fearing that if I did, the little snake head would lash at me with an electric bite. But I never got a chance to choose between the irrational impulses – to touch or not to touch – because a sound behind me made me turn again, and now I glimpsed another man, large and white-skinned – bright white, almost blue-white, it seemed to me in the dim light – holding a baseball bat above his head and closing the distance between us. He grunted and swung the bat. I raised my hand to protect my head – my left hand, bandaged from fingertips to wrist – and the bat cracked through it.

The bat hit me above the ear and a ripping and roaring tore through my head. I knew even as I fell to the floor that, if I lived, a bright pain would come.

Twelve

Lillian

I heard a Fly buzz when I died.

Daniel called at three in the afternoon. He said that when Johnny left the Phelps Paper Company, a security guard followed his car. When Johnny went into Sheneel and Alex Greene's house and stayed for nearly an hour, the security guard decided to check what was happening. When the security guard saw Johnny on the floor with Alex Greene's body, he called the police and then called his boss, or maybe the other way around. Now, Daniel was calling from the highway halfway to Fernandina. I should come too, he said.

My own voice sounded faraway when I asked, 'Did Johnny kill him?'

'The man I talked to told me Alex Greene was cut up and Johnny was there. No one seems to know the details.'

I ran from my office to my car. Would Johnny kill Alex Greene? I saw no reason why, and I hated myself for thinking it. But I also had seen no reason why he would cut up his own hands.

When I got to Fernandina, eight police cars, two ambulances, and a fire truck were parked outside the yellow house. Crime-scene tape stretched across the front yard, and a uniformed cop guarded the front door. Neighborhood kids stood barefoot or straddled bicycles on the street.

I cut across the lawn and asked the officer to tell Detective Turner that I was outside. 'This a family party?' he said, but he radioed into the house.

Daniel came out, looking grim.

I asked, 'Is he—'

'He's going to be all right.'

The little house was crowded and hot, though a window air conditioner blew full. A cop talked with two men in suits. Through the bedroom doorway, two women and a man worked under a bright light. Daniel nodded at one of the businessmen, a thick-chested man, and said, 'His name is Bob Peterson. He found Johnny.' He nodded at the other man – tall, in a pink Oxford-cloth shirt, holding a gray suit coat in his hand – and said, 'Stephen Phelps. He showed up before EMS and the squads.' When I glanced at the bedroom, he said, 'Body's already gone.'

In the kitchen, Johnny was sitting at the table with a detective. The bandage on his left hand was bloody, the arm above it swollen past the elbow. A trickle of blood had dried on his cheek.

The detective said to him, 'He had bright white skin? "Blue-white"?'

'That's what it looked like. I saw him for only a second.'

'Why didn't Peterson see this man?'

'I don't know. Maybe he went out the kitchen window.'

'He was big, you say?'

'Huge.'

The detective looked at the wall above the sink. 'Small window.'

I went to the table and said, 'My husband is hurt.'

The detective looked at me, annoyed. 'Who let her in?'

'He's bleeding—'

His eyes icy, Johnny raised his good hand. 'I'm fine.'

I asked, 'What happened?'

Johnny turned back to the detective. 'I don't know how the guy left. I just know what I saw.'

I said, 'What happened to your hand?'

He looked at me as if *I* had injured him. 'A baseball bat hit it.'

'I'm taking you to the hospital.'

Johnny said, 'Cut it out.'

'What?'

'Cut it out. I'm talking with this man. I'll go when I'm done.'

'Your hand,' I said.

'It's fine.'

'It's not fine. It's—'

'Stop it!' he yelled. Then he lowered his voice. 'Just stop it.'

I walked into the living room. Tears stung my eyes. The hot air smelled like copper and sweat, and I felt nauseous. I went to the couch and sat, and when the man Daniel had identified as Stephen Phelps saw me, he came and sat on the other end. He wiped sweat from his forehead with his sleeve.

'You're Lillian Turner?' he said.

I nodded.

'Sheneel's teacher.'

'Small town,' I said.

'Very.'

'My husband didn't do this.'

'Who says he did?'

The muscles relaxed in my chest. 'Thank you.'

He wiped his forehead again. 'I talked with him a little while ago in my office. I warned him he might hurt himself in this. In Sheneel's part of the family, someone's always getting hurt.'

'Do you know what happened here?'

He hesitated, touched my shoulder, and said, 'I tend to hear almost everything that interests me, but when your husband came to my office, he told me things about Sheneel's death that I hadn't heard before. To tell the truth, I didn't know whether to believe him. Your husband didn't look entirely . . . together. So I sent my security man after him when he left. Bob followed him here, and when your husband didn't come back out, Bob went in after him. He found your husband on top of my cousin's boy.'

'On top?'

'That's what Bob says. Your husband was bleeding from the head, and he was lying on Alex. Bob pulled him off. Alex was dead. Bob called me, and I called the police.'

'Christ.'

'Your husband told Bob that someone else was in the house. He said a man attacked him.'

I nodded at the kitchen. 'That detective doesn't seem to believe him.'

He glanced through the door at Johnny. 'How else could he have gotten knocked on the head? But Bob was outside and saw no one leave.'

Shouting erupted in the kitchen – Johnny and Daniel yelling at each other, Johnny saying something about Daniel covering up Sheneel's murder, Daniel calling Johnny crazy.

Johnny burst into the living room and looked around wildly until he found me on the couch. He said, 'Let's go!'

Daniel followed him from the kitchen and said, 'Here's the secret, Johnny – *there's no secret!*'

Johnny headed for the front door. 'Let's go!'

The cop at the door blocked him and Johnny looked ready to hit him, but Daniel said, 'Let the man out,' and the cop moved aside.

As Johnny disappeared from the front porch, I turned to Daniel. 'Can you get my car back to my house?'

He nodded, and I tossed him my keys and ran after Johnny. He had parked at the curb in front of the house. He glared at me. 'Get in.'

'Give me the keys,' I said.

'Not on your life.'

'If you don't give them to me, I'm not going with you.'

His eyes burned with anger. 'I'm sick of this,' he said. He dropped the keys on the pavement and got in on the passenger side.

He leaned against the door as I drove to the hospital. When I stopped at the entrance to the ER, he got out without a word. By the time I parked the car and went inside, the nurses had him in an exam room, and an hour later

– after the X-rays, the pupil dilation check, and the concentration and coordination test – the doctor, a small, round Asian woman, told us that Johnny had a fractured wrist and a mild concussion. 'We can keep him here overnight, or we can put him in a cast and send him home,' she said.

'I'm going home,' Johnny said.

'That's fine. We'll get you into a cast.' The doctor turned back to me. 'Check on him every few hours and make sure he's alert.'

'Let's go,' Johnny said.

The doctor asked, 'Is he always this way?'

That evening, a layer of clouds covered the sky, and, when we got in bed, a light rain fell against the windows. Johnny lay on his back, the lamp on, staring at the ceiling.

'What are you thinking?' I asked.

He said nothing.

'I'm trying to help,' I said.

He said, 'You're sucking me dry.'

As I fell asleep, the rain ticked against the window glass. I dreamed I was in class, teaching recitation from memory – a kind of teaching almost no one does anymore, not for fifty or sixty years – and two dozen twenty-year-olds chanted lines from Emily Dickinson's 'I heard a Fly buzz.' The students knew the words, and they inflected them precisely, but I felt that a sound was missing, and I realized that the sound was Sheneel's voice. Then I realized that the other students were reciting the poem *for* her.

I willed my Keepsakes – Signed away
What portion of me be
Assignable – and then it was
There interposed a Fly –

With Blue – uncertain – stumbling Buzz –
Between the light – and me –
And then the Windows failed – and then
I could not see to see.

I woke. The lamp on Johnny's side of the bed was on. The clock said it was one thirty-five a.m. Light rain fell against the windows. Johnny was gone.

I got up and went to the kitchen and then to the sunroom. The glass doors from the sunroom to the backyard were open and a cool wet breeze blew into the house.

I stepped out on to the cold, slick grass. Johnny was lying on the lawn chair, wearing only his boxer shorts. 'Hey,' I said.

He said nothing. The cold rain stung my skin through my pajama shirt.

'Come inside,' I said.

He said nothing.

I went to him and stood by him. His eyes were open, staring into the rain. 'The rain will ruin your cast.'

He said nothing.

I thought, *This is the way it ends*. Then I unbuttoned my pajama shirt and let it hang open. Johnny watched the thick dark sky. I slid my underwear down and left it on the wet grass. The rain fell into Johnny's eyes. I stepped over the lawn chair, straddling him, and lowered myself on to him. His eyes focused on mine for several seconds, and he pushed me off of him, on to the grass. I lay on the ground, the cold rain stinging my skin, then got up and returned to him, stepped across him, lowered myself on to him, and when he tried to push me away, I grabbed the wrist of his undamaged hand and held it, and I reached down and pulled his shorts away. He cried out – with anger, pain, desire, I didn't know what – and I took him in my hand until he was hard and I put him inside me. He struggled, but I held him and ground down on him again and again. '*Never*,' I said, and rain spat from my mouth. 'Never, never, never.' I ground down on him deeper and deeper, and his struggling softened until, with a groan of anger or pain or desire, he bucked his hips against me.

'Never,' I said, and he collapsed on to the chair, breathing hard, his eyes closed now against the rain, and I lowered myself against him until our skins touched and the deep warmth of our bodies burned through the cold rain that coated us.

'Never?' he said.

'Never go away from me,' I said.

He lay quiet beneath me, then said, 'I won't.'

But in the morning, over breakfast, with the rain clouds gone from the sky and the grass dry, he said, 'If you treat me like I'm already gone, I don't know what to do.'

'What do you mean?'

'You put me in the hospital. You—'

'You put *yourself* in the hospital.'

'Shhh.' He stared at me hard and said, 'You

116

took my gun from my office. You keep treating me like I'm broken.'

'I'm trying to—'

He held my hand to silence me. 'Maybe I *am* broken. But if you treat me this way, I'm nothing. You understand? Nothing. I won't be able to go away, because I'll already be gone.'

'I—'

'You can't save me from myself. Only I can do that.'

I stared at him, waiting for him to finish.

He smiled a little. 'I give myself about fifty-fifty odds.' He nodded, as if permitting me to speak.

I said nothing. Instead, I went into the bedroom and got his gun from my dresser drawer. I brought it to him and laid it on the table.

'Thank you,' he said.

I stared at it – a piece of squared black metal with a trigger. 'Will you teach me to shoot it?'

'I guess so. Why?'

'Because if you come at me in the middle of the night, I want a fighting chance.'

Thirteen

Stephen Phelps

A seven-year-old's nightmares.

Claws on bark, feet in the leaves, unseen wings in the branches, sex-and-hunger cries of animals.

117

Forest musk. The dark has its own odor. Wisps of night breeze, ghostly webs and nonfingers that brush the cheeks and hands, the threat that closes on the body from all sides.

'A family that grows trees for a living can't be scared of the woods,' Dad said when I turned eight. 'Pine sap rises through your veins as sure as blood.' Around midnight, he parked the pickup at the side of the timber road and led me by the hand into a mid-growth grove. We sat in the dark on the pine-needle floor. He identified an owl cry and the skittering of an armadillo. 'See?' he said. 'Nothing to worry about.' Then, 'Don't come out until dawn,' and he went back to the truck.

I managed ten minutes – *maybe* ten. I scrambled out of the woods and on to the passenger seat.

He slapped me.

I preferred his slap to the forest.

He slapped again. 'Goddamn it. You will *not* be afraid.'

He dragged me into the trees and made me sit. When I ran after him, he dragged me back. 'If you follow again, I'll drive away and leave you here.'

All through the night, I wished I would die. But the sun rose and Dad returned and asked, 'Are you afraid now?'

'No.'

He slapped me. 'You're lying.'

Two nights later, we went back to the woods, and again after a week. My terror swelled, but Dad started to believe my lies or else decided he'd done what he could.

In fact, it was enough. When I was thirteen, I started to long for the night terrors as I started to long for sex. When Dad took me to visit the mature timber tracts in South Georgia, I snuck out after he fell asleep and I wandered among the trees, terrified but feeling as if I possessed the woods as I soon would possess girls and women. In the morning, chainsaws would rip through the trunks. Afterward, the scarred land where the grove had stood would be silent and smell of sawdust and gasoline fumes. But in the dark I touched the trees as I passed – their warm wood on my palms.

Not so different from girls and women. Not so different from Lillian Turner? I had put my hand on her shoulder – a touch, a palm on her heat, no more.

My husband didn't do this.

Who says he did?

Thank you.

She was grateful! To me! If only I'd had a chainsaw. If only I'd had a bed, a kitchen counter, the hood of a car. If I wasn't careful, I would fall in love.

She wore a dress. Silent scars of time on her bare knees where she'd kneeled as a girl or a woman. On what? Gravel? Pavement? Beach sand? A pine-needle forest floor? Knees, scarred. Neck, slender. The tender and the slender. *Not my fault.*

Fourteen

Johnny

We spent Saturday at home – Lillian, Percy, and me. The doctor had told me to rest for forty-eight hours, which I took to mean only that I should avoid getting hit with more baseball bats. So I read the newspaper about Alex Greene's death, which the police were calling *unexplained*, and Lillian checked online for other coverage, which turned out to be mostly the same as in the newspaper. No one was accusing me of killing Alex Greene anymore, and that was good, but I wondered what was *unexplained* about his death. He'd been beaten, probably with the same baseball bat that had hit me, and he'd been cut with a knife.

I looked at Percy and said, 'What's to explain?'

He returned my gaze with his wet black eyes.

Through the morning, Lillian stayed near. 'How are you doing?' she asked every hour on the hour. 'How are you doing *now*?'

'Fine,' I said. 'Fine.'

'How's the hand?'

'Not so bad,' though it throbbed like a pulsing coal. My head, where the man hit me, ached worse.

'Do you want the hydrocodone?'

'No.' But in the afternoon, I swallowed two white tablets, and a dull comfort spread through

120

my arm to my wrist and hand. My head still pounded, but I fell asleep on the sunroom couch with Percy lying on the floor beside me. I woke for a late dinner, slept through the night fitfully, and in the morning the throbbing and aching had become tolerable. With Lillian standing at the stove, I emptied the rest of the hydrocodone into the kitchen sink and turned on the disposal.

'You do know that you're insane?' she said.

I asked, 'Do we have orange juice?'

We spent a second day at home, and when the pain returned just before lunch and brought sweat to my forehead, Lillian left me alone. She drank a vodka and tonic with her sandwich, and in the afternoon we sat together in the backyard – her reading, me staring at the blue of the sky and listening to the breeze in the leaves of the oak tree at the foot of our property.

That night, as Lillian slept, I went back outside to the lawn chair and stared at the stars, which made no noise, though I knew, up close, they would roar like immense incinerators. I don't remember closing my eyes. I would almost swear that I didn't close them. But I must have slept, because sometime later a man's voice woke me, and, when I looked up, the whole sky had shifted to the west. The man was singing in a low voice, just above a whisper. He sang, 'Johnny on the island and I heard him groan—'

'What the hell?' I said, and he stopped. He was an old man, dark-skinned, wearing denim overalls and a blue work shirt. After a moment, I recognized him. Papa Crowe.

121

There was no sense to him being in my back-yard. 'What are you doing here?'

'Singing, mostly.'

I fought to clear my head. 'How did you get through the fence?'

'I open the gate.'

'What do you want?'

'To show you something.'

'What time is it?'

He glanced at the sky, as if he could read it like a clock. 'Late.'

'What do you want to show me?'

'Come with me. I take you.'

'I'm not going anywhere with you.'

He stared at me in the dark. 'Have it your way.' He turned and walked toward the gate.

I called after him, 'What do you want to show me?'

'You come or stay, that up to you, but I go.'

I pushed myself out of the chair. 'Let me get dressed.'

'Leave the gun behind.'

'What gun?'

'Leave it behind.'

We drove north in an old brown Chrysler LeBaron that smelled like wet carpet. Papa Crowe steered with both hands on the wheel, his body tipping toward the windshield, as if his eyesight was bad and he needed the advantage. We left the windows open and the cool night air beat against our clothing. He frowned the way men sometimes do when they're missing lower teeth.

When he saw me watching him, he said, 'When

they ain't no way, sometime you got to make a way out of no way.'

'What do you mean by that?'

'That what I'm about to show you.'

When we reached the exit for Fernandina, he kept his foot on the accelerator. We crossed the Georgia border, and ten minutes later left the highway. We drove down a commercial street, turned, and for another half-hour drove on rural roads, the headlights gleaming off red-bark pine trees that grew in rows as neat and regular as orchard fruit trees. Then Papa Crowe pulled to the side and stopped, angling the car so the headlights shined into the rows.

He nodded into the narrowing light. 'This the land I talk about.'

'What land?'

He leaned across me, the smell of soap on him, and took two flashlights from the glove compartment. Giving one to me, he got out of the car and walked into the rows of trees.

When I caught up with him, he quickened his pace. We walked a quarter-mile or more over a pine-needle carpet. Black-winged night birds, startled by the flashlight beams, flushed from the low branches and disappeared into the dark. The old man stopped once as an animal – an armadillo or a possum – moved through a stand of palmettos ahead of us. He said, 'This land, back to the road and clear a mile on either side, the Greenes and Crowes owned it all. Lived on it, hunted on it, prayed on it.'

A bird dropped from the low branch of a pine tree, made a strangled sound, and flew away from

123

the light. I asked, 'We needed to see it in the middle of the night?'

'Come in the daylight, get yourself in a mess of trouble then.'

Following a marker that I didn't see, he turned left, and soon we walked up a slow incline, and the flashlight beams fell upon the ruins of an old wooden house, the windows all punched out, the front porch roof sagging under the weight of pine needles, the front door gone from the hinges. 'This it,' the old man said. 'A lot of generations live here. My granddaddy. His granddaddy. My Uncle Crowe and his family. We used to call it the Garden House. We have twenty, thirty people here sometime. You don't want to go in there now.' He turned his flashlight so it shined on an open-walled, tin-roofed carport. Under the roof, an old sky-blue Chevrolet sedan – its wheels missing, its hood pried off, its engine hauled away – remained, though thirty or more years of pine growth had rooted into whatever might once have been a driveway.

We went to the car. 'One of the Phelps mills is two miles that way.' He pointed north. 'Night like this you don't know it, but thirty years ago the air make your eyes burn like a dry-leaf fire. Look at this.' He ran a finger along the roof of the Chevrolet. Under the dust, the paint chipped and fell away like a dry canker. 'Fly ash from the recovery boiler. It fall some days like rain and eat the paint off the house and car. My cousin Mary – it eat her skin like this, so she get the cancer.

'My Uncle Crowe leave this car. He fight the

Phelpses, shoot holes in the signs at their mills, get arrested too. But when it come clear that the Phelpses going to take the land and nothing he can do but die on it, he get his wife and children and grandchildren – twelve of them, a little tribe – and they just go, disappear in the night like that. Story my daddy tell the children is they take a bus to the ocean and step right in like the old Ebo king that walk off the Dunbar Creek dock with his family in St Simons all those years ago. My daddy tell the children that my uncle don't drown. He say his family walk across the ocean all the way and they living free.'

I ran my finger across the car and the paint grit clung to it.

'Don't put that in your mouth,' the old man said.

'A Phelps mill did this?'

'Come with me,' he said, and he left the carport and continued into the woods. 'First the garden die, then we start finding dead animals – squirrels, raccoons. Mary and her boy eat them, like they was God's gift, the goddamn fools. Then Mary get sick and her boy too. Now the government come and tell the Phelpses to clean it up, but it too late. Those of us that don't leave, they die right here.'

We arrived at a narrow creek. Under the beam of the flashlights, the water shined clear against the orange-brown bank. 'That where the family get the drinking water. Wasn't sweet, but it was water to live on if you boiled it, and that was sweet enough. The government tell the Phelpses to clean the mill, and now you can breathe the air like you on God's earth, but I wouldn't drink the water if you put a gun to my head, 'cause it amount to the same thing.'

Lillian had told me about the Phelps land grab, but nothing like this. 'It's pretty terrible.'

'Yes, sir, it is that.'

'But what does it have to do with Sheneel Greene's death? Or Alex's?'

The old man held the flashlight beam on the creek. No minnows swam in it. No insects skimmed its surface.

'Sheneel been spitting in the Phelpses' stew.'

'I don't understand.'

He said, 'The Phelpses been whipping the Greenes and Crowes a long time. Sheneel got more fire than water in her. She take it to the Phelpses and threaten them. She know what in this water. I show her myself. She know it can poison the Phelpses too if people find out.'

'The government?'

'Sure.'

'But Sheneel also was a Phelps.'

'Half Phelps. All Greene.'

'So she threatened the Phelpses?'

''Course she did.'

'And they killed her?'

'She dead, ain't she?'

'How do you know they did it?'

'If it look like a snake and it slide through the grass, it a snake.'

'Who's responsible? Stephen Phelps?'

'Or his daddy, Edward. He a mean bastard, Edward, always been.'

I looked at the old man, but in the deep dark

126

of the woods I couldn't read his face. 'So you don't *really* know who killed her?'

'I know what I know.'

'What do you think she wanted from the Phelpses?'

'What she really want, or what she tell them they got to give her? She really want them to suffer for a hundred years like they make everybody else suffer. What she tell them? I don't know. Maybe nothing – maybe she threaten them to make them squirm.'

'So they killed her. What about Alex?'

'Alex know what Sheneel know. Maybe Alex don't talk so much like Sheneel, but the police coming around and you coming around, and who can keep his mouth shut with all these people asking questions?'

'Why don't *you* go to the police with this? Why didn't you report what the Phelpses were doing at the mill?'

'I been to the police ten time and a hundred. No one believe a man like me. Beside, they arrest me for trespassing on Phelps land many time, going back thirty year now, and they arrest me for wrecking Phelps machinery. So I tell them and tell them but no one listen. A lot change in my lifetime but this don't. So that what I got you for.'

When I looked at him, unconvinced, he added, 'My family leave this place. We don't stay and die with Mary and her boy. I like to live, son, and I like to heal. It a weakness, but it mine. I don't say living is better than dying, but some men eat redfish and other men eat crab. Which is better? The one as good as the other. I'm a redfish man, but you definitely is a crab man, eating off the bottom. I think you don't mind dying. So if you want to poke into it, I tell you where it is and you can bring your own claw.'

I looked at the poisoned creek, then shined my flashlight back on the ruined house. 'I want to get out of here,' I said, 'if that's all right with you.'

'Fine with me. Phelpses run security through here sometime, and they worse than the bone of the dead.'

When we drove back to the end of the lumber road, the old man turned left instead of right, and soon we were buried in a tunnel of old-growth trees.

'Where are we going now?' I said.

He leaned close to the windshield as if the dark had thickened. 'A man got to eat.'

'I'm not hungry.'

'Don't matter. We get some breakfast.'

'It's three in the morning.'

'Best time to eat.'

'Take me home.'

'If you ain't reasonably healthy, you don't do me no good.'

'I'm not interested in doing you good.'

He drove.

A flat-roofed, one-story cinderblock building with a tall redbrick chimney appeared suddenly at the side of the road. A string of incandescent bulbs shined on a gravel parking lot full of rusting sedans and pickup trucks. A red cursive sign that said *Tobias Rib* hung over the dirty glass front door. Concrete flowerboxes with weeds growing in them stood on either side.

When we stepped in, the smell of frying food, cigarette smoke, and sweet barbeque hit us. Black men and women, wearing everything from little nightclub dresses to greasy coveralls – partiers finishing the night, shrimpers and crabbers up early before heading out on their trawlers or skiffs – sat at a mix of picnic tables and plywood counters, laughing, shouting, eating, and drinking as if it was happy hour on a Friday evening. A long buffet table stood in the center of the room with aluminum trays loaded with barbequed pork, breaded fried shrimp, fried fish, coleslaw, collards, and biscuits. In the little open kitchen, a fat, potato-faced white man, in a white apron and a green-and-orange head rag, worked a big deep fryer.

As we walked to a picnic table, a woman somewhere in the room started singing in a cracked voice, 'John on the island and I heard him groan. Yeah, Johnny on the island—'

'What the hell,' I said.

'Don't worry about it,' Papa Crowe said.

We ate, and men and women came to our table to say hello to Papa Crowe as if he deserved their special respect. The cook came from the kitchen, and though he probably was forty or forty-five, his skin looked grayer than a ninety-year-old's, grayer than the skin of some of the men I'd seen below deck on the Arabian Sea, and I could have mistaken him for dead except for the smile, big and yellow-toothed, as he told Papa Crowe about a friend who'd gotten drunk and lost his truck. A dark-skinned woman, wearing a brown business skirt and jacket and carrying a leather briefcase, came and kissed Papa Crowe on his cheek.

The voice that had sung about John on the island broke into a new song, about a stray cat, and I thought I recognized its cracked sound.

Papa Crowe leaned toward me and said, 'You eat this food every day and it kill you.' He pointed his thumb at the kitchen where the cook was dipping wire baskets into the deep fryer again as if he was skimming for fingerling baitfish. 'Tobias eat it every day, and he have three surgeries to open the veins. But you eat it once a week or twice, it give you a nice coat for when the winter come or the pain.'

The singing woman started into 'John on the island' again, closer now, and the strangeness and familiarity irritated me. I spun toward the sound.

Felicity, the Philips Highway hooker, smiled at me with drunken eyes. When I'd bought her breakfast three days ago, she'd dyed her hair pink. Now she'd braided in feathers as well.

I said, 'What are you—'

'Hey, you,' she said. 'I saw you on TV. You've been in Fernandina, making a whole lot of hurt.' She was wearing knee-high black vinyl boots and a short burgundy-red skirt, ready for business.

Papa Crowe grinned at me. 'You know Felicity?'

The old hooker said, 'He's my sugar. He gives me cigarettes and I make him groan.'

'You don't – and I don't.'

The old woman laughed. 'Listen to him, the lyin' man.'

130

Papa Crowe said something to her in a language I didn't understand.

She stopped laughing and spoke to him the same.

'She's a messed-up old woman,' I said.

Papa Crowe laughed. 'She family.'

Felicity dropped into a chair between us.

I said, 'What are you doing up here?'

She gave me a cold look. 'You don't think I *live* on Philips Highway.' When she saw my face, she said, 'OK, some of the time I do. But I've got my people here. What're *you* doing here?'

The old man said, 'I show him the Garden House.'

Felicity said, 'Why did you want to see that evil old place?'

'I didn't,' I said.

Papa Crowe said, 'He need to see who the Phelpses is.'

Felicity said, 'I've known them my whole life. Ever since I was fourteen and didn't know better. They like it rough, the Phelpses do. I've seen what the boy does to the girls. I know what Edward's daddy did to me. Have you seen Edward's wife?'

I shook my head.

'You look at her and tell me poison doesn't run in that man's blood. You know, the skin on the outside will heal most of the time, but the inside never does rightly.'

An hour later, as we drove from Tobias Rib, the sky still was dark. The noise of the voices, laughter, and spattering fryer oil hung in my ears,

and though my hand ached, I felt almost pleas-
antly tired. I eased my shoulder into the crack
between the seat and the door and closed my
eyes. 'Home?' I said.

'One more stop,' the old man said.

'It's late,' I said.

'It early,' he said. 'Not even sun-up.'

'Where are we going?'

'When I give you that string and Indian shot
and tell you to put it around your head, you don't
do it, do you?'

'No.'

'Some people got no sense,' he said. He reached
into his pocket and pulled out a small square of
folded aluminum foil. 'Chew on this.'

I unwrapped the packet and peeled away three
bruised leaves. They smelled terrible. 'What is
it?'

'Don't worry.'

'What is it?'

'Jimson weed. I grow it in my garden, but it
grow everywhere – side of the road, if you want
it wild.'

'What's it do?'

'It fix that head of yours so you can think.'

'I can think fine.'

'For God sake, chew it.'

I rolled the leaves into a ball, put the ball into
my mouth, and chewed. It tasted as terrible as it
looked. I rolled down my window and spat it
into the dark. 'Sorry,' I said.

'That all right. You chew it much longer, it kill
you.'

He swung the car around a bend, slowed, and

132

pulled on to a sand-and-oyster-shell road without a sign. By the time he rolled the car to a stop behind a sand dune and turned off the engine, my throat felt hot and dry. He got out of the car, leaving his door open. Ocean waves roared and hushed on the other side of the dune. 'What are we doing?' I asked, and when he didn't answer, I got out too. 'Do you have any water?' I said.

He came close enough to look in my eyes. 'You thirsty? That good.'

A wave of dread passed through my belly. 'What's jimson weed?'

'I tell you already. Come on.' He climbed the dune between the road and the ocean.

I scrambled after him, steadying myself with my good hand. 'Got a flashlight?'

'Stars is plenty bright,' he said.

When we reached the beach, he sat on the sand, and I lowered myself beside him. The air smelled of salt water and the mixture of life and death that it held and always had held. In the corner of my eyes, I saw someone approaching, but when I turned, no one was there.

'Relax,' the old man said. 'Look at the stars. They been burning like the devil since before the world was born, and there no bigger peace than that.'

Again, someone approached from the corner of my vision, and now I saw it was Felicity, but when I turned to face her, she seemed to turn into Lillian. 'Hey!' I said, and struggled to get to my feet, but the old man held me down and Lillian disappeared. I said, 'What's in jimson weed?'

'It is what it is. It been in this world since the world was born.'

Something black and low crept from the waves on to the sand. An animal of a kind. Then another, its flat belly sliding over the sand. A half-dozen more washed in on the next wave. Their black skins glistened under the starlight, and they came up the beach toward me. They were reptiles, black and shiny, without eyes or mouths, sliding up the sand. The next wave brought ten or twelve more.

'I don't like this,' I said.

The old man's voice was steady. 'You ain't supposed to like it. You supposed to hate it. It supposed to chase the fiends from your head. You been hag-ridden too long.'

'I don't like it,' I said again.

'But your hand don't hurt right now.'

'No,' I admitted. 'It doesn't.'

'That right.'

The black reptiles came up the sand. I kicked at them wildly. I got to my feet and tried to step on them.

'You see – nothing there,' Papa Crowe said calmly. 'Nothing but what in your head. You just kicking a lot of good sand around, but it don't mind.'

I kicked one of the creatures. It flew through the air back toward the ocean, and I yelled, 'Hah!'

'That right.' The old man stood up, took me by the arm, and pulled me toward the water. 'Walk right through it. Nothing that can hurt you here. It all in your head. Go all the way if you want.'

When I realized he was pulling me toward the

134

ocean, I fought him. More black creatures were coming from the waves. My legs felt weak, and he drew me down to the water against my will, until my shoes and pant legs splashed in the white foam. The black reptiles lunged at me, though I batted and kicked at them, and still the old man drew me deeper. 'You a tough son of bitch,' he said, and started lowering me backward into the dark water. Hundreds of black animals swam at me. The reptiles that had come for me on the beach now had mouths but no legs. They were eels of some kind, their jaws hooked open. I screamed, and I felt the old man's hands holding me and heard his voice saying, 'Quiet, boy. Quiet.'

He shoved my head under the surface. The black wash of salt water rose into my nostrils and flooded my mouth. Hundreds of black creatures swam at me, slamming against my body and legs, jaws open. I kicked and struck at them with my hands. I screamed. I couldn't breathe.

The old man held me, though I clawed at him and tried to come up. Water sucked into my throat, and I knew I was drowning. The black creatures became a blanket of life or of death – or of something that was neither life nor death but both, woven into one fabric – and it held me and warmed me as if to reassure me that, whatever I was, I was part of the sea – I belonged to it, and it belonged to me. I felt my body relax, the fight leaving me, and I seemed to float under the surface of the water for a long time, neither living nor dead.

The old man must have carried or dragged me

back to the beach. When I opened my eyes, I was lying on the sand, the black creatures gone, the stars shining in my eyes. I breathed hard, rolled to my side, and vomited. I looked at my injured arm. The cast and bandages were a wreck of plaster, salt water, and cotton gauze. I vomited again and tried to sit.

The old man helped me. 'You all right now,' he said.

'Take me home.'

'Sure. I think you ready for sleep.'

On the way back to the city, as the sun rose, animals and insects climbed on to the hood of the car and pasted themselves against the windshield and windows trying to get at me, but I knew Papa Crowe didn't see them. If I told him I did, he might take me back to the beach and try to drown me again, so I said nothing.

The old man seemed cheerful. 'You got to fight the devil with the devil. Some folk call jimson weed *angel's trumpet*. I think the last judgment be gentler,' he said, and he glanced at me. 'You get a new cast for that hand, OK? Unless you want me to splint it for you?'

A wet, black reptile slammed against the windshield. 'No,' I said.

'You all right now, I think,' he said. When I said nothing, he added, 'Now I tell you one more thing. This about your brother-in-law, Daniel Turner. He going to drop the investigation into Sheneel and Alex. He done it for the Phelpses before. I don't know what they give him, but I know they own him.'

'What are you talking about?'

'You wait see.'

I shivered in my wet clothes and looked at him, a strange old man barreling down the highway in a strange car. 'You shouldn't have done this to me.'

He said, 'For your own good.'

I closed my eyes, but that didn't stop the insects and animals.

After a long time, I opened them again to his voice. 'Uh oh, you get some trouble.'

We'd arrived at my street. Two squad cars were parked on my driveway. The sun was still low, and the lights were on in the front windows.

'You *really* shouldn't have done this,' I said.

'A man never do a thing he ain't ready to do.' He pulled to the side two houses before mine. 'I leave you here, son. No sense complicating things.'

I stumbled the rest of the way to my front door, but the insects and animals were suddenly gone, and the early morning sun warmed my wet clothes. I pushed the door open.

Lillian stood in the living room talking with Daniel and three uniformed officers. She wore jeans and a T-shirt. Her hair was unbrushed, her eyes red. All at once she, Daniel, and the officers stopped talking and turned toward me. For a long moment, no one said anything. Then Lillian said, 'Where have you—' and I felt my drugged mind trip over itself again. Her eyes descended over my wet clothes and stopped on the wet remains of the cast and bandages. 'What happened to—' Lillian, Daniel, and the officers moved toward me.

137

Lillian's face turned into the face of Felicity the hooker. I closed my eyes and opened them. Daniel's face and the faces of the officers turned into the featureless faces of dead men I'd processed in the slow-swaying room deep beneath the deck of a hospital ship on the Arabian Sea. I yelled.

For a moment, they stopped. 'It's all right,' said one of the officers, his voice calm. But then they and Daniel – dead men from six thousand miles away – fanned through the living room the way we were taught to do when approaching an enemy combatant, reducing the enemy's choices and increasing ours.

I yelled again, charged along the front wall to the hallway, and sprinted to the bedroom. I slammed and locked the door before they could reach me, and I looked around the room. Wet black animals were trying to come through the closed window. I found my SIG 9mm in the top dresser drawer, aimed at the window, and shot out the glass. The black animals poured into the room. A voice in the hallway yelled, 'Gun!' and I spun and shot a hole through the wooden door. When I spun back to shoot the animals, they were gone, but Felicity sat on the bed, leaning against the headboard, her legs splayed and welcoming. I cracked a bullet hole through the skin between her eyes.

PART TWO

PART TWO

Fifteen

Lillian

The SWAT team parked four RVs in front of the house. A helicopter circled over the trees. An armored tractor with a battering ram backed on to the street from a flatbed trailer. The police cleared our neighbors from their houses, running them to their cars and escorting them to the end of the street. They tried talking Johnny out of the house through a megaphone. When he refused to come, they tried calling him on his cell phone. When he didn't answer, a SWAT team member, dressed in a jumpsuit and helmet, crept along the side of the house and tossed another phone into the bedroom through the broken window. When Johnny answered that phone and the negotiator asked him to come out, he said he was tired. When the negotiator asked him to throw his gun out of the window, he said no. When the negotiator asked what he planned to do next, he said he planned to sleep. When the negotiator said he hoped this would end peacefully, Johnny said he hoped so too, and now if the police negotiator would leave him alone, he would shut his eyes for a while.

At that moment, four SWAT officers kicked down the bedroom door, fingers on the triggers of their automatic rifles.

Johnny was on our bed with the sheets pulled

around his wet clothes, the phone to his ear, his eyes closed, his pistol lying on the floor. They dragged him out, handcuffed and shackled, and, as they shoved him into the back of a police car, he screamed, 'I won't forgive you!'

They took him to the station, charged and processed him, put him in a holding cell, then took him to the hospital where the doctors cut away his clothes and locked him in a room. They kept him for six weeks. During the first three, I got no updates other than that he was medicated and doing fine. During the second three, the doctors said they were trying out different pharmacological regimens.

In that time I replaced the windowpane, hung a new bedroom door, and patched the drywall behind the bed. I taught my classes. My students saw my name in the news and filled in what they didn't know with rumors and disconnected facts. They watched me teach with what seemed to me a profound curiosity that had little to do with the books we were reading. But in the new air and sunshine that had followed Sheneel's death, they had changed too. Sheneel's friend, Samuel Huang, who used to wear khaki shorts and untucked polo shirts, and looked like an overgrown toddler, showed up now with his head shaved and a silver ring through a pierced lip. Students who knew Sheneel, and some who didn't, seemed to take her death as an opportunity to unmask themselves or put on new masks.

When Tom Corfield invited me to a party at the house of one of the other teachers in the History department, I suggested dinner at my house instead. When, after eating, I showed him the patch I was putting on the bedroom wall, he looked longingly at the bed but said nothing. I touched my fingers to his, and the dry heat, thin and invisible as it was, seemed solid. He took my hand in his and said, 'It's been a long time.'

'It has.'

He tightened his hold. 'What happens tomorrow?'

'I don't know.'

'I need to know.'

'I can't say. If that's not enough for you—'

He pulled me to him. For a night – before I turned him away – I clung to him, and the buffeting of my life with Johnny subsided.

Then, one afternoon, Daniel called and said that the prosecutor was dropping the charges against Johnny. A man could shoot up a wall in his house if he wanted to, and the investigators had decided Johnny didn't wish to hurt anyone when he shot through the door.

As for the black creatures coming through the window, Daniel said he had checked with a state game warden and learned that Johnny suffered his breakdown in the middle of the legal hallucinatory-animal hunting season. When I said nothing to that, Daniel said, 'A joke, Lillian. We still can joke.'

'How's the investigation into Sheneel and Alex Greene going?'

'It's going,' he said.

* * *

143

I fixed the house and patched up my life as best I could, wondering whether people who refuse to forgive each other are capable of mending and restoring themselves.

At the beginning of the final week of Johnny's hospitalization, they let me visit. His eyes looked medicated, and he'd lost weight and was pale, though he said the doctors were allowing him to walk outside along the riverfront path if he brought a nurse's aide. We spoke nothing of forgiveness or repair.

I went back to class, and though the syllabus said Melville, we returned to Walt Whitman's 'The Wound-Dresser.' I read a line from the middle of the poem, then asked the students to read a line from anywhere they chose. I read, *'The crush'd head I dress (poor crazed hand tear not the bandage away).'* A girl in the back, who had seldom said a word, spoke without raising her hand, *'Their priceless blood reddens the grass.'* Another girl said, *'I dress a wound in the side, deep, deep.'* A boy read, *'From the stump of the arm, the amputated hand, I undo the clotted lint, remove the slough, wash off the matter and blood.'* Samuel Huang started before the other boy finished, *'I am faithful, I do not give out.'* I started again as Samuel Huang finished, *'But soon my fingers failed me, my face drooped and I resigned myself, to sit by the wounded and soothe them, or silently watch the dead.'* We sewed the pieces into a new poem, a patchwork and discordant thing.

* * *

On a Saturday morning, I returned to the hospital, and Johnny and I walked out together. Johnny looked sluggish, as if he was pushing his legs through sleep. He climbed into the car on the passenger side, and I sat in the driver's seat. His bag of meds lay on the floor at his feet. I'd listened as the doctor warned him about the danger of going med-free, and he'd acquiesced as if a central muscle in him had been cut.

I started the car, then killed the engine. He stared through the windshield at the other parked cars. I took his hand. A nurse had cut off his cast the night before, and he wore a heavy fabric brace on his pale lower arm. His fingers were cold, but they gripped my hand as I gripped them. I asked, 'Can we forgive each other?'

He looked into my eyes as if he was uncertain what lay inside me. 'No,' he said quietly, but still he gripped my hand, as if forgiveness was the least of what we needed.

I said, '*Even though unforgiving, never 'gainst thee shall my heart rebel.*'

For a long time, Johnny seemed to think about the words before saying, 'I like that.'

'Byron wrote it to his wife after he forced her to do anal and she caught him sleeping with his sister.'

Johnny laughed. I loved that laugh, even when it sounded like breaking glass.

Sixteen

Johnny

The doctors injected me with God knows what, and when that only made the monsters grow, they strapped me down and injected me again until they exhausted the monsters and me both, and though the monsters never blew apart into shards of bone, blood, and sinew, they slowed their attack and then froze where they stood like taxidermied beasts collecting dust on a museum floor. I wondered if the medicine had turned me into a taxidermied man too, collecting dust in a hospital bed, and decided that it probably had. The doctors asked me how I had spent the night before shooting up my bedroom, but they seemed to doubt the stories I told them of my trip to a poisoned garden in the woods, my midnight feast, and my drugging and near-drowning in the hands of a Gullah root doctor, as if I'd hallucinated those events as I'd hallucinated the wet black creatures at the window.

I told them about the jimson weed and they doubted that too. They said my blood tests showed tropane alkaloid, which is in jimson, but they also said cocaine is basically pure tropane and they suspected that, whatever else I'd gotten myself into on the night I'd disappeared, I'd dunked my head in a pile of snow. They prodded my body, ran me through dozens of mental health and acuity batteries, shined penlights into my eyes, and brought me little plastic cups with assortments of pills. When the jaws and claws of the monsters went away entirely, the doctors introduced me to a nurse's aide named Gerald, who told me he moonlighted as a bouncer at a strip club by the airport, and the two of us took long walks on the riverbank path and watched seagulls make suicide dives into the brown river only to emerge alive with fingerlings in their beaks. When one of the birds spiraled like an out-of-control jetfighter and then pulled out above the water's surface, Gerald laughed and said, 'Don't you wish you could do that?'

'No,' I said, 'when I go down, I plan to go down for good.'

He said something that surprised me. 'You Icarus, then?'

'Hardly.'

Lillian came and left and came and left. She looked nervous. I wanted to tell her that I was all right and she was all right and we were all right, but the words wouldn't come. So we sat together, staring at each other, smiling a little, as if we'd lit a fuse and nothing had exploded but we knew better than to reach into the hole for it just yet. One morning, after I swallowed my pills, I told her, 'Some things are better left unsaid.'

Lillian nodded. 'I know.'

The truth is I would have forgiven her, but forgiving her would have meant forgiving myself, and I couldn't see an angle from which that would be possible. If, in the safety of a swaying ship hold, I had tagged and processed the bodies of men who had died fighting out in the world, nothing I did now or in the future could undo or change the facts of my existence.

'You know what your problem is?' Gerald asked on one of our walks. 'You've got to lighten up. You can take your medicine, but it won't do any good if you don't lighten up.'

'I'm light,' I said. 'If you don't hold me down, I'll float away on the breeze.'

Gerald shook his head. 'You'd fall like a stone.'

When Lillian arrived to take me home, we went out to the car and sat and held hands, and she told me about Lord Byron having anal sex, and I laughed, and I wondered if Gerald might be right – I needed to lighten up.

But two days later, after Lillian left the house to teach her classes and I was sitting in the sunroom with the newspaper, Percy lying at my feet, a headline on the front of the Metro section made me laugh again, and this time laughing made me feel the way Gerald had described me: like stone. The headline said, *Police Close Fernandina Case*.

The article explained that the Sheriff's Office was ending the investigation into Sheneel and Alex Greene's deaths. The evidence, a spokesman said, pointed to a tragic if unusual double suicide. A forensic pathologist determined that Sheneel had died of an overdose, having swallowed a combination of four prescription and nonprescription drugs. After she died, the police

148

said, Alex – for unclear reasons – had mutilated his sister. 'We've never seen anything like it,' said the spokesman, 'but we're working under the assumption that this was an act of grief.' When the police confronted Alex with the inconsistencies in his account, the grief apparently turned to despondency. The pathologist said that he also died of an overdose, compounded by a head injury most likely sustained when he fell from his bed. Investigation into the source of the drugs would remain active. Additional counseling would be offered to Sheneel's college classmates.

I pictured the bedroom where I'd found Alex Greene. The box spring and mattress rested directly on the green oval carpet where his body was lying – much too close and soft to cause a head injury. I pictured his arm, broken sideways and backward. I pictured a huge man moving toward me in the dim light, swinging a baseball bat.

I felt the fury rise inside me, and, after I'd spent six weeks in the hospital, fury scared me. *Lighten up*, I thought. *Lighten the hell up*. I breathed to ease the pressure. *Lighten. Up.* I went to the kitchen and shook a Xanax from the vial – a tiny gray bullet, little bigger than a BB.

I waited for the drug to mushroom from my head and chest into my arms and legs, and then it did. The drug was a lie, but it was a livable lie. I pictured Papa Crowe driving me home from the ocean where he'd almost drowned me, heard him saying, *I tell you one thing more. Your brother-in-law, Daniel Turner, he going to drop the investigation*. But now I answered, *Lighten up*.

The phone rang. I looked at Percy sleeping on the floor. The ringing phone meant nothing to him. He had the right attitude. The phone rang again. *No one here*, I thought. It rang twice more, and the answering machine picked up.

Lillian's voice spoke on to the recording. 'Johnny?' She sounded worried. She probably thought I'd run off again. I would have to remember to tell her that, with enough Xanax, I didn't need to run off. I was already gone. 'Johnny? Pick up the phone.'

I found the phone in the kitchen. 'Hey,' I said.

'Have you seen the newspaper?' she said. 'Tom Corfield just told me. The police are dropping the investigation. They're saying—'

'I saw,' I said.

'It's bullshit.'

'Yeah.'

'What are you going to do?' she asked.

'What do you want me to do?'

'I don't know. We've got to do something.'

'You don't want to do this to me,' I said.

When we hung up, I took a nap. But I woke two hours later feeling jittery and hyped. *Not good*. Another Xanax would bring me down. And another and another and another. I went to the bedroom, undressed, and took a shower, cranking the heat so it scalded my skin. When I dressed again and walked into the living room, Percy was standing by the front door. 'You think so?' I said.

Fifteen minutes later, I pulled to a meter across from the Sheriff's Office and left Percy in the car. Inside the building, I told the woman at the security desk I'd come to see Daniel Turner, and when she called, he told her to send me back.

As I entered the Homicide Room, Daniel stepped from his cubicle with a big grin and said, 'Glad to see you out, Johnny!'

I said, 'Alex Greene's arm was broken. It looked like someone tried to rip it off.'

Still grinning, he crossed the room, put a loving hand on my shoulder, and said, 'Come on back.' We went to his cubicle, and he said. 'Now, what's this about?'

'You're calling Alex Greene a suicide? And Sheneel too? His arm was bent behind his back—'

He narrowed his eyes, as if trying to be patient. 'The medical examiner said the break happened after he died.'

'Fine. And who broke it?'

'That's a bit of a mystery, right?' he said. 'And with a little prodding from me, we've decided not to look into it.'

'Why is that?'

'As far as we can tell, only one person could have broken it.'

'Who is that?'

Daniel let his eyes rest on me.

I said, 'You've got to be kidding.'

'*You* were there,' he said.

'I didn't touch him.'

Daniel leaned back in his chair. 'When the Phelps security man came into the house, you were lying on top of him. You said someone hit you with a bat, but the security man saw no one and no bat.'

'I told the truth.'

151

'After a fashion.'

'What does that mean?'

Daniel sighed. 'It means you're unreliable, Johnny – *at best*, unreliable. A lot of guys here think worse of you than that. Why should anyone believe you?'

'You know this is wrong, Daniel.'

'I don't know anything like that.'

'Papa Crowe told me you would do this.'

The grin spread across Daniel's face again. 'Who is "Papa Crowe"?'

'He said the Phelpses own you.'

Daniel whispered, suddenly angry, 'Be careful what you say. Crazy man or not, you don't start accusing me. I love my sister and I'm sorry for you, but never try that on me, you understand?'

'I'm telling you what Papa Crowe said. He said you had protected them before.'

'Who is "Papa Crowe"?' he asked again.

'Sheneel and Alex Greene's uncle.'

'And why would Sheneel and Alex Greene's uncle know anything about me?'

'He seems to know about a lot of things.'

'I'm serious, Johnny. Take care of your head. Get healthy. I've done what I can to help you – more than you know. But if you try to bring me down to your kind of craziness, I'll cut you off. You understand?'

'I understand,' I said.

'It's time for you to figure out what matters,' he said.

'Right.' I started to leave, then said, 'What kind of drugs did they overdose on?'

He rubbed his cheek with the flat of his hand. 'The case is closed.'

'I understand,' I said.

When I got back to the car, Percy was sitting on the driver's seat. I shoved him to the side and said, 'I'm going to take you to bite someone. What do you think of that?'

He turned once, lay down on the passenger seat, and closed his eyes.

Thirty-five minutes later, I pulled into the yard outside Papa Crowe's half-painted wooden house. The folding lawn chair on the front porch was empty, but Papa Crowe's brown Chrysler was parked on the broken oyster shells and weeds next to the house.

'C'mon, boy,' I said, and Percy bounded from the car after me.

From the porch, the inside of the house looked dark, but when I knocked on the screen door, slow footsteps approached, and before I could see Papa Crowe, I heard him laugh and say, 'Look what the devil drag home.' The door swung open and he said, 'Come in, son, come in.'

I stepped into the dim room, Percy behind me. On the unpainted walls, rows of wooden shelves held glass jars – mayonnaise jars, fruit jelly jars, old Coke bottles, mustard pots – stuffed with dried leaves and flowers. A glass-fronted cabinet held jugs of strange-colored syrups. The air smelled of cinnamon.

'I should kill you,' I said.

'Truth is I probably have it coming. That's some powerful jimson or your head is weaker

153

than I guessed. But I make a mistake, I own it.' Percy ran among the shelves sniffing at the jars, but the old man looked unworried.

'A bad mistake,' I said. 'Why did you do it?'

'Trying to help.'

'Next time you want to help, let me suffer on my own, OK?'

'Fair enough.' He was having difficulty sounding contrite. 'It good to see you on your feet, that what matters.'

'A little unsteady.'

'That natural. Now, why you come to see me if you ain't going to kill me?'

'To tell you that you were right. The Sheriff's Office dropped the investigation.'

He frowned and turned toward the kitchen. 'They tell the family yesterday. No evidence of murder, they say. Sheneel try suicide before, so she try it again. Alex tell guilty lies to the police about Sheneel, so he must've killed himself too. Straight line of explanation, they say. When fruit fall from the tree, it fall straight down. Don't look for gravity to throw it over the fence.'

I followed him into the kitchen. He went to a half-size refrigerator and pulled out a pitcher. 'Tea?'

'I'll never again put anything you give me in my mouth.'

'Understood.' He poured a glass for himself and took a long drink. 'So now we got to bury two more Greenes in the woods.'

'They say Sheneel and Alex both overdosed. I asked Daniel, but he wouldn't show me the toxicology report.'

'Oh, I seen that. They give us a copy from the coroner. I take care of Sheneel with Indian root, but the report don't mention none of that. It say she got codeine, OxyContin, marijuana, and Rohypnol in her blood. That it.'

'Rohypnol? The date-rape drug?'

'Sure. They say they see it in other suicides. It make it easy. You already asleep when you stop breathing.'

'What killed Alex?'

'A baseball bat crack his head, I think, but they say it is codeine and alcohol.'

'I saw no bottles. I don't think he was drinking.'

'This what they say is all.'

Then, from in front of the house, a car horn blew, once long and once short. Percy barked and jumped against the screen door.

Papa Crowe set his tea on the table and said, 'You wait here, son.'

But I followed him into the living room, where he took a mustard pot from a shelf, and I watched through the front door as he approached a long black town car that had pulled sideways to the porch. The backseat window rolled down and a strange-looking woman peered out. She had high cheekbones and her white skin looked glassy, as if it had melted under high heat. She had no eyebrows, one of her eyelids seemed to hang crooked over her eye, and she'd drawn her thin black hair back tight the way you cinch a string to hold together a splitting bundle. She looked freakishly ancient, though she could have been young. She spoke to Papa Crowe out of one side of her damaged lips.

155

I couldn't hear her words or Papa Crowe's response, but saw that he spoke gently before touching her glassy forehead with his fingers. She drew back as if his touch stung her, then seemed to will her face back to his fingers. After saying a few words, he lifted the lid from the mustard pot, dipped a thumb deep into a muddy substance, and drew a thick cross on to the woman's forehead.

She said something more, he nothing. The window went up and the town car rolled slowly out of the yard. Papa Crowe turned away, frowning.

When he came into the house, I said, 'Who was that?'

He looked distracted as he returned the pot to the shelf. 'That Mrs Cecilia Phelps. Edward wife. Proud woman, too bad for her.'

'And she comes to *you*?'

'Lot of people come to me, and I don't dose them all with jimson.'

'What happened to her?'

'You like that? Long time ago, she get burn in a house fire. Gas stove blow up. She get her boy Stephen out, but when she go back for Stephen's little brother, the house fall down on her.'

'It's terrible.'

'Better it be Edward that got burnt.' He went back to the kitchen for his tea.

'I still don't get it. Why does she come to *you*?'

'I got the only medicine that take away the pain.'

'The muddy cross?'

'It cow dung. Put it on a burn and it take

156

down the pain and swelling. Thirty year after the fire, she still think it do her good, so it all the same.'

Percy came into the kitchen and lay by the table.

I said, 'You know what, I will take some tea.'

'I figure you would sooner or later.' He got the pitcher from the refrigerator and poured me a glass. 'You want jimson for that?'

I gave him a look.

'Was a joke,' he said, and handed me the tea.

'I've been told I need to lighten up.'

'It OK to be heavy, but a man got to laugh. He don't laugh, he split down the middle.'

'What did Cecilia Phelps tell you that made you frown?'

'You see that? You got the vulture eye too much.'

'What did she say?'

He considered me. 'For some people, time don't pass,' he said. 'Something bad happen, and time stop. It like that for Cecilia Phelps. Time stop thirty year ago, the day of the fire. She living that afternoon still. She running out of the kitchen with Stephen in her hands and her hair burning. She running back for the baby, and the ceiling coming down on her. It a terrible thing when time don't pass.'

'So what did she say?'

'She say she never forgive me.'

My own words to Lillian stabbed at me. 'Why would she say that?'

'She blame me for the death of the baby.'

'Did you have anything to do with it?'

157

''Course not. I tell you – the gas stove blow up. But a woman like that, she think I got the power to make fires like I heal them.'

'It seems like there's a lot of blame around here.'

He looked at me. 'Yeah, it do. So, I got a question for you. What you do now?'

'Nothing. I'm done. Six weeks in a hospital. No more for me.'

'Then why you drive here to talk with me?' He shook his head. 'I know what you going to do now. You go talk with Edward Phelps. You ask him what he do when Sheneel threaten to tell what the paper mill putting in the water.'

'Not me. I'm going home.'

'Maybe you also ask him why his wife's driver is a big pale man, look like the man you say hit you with a baseball bat.'

'That's what he looks like?'

'He do five minutes ago.'

'A lot of men are big and white.'

'True enough.'

I called Percy to me with a pat on my leg. 'Thanks for the tea,' I said.

'I know another thing you going to do.'

'Yeah, what's that?'

'You go fishing with me tomorrow.'

That made me smile. 'Why would I do that? I don't like fishing.'

'I show you the islands. We catch dinner for you and your wife.'

'Last time I went on a trip with you, it turned out bad.'

'We get the bad one out of the way. Tomorrow

158

be the good one. I show you things you never see before.'

'That's what worries me.'

'The redfish is running. You like oysters? We dig some.'

'I don't think so.'

He shrugged. 'You change your mind, be here at five a.m. We be pulling out crab pots when the sun come up.'

Seventeen

Lillian

Daniel stopped by when his shift ended. 'Is he home?' he asked, and, as if Daniel had conjured him, Johnny stepped into the living room from the kitchen.

'Ready for duty,' Johnny said.

Daniel looked exhausted, listing to the left, his thin hair pasted against his forehead. When he saw Johnny, he seemed to want to back out of the house. He said to me, 'I want to explain—'

Johnny said, 'The drugs in Sheneel Greene's body included Rohypnol. No one takes roofies for fun. And people don't kill themselves with it. It's used to rape or rob or maybe kill someone.'

Daniel's voice was heavy and weary and slow. 'See, you're wrong again. Kids take it at parties, and we see it a lot in intentional overdoses. Look it up on your damned computer before you open

159

your mouth.' He turned back to me. 'I want to explain what happened with the—'

'The Phelps mills are poisoning the water and the land,' Johnny said. 'Sheneel was going to expose them.'

Daniel shook his head. 'Shut the hell up, Johnny. All right?'

I said to Johnny, 'It would be a good idea.'

But Johnny had already done the damage. Daniel asked him, 'Do you really know who the Phelpses are?'

'I know they've bought some cops,' Johnny said.

Daniel said, 'I've warned you about that.'

'What will you do? Lock me in a mental ward? I've done that. Put me in jail? Take me out back and fight me?'

Daniel looked at me. 'Your husband needs serious help.'

I said, 'You told me the investigation was still *going*.'

'It was. But it turned out that it was going nowhere. Look, this is my job. I can't tell you everything. But we're confident about Sheneel Greene. No one knows for sure what happened with her brother. The Gullah sometimes take care of their own problems. Alex cut Sheneel's arm, and that might have been too much for them. If he didn't kill himself with drugs, he did it by breaking the rules and bringing this on himself.'

'Why would he cut off Sheneel's arm?' I asked.

'Why would anyone?'

'That's not an answer.'

160

He said, 'It's the only answer I've got.'

Johnny said, 'It's time for you to leave.'

Daniel stared at him.

'Out of the house,' Johnny said.

'I came to explain to Lillian—'

'To tell lies? We've had enough already. Time to go.'

Now Daniel was angry. 'You've got to back off, Johnny.'

'I want to,' he said. 'I'm doing my best to. But every time I take a step back, you take two steps toward me. Or someone else does.'

'I'm telling the truth,' Daniel said.

'That's another lie.' Johnny got in close to Daniel, and Daniel stayed where he was. Percy growled.

'Johnny!' I said. 'Daniel!'

'You never learn, do you?' Daniel said to Johnny.

Johnny laughed at him again. 'For the last six weeks, doctors and nurses have been bouncing me off the walls – telling me when to eat, when to sleep, when to piss, when to watch TV, when to talk, when to shut up – and if I've done it wrong, they've drugged me into doing it right. I've learned a few things along the way.'

Daniel moved closer to Johnny. 'Then act like it.'

Percy barked.

Daniel spun toward the dog. 'Don't you start too!'

Johnny punched Daniel in the jaw.

Daniel fell back but stayed on his feet. He lifted his fingers to his face, checking for blood.

'You've gone too far,' he said, and went for Johnny.

I screamed.

Daniel stopped. Johnny stopped.

I told Daniel, 'Just leave, OK? Get out. I'll take care of it. Johnny will stay out of the way.'

Daniel opened his mouth to speak.

'Go,' I said.

He went.

The house was silent.

Percy wagged his tail uncertainly.

Johnny looked at me and burst into laughter.

'Not funny,' I said. 'Not funny at all.'

'I know.' But he kept laughing. 'I've wanted to do that for so long.' His eyes teared he was laughing so hard.

'He's my brother,' I said.

'I know,' he said. 'I know.'

His laughter died a slow death, and he stared at me with wet eyes and I stared at him. He already knew everything I could tell him: the point-by-point arguments for why he needed to calm himself, why he needed to back off, why hitting Daniel would come to a bad end. What was there to do? I could pack a suitcase and leave him to himself. But his erratic violence drew me to him in spite of myself. And, after all, he was right about Daniel. Daniel was walking the line between honesty and lies, or maybe he'd already fallen hard into corruption.

Johnny stared at me, eyes wet, and said, 'What?'

What was there to say? What was there to do? I shrugged and said, 'You want to eat in or out?'

* * *

La Nopalera ran a chain of restaurants in North Florida and South Georgia. They fried good chips and served two-for-one margaritas on weeknights. Before Johnny's last deployment, we ate there once or twice a week, and the waiters still recognized us and brought me my first margarita and Johnny a beer before they gave us menus.

We ate, and, as I finished my second drink, I said, 'When I was thirteen and Daniel was twenty, I would sneak into his bedroom. He had dropped out of college and was living at home. This was before he decided to become a cop.

'I would open his dresser drawers and pull out a T-shirt or a pair of shorts. Ever since I can remember, he's been big – bigger than my parents, so much bigger than me – and if I held a T-shirt under my chin, it fell to below my knees. I would open the desk drawers. I don't know what I was looking for – notes from Daniel to a girl or from a girl to him, secrets of any kind.

'One afternoon, I found magazines. *Playboy*. *Penthouse*. I took them to my room, and for the next two weeks they were mine to look at when I got home from school and sometimes at night with a flashlight. When I wasn't looking at them, I hid them under my mattress.'

Johnny chewed a bite of chicken taco and said, 'Why are you telling me this?'

I said, 'One day after school I locked the door and lifted the mattress, but the magazines were gone. I panicked. What if my mom had found them? Or my dad? But that night at dinner neither of them acted differently, and then neither of them came to have a private talk when I went to

163

bed. For nearly a month, I was sure that they had found them. But then I snuck back into Daniel's room and checked his drawer, and there were the magazines. He had found them and taken them back.

'I knew I should leave them, but instead I took them to my room again and hid them as I'd hidden them before. Three days later, they were gone, and a week after that I took them again. We went back and forth that way for months. And all that time, we never said a word to each other about the magazines. We never even glanced at each other over the breakfast table to acknowledge the strange dance we were doing.'

'Did he ever try anything with you? Ever put his hands on you?'

'No. Never. That's part of what I'm saying. It wasn't like that.'

'And yet it was.'

'No.'

'So, what happened?'

'When I was fourteen, he joined the police academy and moved into an apartment with a friend.'

'He took the magazines with him?'

'No. The morning after he left, I checked his drawer and they were gone, and so – I don't know why – I checked under my mattress, even though he'd had the magazines for the past couple of weeks. He'd put the magazines under my mattress as a farewell present.'

Johnny ate his taco and drank from his beer. 'Kind of creepy.'

'And yet not.'

'He was twenty when this started? And you were thirteen?'

'Maybe it was wrong. Maybe it was weird. But he never touched me or suggested that he wanted to touch me. Maybe it was just part of the messiness of being human.'

'But you were only a kid.'

'Yeah. I'm not excusing it. I'm trying to explain it.'

'*I* can explain it.'

'Daniel and I have still never talked about the magazines. I know that when he looks at me, the magazines are part of what he sees, and they're definitely part of what I see when I look at him. But I also see the rest of him. The man who became a cop. The brother who took care of me. The guy who set you up in an office when you came home. The one who has saved you from yourself a couple of times. I see a complicated man but also a good man.'

'So you're excusing his cover-up of Sheneel and Alex Greene's killings?'

'*Is* it a cover-up?'

'Yeah.'

'I'm not excusing anything. I'm trying to understand it. I'm trying to avoid condemning him too quickly.'

Our waiter, a tall thin Mexican who never stopped smiling, brought a third margarita. 'On the house,' he said.

'I don't need another drink,' I said.

He smiled. 'I think you do.'

When the waiter left, Johnny said, 'You liked the magazines?'

165

'I was thirteen. It was sex. Of course I liked them.'

When we went home, we kept our hands to ourselves. Percy climbed under our bed, where he sometimes hid during thunderstorms, though the night sky was clear and a full moon was rising. I lay in the bed covers, grading student essays through the margarita haze. Johnny lay on his back, staring at the ceiling. He rolled on to his side. 'So you liked looking at pictures of nude women?'

'At thirteen? Yeah.' I put down my pen and looked at him. 'Are you getting off on that?'

'You're not thirteen anymore. I'm not your brother. Of course I'm getting off.' He rolled on to his back. When I turned out the light, he was still staring at the ceiling.

I woke later in the dark and felt his body cupped around mine, holding me.

A couple of hours passed and I woke again. Now he was sitting on the side of the bed, tying his shoes. The clock said three forty-eight.

'What are you doing?'

'Getting dressed.'

'Don't be a jerk. Where are you going?'

'Fishing.'

I felt a flash of fear. 'What do you mean, "fishing"?'

'Hook on the line. Bait on the hook. *Fishing*.'

'Don't do anything—'

'What am I going to do to myself with a hook and bait?'

'You're really going fishing?'

166

'That's what I told you.'
'But you don't fish.'
'I do now.'

Eighteen

Stephen Phelps

Blue moonlight on our white bed sheets. Blue moonlight on her white nightgown and her tennis tan. Kathryn, wife of mine – no more mine than the photograph that I kept on my desk, a stool that I shifted to rest my feet on when I was tired. And if I waited for the moments between her breathing in and breathing out, she looked . . . not quite dead, but not quite living either. I put my hand on her bare shoulder, and, in the air conditioning, under the ceiling fan, her skin was cold.

Kathryn sleeping, me sleepless. Most nights. Not my fault.

Time to think.

Bob Peterson's report: Johnny Bellefleur left Lillian Turner alone – most nights. Sad for such a woman to be alone. Easily remedied. What color of moonlight fell on her skin? What quiet fell between her breathing in and breathing out? What unlocked doors, what windows left open to catch the breeze?

My hand on Kathryn's tan thigh in the blue moonlight.

167

If I had my way, I would break every pane of glass from every window in their house. I would rip every door from its hinges.

Why shouldn't I have my way?

I put my hand under Kathryn's nightgown.

'No,' she said. Asleep. Mostly.

I would wander their halls. I would come to their bedroom. She would be sleeping. Mostly waiting for me.

I shoved my fingers inside Kathryn's underwear.

'Sleeping,' she said.

'Present tense or past?'

'No,' she said.

I pulled her underwear from her legs.

'No,' she said.

'Yes,' I said. 'Yes.'

Nineteen

Johnny

We motored from the Fernandina harbor dock into the Intracoastal Waterway, north toward the end of Amelia Island and the Atlantic Inlet, and then back toward the dark marshes where narrow rivulets and creeks emptied into the larger water. With the moon hanging in the western sky, Papa Crowe sat at the back of the aluminum skiff, a hand on the throttle of a thirty-horsepower Evinrude. We pounded over the sloppy waves, the brackish spray snapping against my cheeks and arms and filming my lips with salt. Fishing rods rattled against the hull. A night bird shadowed through the moonlight.

An hour earlier, when I arrived at Papa Crowe's house, he was sitting in his car, the windows open, the engine running, the radio on to AM Talk. I got in on the passenger side, and he said, 'You late.'

I asked, 'Do you ever sleep?'

'Not tonight. You?'

'Here and there.'

Now, as he cut back the throttle and the skiff glided into the mouth of a creek, the difference between sleep and waking seemed unimportant. With my eyes open or shut, the night was gentle and the warm breeze blew with the pleasant dizziness of a happy dream.

Papa Crowe killed the engine and dropped a little anchor overboard. He baited the fishhooks with live shrimp, handed me a rod, and cast his own bait toward a mudflat that was gleaming in the blue moonlight. He lay on the thwart so his head rested against the gunwale, and closed his eyes. I cast my shrimp toward his and watched the water.

Fifteen minutes passed. Twenty. Thirty. 'Do you catch much?' I asked.

'This time of night, no.' His eyes stayed closed.

I started reeling in my bait. 'Why bother?'

'Can you think of a better place on God's earth than right here before the sun come up?'

'I don't like fishing,' I said, 'and I really don't like pretend fishing.'

169

'Then why'd you come?'

'I couldn't sleep.'

As the moon closed on the western horizon and sunlight filtered into the sky from the east, the water surface turned slate-gray, then began to glow orange, and, as if Papa Crowe had known the timing of the world, the tip of his fishing rod bent down. He gave me a tired smile, snapped the rod to set the hook, and reeled in. When he pulled the redfish on to the aluminum floor of the boat, he struck it once on the head with a wooden club darkened with age and blood.

'That it then,' he said.

He put the fish in a cooler, stowed the rods, and pulled the ripcord on the engine. For the next hour, as the sun rose orange and enormous, we collected crabs from pots that Papa Crowe had set in the estuaries. When he dropped the crabs into the cooler, he opened a gallon Ziploc bag, pulled out a sealed plastic container, and opened that too. The smell of putrefying meat, as bad as anything I'd smelled in the ship hold on the Arabian Sea, filled the air.

Papa Crowe grinned at me. 'Rotten chicken get the sweetest crabs.'

I breathed in the death and corruption and tried to keep my mind on the gentle morning off the Florida coast instead of the nauseous underbelly of a hospital ship.

After Papa Crowe lowered the last crab pot into the water, he turned the bow of the skiff toward the Intracoastal and opened the throttle. As we topped the swells and a salt breeze stung my face, I felt a happiness unlike any I'd felt

170

since before my last tour of duty. The sun was rising, warming the early morning, and the light danced on the water in strange patterns. Gulls crossed the sky high above, seemingly oblivious to all but the breeze.

For a half-hour or more, we skimmed across the Intracoastal, and then Papa Crowe hooked the boat through a gap that led to the open Atlantic.

I yelled over the sound of the engine and the skiff-pounding water, 'Where now?'

He squinted into the sun and pointed toward a barrier island.

I turned again to face the salt spray and the early morning sunlight. If we rounded the island, the sea would open for thousands of miles. I felt again the excitement that I'd felt on my first deployment, when I'd stood on the deck of a destroyer so powerful that it felt more like a monstrous machine than a boat and I'd watched the sun rise over the rolling surf.

Now, the fins of two dolphins surfaced in the water to our left, and another to our right, and though I'd watched – from the same ship where I'd seen the sunrise – as pods of dolphins had corralled and butchered shoals of fish, these three looked as far from battles and butchery as they would if they were escorting us from dry land into a world without conflict or bloodshed. When I came back from the Arabian Sea, I thought I would be happy if I never stepped on to a boat again. But this morning, as we motored from shore, the expanse of the ocean brought me as close as I expected to come again to peace.

Instead of continuing toward the open ocean, though, Papa Crowe angled the boat toward a densely wooded island shoreline. A mile or so up the beach, a structure that might have been a dock protruded into the water, but no other signs of human life appeared. The old man cut back the gas and we idled alongside a mudflat.

'This a Gullah island,' he said. 'Lot of Greene and Crowe family live here still.'

'I don't see anyone.'

'No, you don't.' He angled the boat close to the shore. 'Used to be, after the Civil War, a Confederate general own the island. Then the general's son shoot his own boy and kill himself too, and the general say the island got too many ghosts for him and he sell it to the Carnegie family – Carnegie steel, you know. The Carnegie, they immigrant from Scotland and no one like immigrant, even immigrant with money, and the other people with money, they say the Carnegie can't join their club, so the Carnegie buy the island and start their own club. Everybody want something someone else got. They take it or they make it. But I tell you, the whole time, the Greene and Crowe live here and work the fields when there're fields to work and fish when there're fish to fish. The general's son and grandson die, and then the general die too, and the Carnegie, they gone long time, most of them, except some grand-children and bastards. But the Greene and Crowe still here.'

Without warning, he hit the throttle and cut the skiff hard toward the beach. The boat shot on to a sandbar, and he killed the engine. 'We here.'

172

'Where?'

'Come with me.' He tossed the anchor over the side, climbed into knee-deep water, and trudged toward dry land. I followed and soon we stood together on the beach, the breeze bending the grass and hushing through the tall trees beyond the dunes.

I said, 'What are we—'

'Shhh.' He pointed at the edge of the woods. From between two longleaf pines, a tall brown animal stepped on to the sand, followed by a smaller animal. Horses – a mare and her foal. The sun glinted off their brown coats, as if they were wet from running.

'What are they doing here?'

'They wild.'

The mare trotted on to the dune and the foal followed her. Then another five horses, all of them brown or gray, most with a streak of white running from their foreheads to their muzzles, emerged from the woods. Two bolted over the dune and on to the beach.

'C'mon,' Papa Crowe said, and he crossed the sand to a bleached driftwood log. We sat facing the ocean as the rest of the horses came across the dune on to the beach. Soon, four more joined them. The mare and another stood with their foals, and the others ran on the beach or nuzzled and rubbed against each other.

'How many of them are on the island?' I asked. 'A hundred? Two hundred?'

We sat, and again something like peace descended on me.

Papa Crowe said, 'Why you think I bring you?'

Beyond the horses, the gentle morning surf rolled white, dropped softly on to the beach, receded, and rolled again. 'To free me from myself?'

'This place do that for you?'

'Maybe it could.'

'I think you mistaken. Everybody want something.'

As he spoke, a hand reached from behind me and cold metal pressed against the skin of my neck. I jerked and tried to pull away, but the metal was a blade and the blade cut into me. I froze. I tried to speak but couldn't.

'Don't move,' Papa Crowe said, 'else you cut you own fool throat.'

I couldn't turn to see who held the blade. 'What the hell—'

'Shhh,' said Papa Crowe. 'Now you know this ain't your place. This *my* place. If you want to get free from yourself, you find your own place. You understand?'

Blade against my throat, I said, 'You're insane.'

'Do you understand?' he asked again.

I wanted to run. I wanted to fight. 'Yeah.'

'Yeah. 'Course you do.'

The blade moved from my neck, and I spun. A woman stood behind me, holding a knife loosely in her fingers. Her skin had the kind of deep tan that comes from a life lived outside. Her stringy brown hair fell to her shoulders. She looked forty or so. She wore jeans and a pink cotton blouse that she'd knotted in front so that her belly showed. She was barefoot.

'Johnny Bellefleur,' Papa Crowe said, 'meet Laura Greene.'

174

'Glad to know you,' the woman said. Her face was hard-featured.

'You're Sheneel and Alex's mother?'

'Yeah.'

'Alex said you were in New Mexico.'

'I'm not.'

'Laura come home when she hear about Sheneel in trouble,' Papa Crowe said. 'Then Sheneel get killed and Alex get killed. So Laura stay here and she still alive so far.'

She had intensely focused gray eyes, desperate eyes. I said, 'Do you always introduce yourself by threatening to cut someone's throat?'

'Lately, it seems like a good idea to let people know what to expect if they come too close to me.'

'I was just sitting here.'

'And I didn't cut your throat either, did I?'

Papa Crowe said to her, 'Johnny a good man mostly. Don't take to jimson weed and don't know his own place, but he a good man.'

She said, 'Let's go somewhere else, get out of the open.'

'What's wrong with here?' I said.

But she was already climbing over the dune, heading toward the trees, her knife in her hand.

We went after her, walking into the woods between the longleaf pines. We came to a rough path of pine needles and sand, pocked with hoof prints from the horses. Pine trees and cabbage palms shaded us and palmettos brushed our sides. As we moved inland, the path widened and we entered a grove of magnolias and live oaks with muscadine vines clinging to the trunks and

175

Spanish moss hanging from the branches. A brown horse stood in the shade of an enormous oak as if it were sleeping. Except for the sound of our footsteps, the woods were quiet.

'Does anyone live here?' I asked.

'Sure,' said Papa Crowe, but he said no more.

The path opened on to a large plot of weed- and grass-covered land out of which rose a big white house, pillared from the long front porch to the broad eaves, the first-floor windows and grand front door covered with plywood, the second-floor windows dark. A small white outbuilding was attached to the main house by a vine-covered breezeway.

'One of the Carnegie girls live here till she die,' said Papa Crowe.

Laura Greene cut across the yard toward the outbuilding. She went around the side and opened an old door with a broken lock. The building housed an empty marble-tiled swimming pool. Gray, unpainted stucco walls rose to a gray, unpainted ceiling. On the narrow strip of floor next to the pool, Laura Greene had set up a camp with a pile of green-and-white striped cushions that looked salvaged from old chaise longues, a wicker basket stuffed with personal possessions, and two folding wooden chairs.

'When I was a boy, I sometimes sneak in here,' Papa Crowe said. 'Back then, they cover the walls with pretty pictures, but they fill the pool with water from the well, and they so much sulfur in it, the air eat the paint off. Terrible smell, but I swim like a rich boy.'

'Sit down if you want,' Laura Greene said.

Instead, Papa Crowe went to the pool, lowered himself on to the marble ladder built into the side, and climbed down.

I remained standing. 'Do you know why someone would kill Sheneel and Alex? Or why someone would cut Sheneel's arm?'

She glanced at Papa Crowe, who shook his head, and she turned back to me. 'I know who cut it off. I did. I cut it and buried it.'

I felt ice in my chest. 'Why would you do that?'

She looked at me with those desperate eyes. 'I hadn't seen her for three years,' she said. 'I talked with Alex on the phone, but I hadn't even talked with her. When Alex called and told me the trouble she was in, I got on a bus. But it was too late.'

'Why did you—'

'I'd just moved into this place when she died. Alex called and told me she was dead and so I went out to see her—'

'This was before the police?'

'Of course. I brought my knife—'

'Alex knew where Sheneel's body was before the police did?'

'How else would he have told me where to find her?'

'How did he know?'

She glanced down at Papa Crowe, who was pacing in the bottom of the empty pool. 'Will you tell him to shut the hell up and listen?'

Papa Crowe said, 'Shut up and listen.' He lay down on the marble tiles and looked at the gray ceiling as if it were the sky.

'I went out to Little Marsh Island,' Laura

Greene said, 'and I saw my baby. I saw what they did to her. Animals hadn't gotten to her but insects had. There wasn't much I could do. I couldn't bury her. She was too big – I only had my knife. But she was holding one of her hands in front of her face, as if she was trying to keep the insects from her eyes and mouth, and I saw the snake that Papa Crowe had tattooed on her wrist, and I thought, I can do this much. So I used my knife and I put that part of my daughter into the ground.'

'That's kind of messed up.'

'What would you know?'

For eighteen months I had assembled the bodies that had come to a ship's hold in vinyl bags, and had tagged the assemblages with individual soldiers' names that I found on the dog tags in the boots if the boots hadn't been blown away or burned. I'd done my job as if the broken bodies still had separate identities. 'Nothing,' I said.

'That's right,' she said. 'So I gathered what I could. She had ten dollars and her cell phone in her pockets. I bought cigarettes with the ten dollars and smoked them, and that's how I mourned her passing. Is that messed up too?'

'You got her cell phone?'

'Yeah, I got that too.'

'Someone called my office with that phone. That was you?'

She shrugged. 'Alex told me you'd come around asking about Sheneel. I wanted to know who you were.'

'So you came back here and smoked cigarettes and played phone games?'

'More or less.'

'And you didn't report her death to the police?'

'Why should I? She was gone. Nothing they could do about that.'

'But they could get the person who did it.'

'Oh, they already know who did it,' she said. 'Or if they don't and I told them, they would do nothing about it.'

'Who?'

'Stephen Phelps.'

Again, I felt the ice that I'd felt when she'd told me she cut off Sheneel's arm. 'How do you know?'

'I'll tell you who he is. When he was ten years old, his father – my Uncle Edward – sat him down and told him he had six or seven years to do anything he wanted. The Phelps money could buy him out of just about any trouble he found for himself until he came of age. Edward told Stephen to fool around with as many girls as he could, run as wild as he liked, take what he wanted, because time was short and, until he turned seventeen or eighteen, sixteen at the earliest, he would be innocent in the eyes of the law.'

'How do you know this?'

'Because when Stephen was fifteen, he told me so himself. I was twenty and already had Alex. I was living in Jacksonville, near the river. Stephen came to my house one afternoon when he should have been in school. Alex was playing in the backyard, and Stephen sat at the kitchen table and I offered him food and soda, but he just sat there with a dumb look on his face like he was thinking about something faraway.

'I stood at the counter, making him a sandwich anyway, talking about this and that, when I felt him behind me – his hands on my waist, his body pressed against me. I laughed, you know? We were cousins, though we hadn't seen each other much since his father pushed my dad out of the paper company, and less after my dad died. So I laughed when he came up behind me, until he reached under my dress and put his hand on me. I hit him, or tried to. I should've used the kitchen knife. He pulled down my underwear and raped me. My fifteen-year-old cousin.' Her anger still burned in her eyes. 'When he finished and let go, I fixed my dress. Alex was standing in the door, watching. He wasn't even three. He didn't understand what he'd seen, but he knew this was no good.

'I told Alex to say goodbye to his cousin. I told him that Stephen wouldn't be coming around anymore. But Stephen took the sandwich from the counter and sat at the table and ate it, and while he ate he told me about the lesson his father had taught him when he was just ten. He told me I could do what I liked. I could call his dad. I could call the police. It didn't matter to him. He finished his sandwich and left the house, saying he'd come again soon.

'I missed my next period, and sure enough I was pregnant. I called Uncle Edward and told him what his boy had done, but Edward laughed and said to send him the bill. That was enough to make me want to keep the baby, and I did.'

I said, 'Pregnant with Sheneel?'

She nodded. 'Papa Crowe helped me raise her.

180

We gave her a Gullah name too. *Ngafa*. Bad spirit. Because if anyone ever tried anything with her, I wanted her to bite into him like a devil.

'For sixteen years, I didn't tell her who her father was. Then, about three and a half years ago, he started coming around again. Now he took interest in Sheneel. At first, I wouldn't let him in, but he offered to help, and I needed money and he gave me some. If he wanted to pay me to get to know Sheneel, I saw no harm in it, and Sheneel, at that age, appreciated the attention. Then I saw him put a hand on Sheneel and I understood what this really was. That's when I told Sheneel who her father was.'

'He a sonofabitch,' Papa Crowe said from the bottom of the pool.

Laura Greene said, 'Sheneel was furious. At me. At Stephen. I'd tried to protect her, but she thought I'd betrayed her. She moved out of the house that night. Alex was renting his place on Gum Street and he let her stay with him.

'Stephen kept coming to my house. I don't know what he wanted. I don't think he knew either. He talked to me. I couldn't stand hearing his voice. I told him to leave. But he talked and kept talking, like he owned my house and owned *me*.

'He talked until all I could think about was sinking a kitchen knife into his chest. So I left. I packed a suitcase and got on a bus for New Mexico. I spoke with Alex from time to time on the phone. For a while, everything seemed fine. But, last spring, Stephen started coming around Alex and Sheneel's house. Alex wouldn't tell me exactly what was going on between Sheneel and her father. I knew I should come back, but I couldn't get myself to do it.

'Then, last June, Sheneel stabbed Stephen.' She smiled, and her mouth was crooked. '*My* girl. That's what Stephen needed, I thought. But maybe it's what *I* needed. Stephen refused to testify against her, the charges were dropped, and I hoped it was over.

'But Stephen kept coming around, and then Alex told me on the phone that Sheneel had threatened to report what the mills were doing. That's when I decided to come home. I knew the Phelpses wouldn't allow it.'

She looked hard at me, as if her story had been a kind of challenge. I glanced down at Papa Crowe, who'd closed his eyes at the bottom of the pool.

I said, 'So Stephen killed Sheneel because she was threatening him.'

'Because she was threatening him and because he wanted her but couldn't have her. I know it.'

'Do you have any evidence?' I asked.

'What evidence do I need?'

'The police won't arrest a man on what you've told me.'

She nodded down at the pool. 'Papa Crowe said you would help.'

'Not me.'

She screwed her lips. 'You don't want to be a coward. That's what Papa Crowe says. He says you want to be a hero.'

I shook my head. 'All I want is a good night's sleep.'

'Is that any different?'

'Alex didn't tell you that Stephen Phelps killed Sheneel?' I asked.

'He didn't need to. When he told me she was dead, I asked where she was. He told me and I went.'

'And he didn't tell you who told him she was there?'

'I knew and he knew that I knew.'

'Why would Stephen have shown him her body?'

'So Alex would know what Stephen would do to him if he didn't behave. It's always been this way. You do what the Phelpses say or they burn you or rape you or take what you value most in the world.'

I glanced again at Papa Crowe, lying with his eyes closed. 'I don't see what I can do that the two of you can't.'

'No one listens to us. I'm the girl who got pregnant when I was seventeen and again at twenty and whose own family won't talk to her. Papa Crowe is a crazy old Gullah who they keep arresting for trespassing on land he says he owns but he's got no title to, and who crams the shelves in his house with bottles of weeds and animal blood. You're from outside. They'll listen.'

I laughed at that. 'I just got out of the hospital where they shot me full of drugs every time I tried to talk. No one listens to me either.'

For the first time, her intense eyes dimmed. 'That's what I told Papa Crowe.'

'Sorry.'

'You won't help?'

183

'Nothing I can do that you can't.'

She shook her head, picked up one of the wooden folding chairs, carried it to the edge of the pool, and dropped it to the pool bottom. The chair shattered by Papa Crowe's head. He opened his eyes. Laura Greene said, 'He says he can't help.'

Papa Crowe pushed himself to sitting and then stood stiffly. 'I ain't deaf.' He climbed the ladder, brushed the dust off his pants on the poolside, and stepped close to Laura Greene. 'But you,' he said to her, 'you got to listen better.'

As we motored back across the water toward the harbor, the morning sun hung in a cloudless sky and glared off the rippling surf. Two gulls soared above the skiff.

I yelled above the sound, 'Why did you tell her I could help?'

''Cause you need this. 'Cause you been helping already and I reckon you will.'

'You reckon wrong.'

We rounded an island that was mostly submerged under the rising tide. One of the gulls banked to the left and disappeared, the other lowering over the skiff as if it expected to be fed scrap fish or bait. Papa Crowe opened the throttle.

'Where to now?' he said. I said nothing. We crossed an area of flat water and I looked into its depths for fish but saw only ribbed sand. 'You a useless man now?' Papa Crowe said. 'You go home and lie on the floor with your dog?' As we approached shore, the water turned gold and brown, stained with tannin from the same pine trees that the Phelpses pulped, bleached, and pressed into paper. 'You sit on the branch of a tree and sing of nothing like the bird?' he said.

'You're a bastard,' I said.

'You sleep in a hole in the ground like the tortoise?'

When we entered the Fernandina harbor, he cut back on the throttle, and as we approached the dock he let the engine die and we glided alongside the weather-beaten wood until he threw a line around a cleat.

'Get out,' he said, and there was a mean edge to his voice that I hadn't heard before.

I said, 'Do you know where Stephen Phelps lives?'

'Sure. Everybody do. He live in the big house built by his grandfather.'

'You expect he would still be there, or would he be at the mill?'

'He a boy with a lot of money and don't like to get out of bed over early.'

'OK, then,' I said.

'Yeah?'

'Yeah.'

He smiled. 'It the right choice, son.'

'You're coming in with me, though.'

'You think?'

'I do.'

'Then how can I say no?'

Stephen Phelps lived with his wife and two children near downtown Fernandina in a large yellow Victorian house with a walled-in front garden. The front path, made of crushed and raked coquina, circled around a central fountain and led up three broad steps on to a veranda.

When we knocked, a small girl with blond hair answered. I'd seen her in a photograph on Stephen Phelps's desk when I'd visited his office. She wore white cotton pajamas and gazed up at Papa Crowe and me with what looked like astonishment.

A voice spoke from behind her. 'Sammie! Get away from there.' The child disappeared, and a black woman, about fifty years old and wearing the kind of black-and-white maid's uniform that I'd thought was only used in old movies, opened the door wider. She gazed at me, then Papa Crowe, and then me again, seeming to appraise our wet pant legs and dirty, night-worn faces.

'Hello, Toya,' Papa Crowe said.

But she spoke only to me, through sour lips. 'What can I do for you?'

'We're here to talk with Mr Phelps,' I said.

'He's expecting you?'

'No, but he should be,' I said.

'Your name?' she asked, as if she imagined it would be something unpleasant.

But footsteps approached from behind her, and Stephen Phelps, dressed in khakis and a blue Oxford shirt, holding his daughter in one arm, said, 'It's all right, Toya. I know these gentlemen.'

'They—' she started.

He repeated himself. 'It's all right.' He put a patronizing hand on her shoulder, and I imagined him putting that hand up Laura Greene's dress and on Sheneel Greene's leg. 'Will you please help Kathryn with breakfast?'

186

The maid gave Papa Crowe a distrustful glance and disappeared down the front hall.

Phelps looked at Papa Crowe and then at me. 'How does that saying go? A man is judged by the company he keeps.'

I said, 'You two know each other?'

Phelps said, 'I've had many encounters with Mr Crowe. They often have involved trespassing and sometimes destruction of machinery or other property.'

'Those were accidents, sir,' Papa Crowe said.

Phelps asked me, 'What can I do for you?'

'When we talked last time, you said I should let you know if I had more questions.'

'I meant at my office,' he said.

'But you weren't at your office this morning.'

'I haven't even eaten breakfast.' He looked at his watch.

We stared at him.

He said, 'Fine. Come in, then.'

Inside, the house smelled of scented cleansers and furniture polish the way a closely kept old hotel does. Wooden stairs, covered with a paisley carpet runner, led to the second floor from the front hall. The furniture in the living room looked as old as the house, but newly upholstered and clean.

As Phelps walked to the breakfast room, his daughter watched us over his shoulder. His wife stood at the table, spooning scrambled eggs on to three plates. She wore her blond hair in a ponytail and had the kind of face that thins rather than widens with age. She wore a tennis skirt and a white V-neck T-shirt with a pink heart logo.

187

Phelps asked the maid to get coffee for Papa Crowe and me, introduced his smiling wife as Kathryn and his daughter as Samantha, and said, 'You just missed my boy. He's left for school.'

I said, 'Do you teach him what your father taught you?'

He smiled. 'What was that?'

'You know, the world is your oyster? Take the pearls where you find them?'

'I'm sure I don't know what you're talking about.'

I hadn't expected Phelps's wife and child at the table. But I said, 'Laura Greene says you raped her.'

The surprise on his face turned hard to anger. His wife looked stunned and confused, his daughter only confused. Papa Crowe grinned.

Phelps said, 'What the hell are you talking about?'

'Sorry,' I said, and sipped the coffee. 'She also says you killed Sheneel and Alex.'

Kathryn Phelps stared at her husband.

He said, 'I've invited you into my house, and you've insulted me. You've told terrible lies in front of my—'

'I said I was sorry.'

The Phelps family watched me drink from the coffee cup.

Phelps took a deep breath and let it out. 'It's time for the two of you to leave.'

I said, 'She told me you were only fifteen when you raped her, long before you and your wife got together, I'm guessing.'

Phelps said to his wife, 'Honey, will you take

188

Sammie—' And he pointed a thumb up the front hall.

She forced a smile, took her daughter's hand, and pulled her from the table.

Phelps lowered his voice to a whisper, but the force and threat were clear. 'You don't know what you're doing.' He pulled a phone from his pocket and fumbled trying to dial it. I figured he was calling either the police or Phelps security.

I said, 'Is it true that Sheneel was your daughter?'

He slammed the phone to the table. 'Get out!'

'I hear that you were bothering her last June and she had to cut you.' I reached for a basket of muffins, but he knocked the basket from the table. 'Pathetic,' I said.

He lunged at me. But I rose and met him halfway. He was a tall man and strong, but he was used to a life of soft comforts, and I didn't care whose skin split, his or mine, or whose bones broke. My hand found a knife on the table, and I brought it to his chest.

He whispered, 'A bad, bad mistake.'

Hands pulled me away – Papa Crowe's hands. 'Enough,' he said. 'Nothing good come from killing a man in his own house.'

I dropped the knife on the floor and let Papa Crowe draw me back.

'We get what we come for,' he said.

Phelps stood at the table, panting, his eyes full of fury and humiliation.

'Goodbye, Stephen,' Papa Crowe said, and he stepped toward the front hall.

Kathryn Phelps must have put her daughter in her room or left her with the maid, because she'd returned and stood in the doorway.

'Thank you for the coffee,' Papa Crowe said. 'We about dying with thirst,' and he brushed past her into the hall.

She said nothing, but watched her husband with strange curiosity, and I said nothing either, but followed Papa Crowe out of the house.

Papa Crowe drove me home, grinning as if he was demented.

'What?' I said.

He said, 'You make him worry like a snake in a fire.'

When he dropped me off, Lillian was in the backyard with Percy. Papa Crowe gave me the redfish he'd caught, and I took it outside to show her how I'd spent the night and early morning. I felt good. The saltwater spray had stung me out of myself. Confronting Stephen Phelps had given me a charge of adrenaline. Maybe the meds that the hospital had prescribed for me were giving me a boost too.

Percy wanted the fish, but Lillian seemed unimpressed. She said, 'You have a counseling appointment in forty-five minutes.'

'OK,' I said.

'Yeah?' My easy acquiescence softened her. She looked at the redfish again. 'I didn't think you liked fishing.'

'I didn't used to.'

'I'll cook it for lunch,' she said. 'But I won't clean it.'

We went inside to the kitchen, and she gave me a knife, sharper than the one I'd held to Stephen Phelps's chest. I flipped the redfish on to its back and drew a deep slit from the base of its gills to its anus. I ran my finger through the slit, scraping against the inside of the ribs, pulling the slop of organs and guts on to the counter. Percy danced hungrily at my feet, and my memory flashed to the underbelly of the ship on the Arabian Sea and the slop of bodies, bones, and blood. I forced the picture from my head.

The outpatient psychologist they assigned me at Baptist Hospital had a performer's shtick, complete with finger-on-the-tabletop drum rolls. We sat in his office, with putting-green-colored carpet, a polished wood table between us, and a floor-to-ceiling window facing over the St Johns River.

He said, 'What is it you *want*? What do you *really* want?'

I thought about the question. 'A lot of the life we live is about ignoring the obvious truths. I don't want to live like that.'

'Why not?'

'I want the truth.'

'Even if it's unbearable? Unlivable? What good is a truth like that?'

'It's better to lie to ourselves?' I said.

'Absolutely.' Drum roll.

Twenty

Lillian

A half-hour after Johnny left for his appointment, I put Percy in the backyard and got into my car. Johnny's story about Laura Greene had spooked me. Sheneel's pale face, blue with veins on her forehead and temples and her paper-white hair, hung again in my imagination.

Desire. Like an empty casket. A need in my head, between my legs, in my heart.

I drove out Heckscher Drive to Little Marsh Island. The day had warmed and I kept the windows up and the air conditioner on, though the cool air on my skin made me think of hearses and the futility of resisting bodily corruption. I drove over a narrow bridge, where three black men stood fishing with bamboo poles, and on to Little Marsh Island, past clean stucco houses with neat lawns and gardens, and along a stretch of road with more houses on one side and trees and scrubland on the other. I drove by a newly cut service road, which was blocked with a single chain, and, after the road, a new chain-link fence topped with razor wire.

I realized only when I reached the end of the fence that it closed access to an area just beyond the spot where, according to the first news reports, a man named Peter Lisman had found Sheneel's body while looking at a fifteen-acre plot of real estate.

I turned the car around and drove back along the fence to the chained-off service road, pulled on to the grassy shoulder, and got out. The road cut around the back of the fenced property, and, as I walked, the sounds of Heckscher Drive fell into a silence broken only by the hum and whine of insects. The road bent and led to an open gate in the fence. Large signs on either side said, *No Hunting – No Trespassing*. Another large sign said, *Douglas Commercial and Industrial Development Corp.* A smaller sign, under the developer sign, said, *Phelps Paper Company*.

I stared at the Phelps Paper sign, yanked out my phone, and called Daniel. The news reports had said only that Peter Lisman found Sheneel's body while looking at real estate. When Daniel picked up his phone, I said, 'Does Peter Lisman work for Phelps Paper?'

'Who?'

'I mean it.'

He said nothing, and then, 'You don't want this, Lillian.'

'What have you done?'

'Nothing. I've done nothing.'

'The Phelpses bought the land where Sheneel's body was found?'

'I've let things take their course.'

'That's doing something too, though, isn't it?'

'Leave this alone,' he said.

'Christ, Daniel, if you're mixed up in this—'

'I'm trying to stay as far from it as I can.'

I had to think about that. 'That's a problem.'

'I'm doing the best I can.'

'And what's that?'

'The best I can.'

'What have the Phelpses given you?'

'I didn't like Johnny saying that. I hate it from you.'

'What have they given you?'

'Goodbye, Lillian.'

'It's not too late,' I said, but he had already hung up.

I looked at my watch. Almost four p.m. Johnny would be done with his counseling session and wondering where I was. I looked at the sky – the thin clouds overhead, the sun tipping toward the west. A locust keened high in a pine tree. I walked to the gate. A car had left fresh tracks in the sand. Had it driven in or out? The gate was open. *In.* The *No Hunting – No Trespassing* signs said offenders would be fined up to five hundred dollars or sentenced to sixty days in jail. Daniel's voice sounded in my memory: *You don't want this.*

I went through the gate, following the tracks.

The road cut over a small rise and dipped again on to a wide sandy plot that ended in a grass marsh. Overhead, three turkey vultures, tilting their wings side to side, glided in lazy circles. The road bent around a stand of pine trees and opened on to a construction site. The land was scarred – cleared, filled, flattened. Trees that once grew in the center of the site lay broken and splintered on the periphery, their yellow-white insides exposed like shattered bone. Two white construction trailers stood at the far end. An idle bulldozer stood nearby against a bank of live oaks. Pink landscaping cord, stretching between stakes in the ground, laid out the shape of a large building. A green Land Rover, the driver's door open, stood where the gravel road ended.

I walked to the pink cord, strung so straight and tight it would have thrummed if I'd plucked it. Along one side of the staked-out area, the marsh grass extended a few hundred yards into a body of green-brown water. A mile or so away, two white smokestacks pumped white lines of smoke into the sky.

Across the construction site from the marsh, the white trailers gleamed in the sun. Blinds covered the windows.

I didn't see the men until they were nearly beside me. They must have come from the woods. The tall, thin one had gray hair, parted at the side and thinning but well cut, and a country-club tan. He looked in his mid-sixties and wore a blue tailored suit and black leather ankle boots. The other, much younger, was enormous and balding. He wore black trousers, a white polo shirt that stretched over his belly, and white tennis shoes. He carried a surveyor's wheel in one big hand. His skin was bright white, almost blue-white, almost as translucent as Sheneel's. He looked, I realized, like the man Johnny said hit him with a bat after he found Alex Greene dead.

'Hello,' said the older man.

I tried to smile.

They moved close to me, one on either side. The older man said, 'You didn't see the *No Trespassing* signs?'

'I saw them.'

He looked me over with the whole-body judgment some men use. 'You don't belong here,' he said.

'Nor do you,' I said.

Now he smiled. 'I own this land, miss.' His teeth looked artificially whitened.

'That doesn't mean you belong here.'

'What's your name?'

'Lillian Turner.'

'Ah,' he said. 'Sheneel's teacher.' My surprise at his knowledge seemed to please him. 'Detective Daniel Turner's sister. And, I regret to say, wife of a particularly troublesome man.'

'That's scary.'

'Perhaps it should be. I certainly don't want strangers knowing so much about me. I would worry about what they might do with that knowledge.'

'What's your name?'

'Edward Phelps.'

'Ah,' I said. 'And your friend?'

'You can call him Peter.'

'Peter Lisman?'

'Very good,' Phelps said.

Lisman's face was pale and strange. I asked, 'Are you related to Sheneel Greene?'

Phelps answered for him. 'Of course not.'

I still spoke to the big man. 'But you found Sheneel's body?'

Phelps answered again. 'We were in the last stages of buying this property. Peter was checking land boundaries.'

Lisman stepped closer to me.

I wanted to run. 'Are you capable of talking, Peter?'

'He's my assistant,' Phelps said, as if that was an answer.

'But you talked to the police after you found Sheneel. You showed them where she was.'

He stared at me impassively.

'You kept your mouth shut when you hit my husband at Alex Greene's house, though.'

Phelps said, 'To my knowledge, Peter has never met your husband.'

'A brief encounter?' I asked.

Phelps nodded to Lisman, and Lisman stepped to my side. I stepped back so that I could see them both. Phelps asked, 'Why are you here? This is private property. It's fenced in. Signs tell you to stay out.'

'Sheneel was here.'

'Yes, she was, but that changes nothing.'

Lisman moved again, so I couldn't see him and Phelps at once. If I backed away, I would back into him.

'I'll leave,' I offered.

'No, not anymore.'

'What do *you* want?'

Phelps spoke to his companion, 'What do we want, Peter?'

Lisman said nothing. If I ran, would he catch me? I could outrun Phelps. But the Land Rover stood fifty yards from us, and I would be lucky to get through the fence gate before they caught me. I said to Phelps, 'You got right back to business after Sheneel died.'

'You think I'm disrespectful?'

'You might be worse than that.'

'Why did you come here?' he asked again.

I felt the closeness and the threat of the men. 'Honestly? I wanted to see Sheneel's blood on the ground.'

The smile returned but gentler. 'You're a little late for that.'

'You've plowed everything under, haven't you?'

'If you own the machine, you use it, right?'

'Not necessarily.'

Again, the smile. 'Clearly, you don't own the machine.'

'I would like to leave now,' I said.

'I'm sure you would.' Then he spoke to Lisman behind me. 'Will we keep the young lady here?'

Lisman answered for the first time. 'No, sir.'

His voice was strangely high and pinched, and I turned to look at him. He stared back without expression.

'Be on your way, then,' Phelps said.

I backed away and started toward the gate.

Phelps called after me, '*Or* you could join me and my family for an early dinner.'

I stopped and already felt the grip of his words. 'Why would I do that? Why would you want me to?'

'We have more to talk about – more matters to consider.'

'Like?'

'Let's talk over dinner.'

'I don't think so,' I said.

'With the work I do and in my social life, I meet many others in positions of power.'

I had no idea where he was going. 'That doesn't surprise me.'

'For instance, the provost of your college.'

'So?'

'What's your provost's policy concerning inappropriate relationships between faculty and students?'

My face was hot. 'I don't know. I've never had any.'

'What's the policy concerning affairs between a member of the English Department and, say, a man in History? And what's your husband's policy?'

'You asshole—'

'I don't pretend to understand higher education,' he said. 'When I was young, I attended Princeton for only a year and a half. But I do understand something about how universities govern and police themselves. You see, I left Princeton by mutual agreement with a disciplinary committee. I agreed that I would withdraw from the university and they agreed that they wouldn't report my activities to outside law enforcement. But that was a long time ago. Do universities still work that way?'

'I've done nothing against the law.'

'I'm not suggesting you have. But I'm guessing that at a minimum you've broken the trust of people you care about.'

'What do you want from me?'

'As I've said, I'm inviting you to dinner. I'll feed you.'

I followed the Land Rover in my car as it drove out to the Interstate and then south toward the city. Afternoon traffic was thickening, but Lisman, at the wheel, maneuvered among the cars and trucks with fluid speed, slowing only when I got blocked in and couldn't tail him. Heat from the sun radiated from the windshield and I dropped the visors and turned the air conditioner on full, but I sweated anyway. My cell phone rang, and I checked caller ID. Johnny was calling. What could I say to him? That I was driving to Edward Phelps's house because Phelps had threatened to tell him about the nights I'd spent with Tom Corfield?

I silenced the ringer.

Phelps lived in the old Ortega neighborhood on the west side of the river. A long black driveway wound from the road to a cul-de-sac from which a car could pull into a triple garage or drop passengers by a front door that rose halfway into the second story. Wisteria vines climbed the brown brick walls and clung to the chimneys at both ends of the house.

Phelps got out at the front door, and I parked behind Lisman at the side of the driveway. When I met Phelps on the front steps, he said without any irony that I could hear, 'I'm glad you can join us.'

Inside, the high-ceilinged front hall opened to a double balcony. Behind the front hall, a wide entrance led to a dining room with glass doors looking out over a long backyard that sloped down to the river, where a narrow dock protruded into the water. Halfway down the sloping yard, landscapers had created a terrace and sunk a swimming pool shaped like a teardrop.

Lisman disappeared through a hallway, and Phelps led me into the living room where Stephen Phelps sat with a thin blond woman, drinking from cocktail glasses.

'I believe you met my son Stephen when Alex Greene died,' Phelps said, 'and this is his wife, Kathryn. This morning, your husband insulted them, though I'm sure they won't hold you responsible for his behavior. I thought that we could clear the bad air through civilized conversation and a nice dinner.'

'Which you've forced me to attend.'

He nodded his acknowledgement. 'In my experience, civilizing forces are rarely gentle.'

Lisman entered through another door, carrying a tray of five drinks.

'Scotch and sodas,' Edward Phelps said, 'every afternoon when the heat is high.'

As Lisman exchanged full glasses for the ones that Stephen and Kathryn Phelps already had, the blue-veined skin on his big hands looked strangely delicate – almost glasslike.

'They have you do all kinds of jobs,' I said to him. 'Real estate surveyor, driver, household servant.'

Stephen Phelps laughed. Strangely. He stared at me as if we shared an inside joke, as if he knew me well.

But his father said, 'Peter is completely reliable.'

Lisman brought the tray to me and I took a drink. 'You look just like Sheneel,' I said. 'But taller and fatter.'

201

He said nothing and left the room.

Edward Phelps said, 'You and your husband are ruder than you need to be.'

'I don't like to be coerced.'

'Then don't act as if you need to be. I'll tell you this only once. I'm bigger than you. Smarter. Stephen is too. Even Kathryn, who spends her days playing tennis and doles out childcare to two nannies and a babysitter – she's bigger than you. You will do well to recognize that. Life will be easier for you and your husband if you do.'

Lisman came back into the room and said in his pinched voice, 'Dinner is ready.'

We went back through the front hall to the dining room. Already sitting at one end of the table, with her back to the windows, a woman watched us come. She wore a teal-and-gold dress with long sleeves and a collar that came high to her neck. Her face was a mass of scars. The skin on one side of her forehead had grown over most of an unmoving eye. She had penciled in eyebrows where none grew. Her skin stretched tight over bony cheeks. She had pinned her remaining strands of black hair behind her head. Her right hand looked healthy and had the skin of a woman in her mid-fifties, but the pinky and the ring finger on her left hand seemed fused together and the index finger was gone, a knot of shiny skin where it should have been.

Edward Phelps directed me to a chair next to the scarred woman and introduced us. 'My wife, Cecilia,' he said. 'Cecilia, this is Lillian Turner. You've met her brother, Daniel.'

The woman smiled from one side of her mouth.

Two servants brought platters of fish and steak from the kitchen. As we ate, Kathryn Phelps told the others about the change in management at one of the clubs where, it became clear, she was the top tennis player in her age bracket. Stephen told his father about his progress in getting a piece of land re-zoned for heavy industrial and industrial-water use. But he kept glancing at me as he talked. Cecilia Phelps picked at her food with a fork.

Then Edward Phelps said, 'We're ignoring our guest. What interests you, Lillian?'

I asked, 'What did they catch you doing?'

'What?'

'At Princeton. You said you went for a year and a half. Why did they kick you out?'

Cecilia Phelps said, 'Edward has always been known for his sense of fun.'

He said, 'They didn't *catch* me doing anything. It involved a misunderstanding with a young lady.'

'What kind of misunderstanding?'

'The kind that ends a college career.' He smiled with his hard white teeth.

'OK,' I said. 'And what are you building on the land where Peter Lisman found Sheneel?'

He cocked his head to the side. 'If the zoning changes go through, as Stephen assures me they will, a waste refinery for high-grade pulp. The land has freshwater sources and is close to our other facilities. Are you interested in paper processing?'

Cecilia Phelps cleared her throat.

Her husband turned to her. 'Yes, dear?'

The scarred woman looked at me. 'Do you have children?' Her voice was clear and soft.

'No,' I said.

'Why not?'

'Pardon me?'

'Why not? Choice or incapacity?' When I said nothing, she added, 'It's a simple question.'

Edward Phelps said, 'Dear, you're embarrassing her.'

'My husband has been in the Navy,' I said. 'We were waiting until he got out.'

'In case he died?'

'Or something,' I said.

'Now he's out?'

'We're taking time to heal.'

She stared at her plate. We watched her. 'A woman should have children,' she said. 'Even if they turn out to be little bastards.'

'Who would like more wine?' her husband said.

When the servants cleared the table, he said to me, 'I'll give you a tour of the house and then we can walk outside.'

Stephen Phelps said, 'I can do it.'

His father fixed him with a stare. 'You take care of Kathryn.'

'I'd like to go home,' I said.

'Soon.'

He showed me through the downstairs rooms – a sitting room with oil paintings, some recent and some old, depicting the faces of various family members and ancestors; a media room with a large screen on one wall and windows blacked out against sunlight; a library with shelves lined closely with books.

'Come,' he said, and led me into a room with dark leather easy chairs, a dark leather daybed, a large wooden desk, and more books. 'This is my room, my escape.' He went to a cabinet and found a bottle of Maker's Mark and two glasses. 'Drink?'

'No.'

He poured me one anyway. 'Cecilia must eat early for health reasons that you don't want to know about. So I often drink through the rest of the evening.' He handed me one of the bourbons, but left his hand on the glass so that our skin touched. When he let go, he stayed close to me. 'She's incapable of pleasure. Did you know that? If I touch her, she feels only pain. The doctors say that burns can be like that, even old burns.' His breath smelled of whiskey.

'What happened to her?'

'It was a long time ago, when Stephen was little more than a baby.' He reached for my hand, but I pulled away. 'It involved your husband's friend. He calls himself Papa Crowe, but back then we called him Jacob. He did small jobs for us. He took care of the gardens. He carried the dirty clothes to the laundress. He changed the oil in the cars. That's what he did before the fire. Then the stove blew up.' He showed me his white teeth and reached for me.

I stepped around him. 'I'm leaving.'

He said, 'I've told you what I can do *to* you. But I've said nothing about what I can do *for* you.'

'I want nothing from you.'

'Nothing?' He looked perplexed. 'There was a

time when I wouldn't have accepted that as an answer. I expect Stephen still wouldn't. But we grow old – and such things diminish. Walk with me a little, and then you can go back to your faithful husband and your relationships with your students and fellow teachers, whatever they might be.'

We went out through the dining-room doors on to the patio and down a set of broad concrete stairs toward the swimming pool and river. We stopped on the pool deck. Below us, two large live oaks, their lower branches draped with Spanish moss, framed the green lawn. The river, more than a mile wide, shined golden in the early evening sunlight.

'Look at that,' he said.

Across the water, a sailboat moved in the gentle breeze. A pair of brown pelicans cut across the middle distance.

He said, 'Did you know that sunsets wouldn't happen here without the particulates from my mills? The air would be too clear. Nothing to refract the light. Three hundred years ago, if you canoed up this river in the evening, you would have seen dull skies.'

I said, 'I don't understand why you've brought me here.'

'I wanted you to see how much I have to lose. I live a good and happy life. It's not without hardships – my wife, of course. But I'm comfortable. With very few limits, I do what I want. Few people in the world can say as much. If anyone threatens me, I'll do everything necessary to protect myself. Do you understand that?'

'I think I do.'

'I'm glad. You and your husband need to stop interfering.' He watched the pelicans as they flew downriver, dipped toward shore, and disappeared. 'I take no pleasure in protecting myself.'

'Did Sheneel threaten you?'

'I'm not talking about Sheneel. I'm talking about you.'

He spoke quietly, and I asked as quietly, 'Did you kill Sheneel?'

He rubbed his chin with his hand. 'No.' He gave me a tired smile. 'But I protect what's mine.'

'Did Stephen?'

His voice remained quiet. 'I know you're smart, but my message isn't getting through.'

'I'm not afraid of you,' I said.

'You should be, dear,' he said. 'You should be.'

Twenty-One

Stephen Phelps

I smelled the sour odor of fear on Sheneel. On Laura. Among others. I smelled it on their bodies, the bed, the kitchen counter, the hood of a car. So thick I could lick it. I didn't. Could.

What would the midnight sex-and-hunger cries of forest animals have over me? Would Dad have slapped me? Would Kathryn have wiped her tender lips on her napkin and left for the club? Would Mom have smiled her crooked smile and said, *My son is a wolf. He's a panther. As all children are. You should have one of your own, even if he eats you* – saliva streaming from her half-mouth?

Lillian Turner's eyes darted from Dad to Mom to Kathryn. Why not to me? She knew she was a caged animal. She knew iron bars are weaker than the ones this family raises around its dinner guests. Also anger in those darting eyes. Fear and anger. Anger has no smell. Stand downwind of it. Lay your tongue on it. Nothing. Antiseptic. But you can break anger. You can turn it into fear. You can even turn it into desire with its own sweet odor.

Twenty-Two

Johnny

Lillian came in at seven thirty. Percy and I were sharing a frozen sausage-and-mushroom pizza, and she walked into the kitchen, watched Percy suck a piece of sausage into his mouth, and said, 'That'll make him sick.'

'Where were you?' I said.

'At school. I told you I had a late meeting.' Her eyes looked wild.

'No, you didn't.'

She said nothing.

'You hungry?' I asked.

'No, just really tired.'

I pushed a kitchen chair from the table. 'Sit and talk?'

'I'm tired of sitting and talking.' But she came to the table and sat.

'Long meeting?'

She nodded but didn't look at me.

I fed Percy another slice of pizza. 'Where were you?' I asked again.

'I told you—'

'Where were you really?'

Her face broke. She didn't cry. But the disintegration in her eyes and mouth was worse than tears.

I took her hand and she gripped me as if she wanted to tear the skin from me. 'Tell me,' I said.

'No.'

Anger and fear welled inside me. 'What happened?'

She told me. She'd gone to Little Marsh Island and found a Phelps Paper Company construction site. Edward Phelps and Peter Lisman had threatened her and made her follow them to Phelps's house. They hadn't touched her. They'd made her eat.

'They what?' I asked.

They'd made her join the Phelps family for dinner.

'Strange,' I said. 'How did they threaten you?'

Her face broke again. 'You'll hate me,' she said.

'I could never hate you.'

She told me she'd had an affair with Tom Corfield when I was on my first tour.

'This happened ten years ago?' I asked.

'Yes.'

'And nothing since then?'

'Not really. No.'

I looked up at the kitchen lamp. I looked down the floor. I took a deep breath. 'OK, then.'

Lillian looked hopeful, even grateful.

The affair happened a long time ago, just after Lillian and I moved in together. It hurt, but if I could heal from all I'd seen on the Arabian Sea, I would figure out how to heal from this. I forced a smile.

She said, 'Except one night when you were in the hospital.'

'What?'

'He came over. He spent the night.'

'You mean last week?'

'Last month. I was hurting. I was scared.'

I was breathless. 'Yeah, you and me both.'

'I'm sorry.'

I wanted to strike out with my fists and legs, but my muscles felt weak. 'I know.' I could hardly move.

'Do you hate me?'

'Yes.'

I got up and stumbled away. As I went out the door from the sunroom to the backyard, Percy retched and vomited pizza on to the kitchen floor.

Lillian didn't come to me that night. I sat on the lawn chair, the moon almost full above me, and though the heat of the day had carried past sunset and the fiery light of the moon was so bright I needed to turn my eyes away, I shivered with cold.

When I went inside in the morning, Lillian was gone. Had she run to Tom Corfield's house and spent the night with him? No, our bedcovers lay at the bottom of the bed. She'd slept at home and had left to teach. She had written no note explaining, apologizing, or accusing.

What was there to say?

Although words were her life, she'd always been sparing with them, as if each one weighed so heavily that she feared overburdening the air with them. But she'd never been *without* words. She had carefully chosen ones for every occasion. But now she'd said nothing.

I burned an egg in the frying pan, so I put it in Percy's dish and set it outside in the yard, then poured a bowl of Cheerios because I seemed incapable of anything more.

I needed to do something. But what was there to do? Nothing. I should take my meds, practice deep breathing, and learn to accept the imperfect world.

I took my meds.

I lay on my back on the sunroom floor and breathed deep.

Percy stood outside the glass doors and whined to come in.

He wanted to do something.

'Sorry, boy,' I said.

I breathed deep.

I considered emptying the rest of the meds into a coffee cup, stirring them with orange juice, and chugging.

I breathed deep.

Something.

I went to the bedroom and found the box that I'd brought home from my last tour. It contained my tags, my service and discharge papers, my small-change ribbons and medals, a pair of dress shoes that I'd worn to a Navy dance with Lillian, a pair of combat boots that I'd worn only in training exercises, a set of binoculars that I'd bought years ago on a shore leave in Bodrum, and a pile of T-shirts each naming a ship that I'd served on.

I laced the boots and hung the binoculars around my neck.

A half-hour later, I parked next to the wooden porch at Papa Crowe's house. The hawk that had perched in an oak tree when I first visited Papa Crowe nearly two months earlier sat again like a sentinel at the end of a branch, its head ticking in degrees as it scanned the sky and ground. The house was quiet but the door behind the screen door was open.

Papa Crowe came from a back room when I knocked. 'Can't get enough of me now, can you, son?'

I said, 'Do you own a gun?'

He opened the screen door and let me in. The room smelled of cut grass and an herb of some kind, sharp like basil. He shuffled toward the kitchen. 'I don't shoot. I don't need no gun.'

'That's not what I asked. Do you own one?'

'What happen to yours?'

'Someone made me bat-ass crazy on jimson weed. Then the police took it away.'

'Don't know what kind of sonofabitch would

do that to you,' he said. He disappeared into the dark of the kitchen, went to a broom closet, and pulled out a rifle. It was a thin-stocked, narrow-barreled .22, little more than a pellet gun.

'That's not a gun. It's a toy,' I said.

'It all I got.'

'Shells?'

'No.'

I shrugged and took it. 'Thanks.'

He watched as I went out through the screen door on to the porch.

I stopped and said, 'You aren't going to ask?'

'It your business, not mine.'

I drove two miles to a Walmart, bought a box of a hundred Remington long-rifle cartridges and a little bottle of Hoppe's gun oil, and drove back toward the highway. A side road cut through a commercial grove of slash pines, and I turned on it and came to a defunct sand quarry. I parked by the quarry lake and waded through knee-high grass into the grove. No one had tended the grove for a long time, and ferns and palmettos grew between the rows of trees. A hundred yards or so from the quarry, I set three targets that I made from leaves and bark against the trunk of a tree. Then, twenty paces away, I sat on the pine needles, cleaned the bore of the .22, and oiled the bolt action until it slid and snapped. I loaded the gun, lay on my belly, sighted, and shot. In training exercises, I'd shot guns that bruised my shoulder with their kick and others that made hardly a sound as they sent a piece of metal ripping through the air. None shot with truer aim

213

than Papa Crowe's .22. One, two, three – I put holes in the leaves and splintered the bark. I made new targets and stepped away forty paces. One, two, three – I hit the first two targets and splintered the tree trunk next to the third. I pulled the trigger again – four – and the last piece of bark burst into pieces.

An empty log truck, heading toward the highway, passed as I drove to the Phelps pulp mill. Convincing the security guard to let me in might be harder than when I first visited, and I tucked the rifle behind the front seat in case I needed it to get through the gate.

But as I pulled close to the security station and breathed the sweet chemical stench of the mill, a red Audi sedan sped out, heading toward town. Stephen Phelps was driving it.

I pulled on to the shoulder, turned around, and went after him.

Edward Phelps had threatened Lillian and had exposed us to each other. Stephen Phelps had raped Laura Greene, might have killed Sheneel and Alex Greene, and had done God knows what else besides. The police were doing nothing about them. If I went down with them, I would count the cost as worthwhile.

The Audi drove south toward town, then looped back and headed north on a county road. After ten minutes, we crossed into South Georgia and the Audi turned on to another rural road that took us past trailer homes with plastic children's picnic tables and toys in the front yards and roof-top satellite dishes cocked to the sky. If Stephen Phelps knew a car was following him, he showed no sign of it. He turned on to a lumber road, and I realized that he'd come to the same area where Papa Crowe had brought me on the night he drugged me with jimson weed. We flew past the cinderblock Tobias Rib restaurant, the front door propped open, the gravel parking lot full of rusting pickups.

Three miles farther, the Audi turned on to a winding road marked with a *No Outlet* warning. I dropped back, letting Phelps disappear around a bend, and followed slowly past a mix of little ranch houses and trailers set back in the trees. Branches shadowed and reflected on the windshield, and I drove past a green doublewide before I realized that Phelps had parked the Audi outside of it and stood on the aluminum front steps waiting for someone to answer the door. A quarter-mile up the road, I turned the car around, drove back past the doublewide, and pulled to the shoulder. With Papa Crowe's .22 at my side, I slipped into the woods and worked through the trees.

The doublewide stood on a plot of weedy sand, cleared of trees to about ten yards. A rusty swing set with a slide but no seats stood behind the house, and a stack of firewood stood between the swing set and the woods. I cut through the trees to the woodpile.

The windows on the doublewide were open, as was a sliding glass door that led to an unpainted wooden deck. A ragged tabby cat lay in the sun on the deck and watched me. Inside the house, a woman laughed. Phelps spoke to her, but I couldn't make out his words.

215

I drew my binoculars from window to window. There was a cheaply furnished bedroom and a kitchen with a dirty refrigerator. Inside the open sliding door, there was a sofa and, on the wall behind it, a framed poster of a horse standing in a flowering meadow. The last window opened into another bedroom. Stephen Phelps stood in it, his back to me. A black woman in black shorts and a white cut-off T-shirt faced him. Her hair was dyed a color between pink and henna. 'It can't be,' I muttered, and I thumbed the focus dial. A sound came from my throat – Stephen Phelps stood in the bedroom with the old prostitute, Felicity.

As I watched, Phelps stripped off his clothes and stood naked in front of her. Then she stripped off her clothes too. Her breasts hung low with age, and her hips sagged with fat. In the half-light of the bedroom, her body looked gray.

With all his money, Phelps could buy any hooker he wanted – a high-priced escort or a model with a drug habit – instead of a woman who, most nights, couldn't find a customer even among the addicts and lowlifes who looked for pleasure on Philips Highway. But I knew that must be the point. He was seeking self-abasement. He had his pretty blond wife at home and together they'd made pretty blond children. And, on the side, he had *this*. I put down the binoculars and sighted the .22 on the cross where his shoulder blades met his spine.

He sat with his back to me on the far side of the bed, and Felicity, naked in front of him, kneeled on the floor between his knees. He ran

216

his fingers through her pink hair as she took him in her mouth.

Did I want to think this through more fully?

No. I tightened my finger on the trigger.

But Felicity rose from the floor and mounted him, straddling him where he sat, her thighs wrapping around his thin white torso. His back rose and fell with the rhythm of their sex. If I shot him now, would the bullet pierce his body? Would it rip into the tender skin of the old prostitute and kill her too? No. The .22 shells carried only forty grains of gunpowder – enough to tear through one person but one only.

But then Phelps stood from the bed, clutching the hooker's body to his, turned, and lay her on her back.

I lowered the rifle and brought up the binoculars again. If Phelps raised his eyes to the window, he would look across the space of thirty feet and see me watching him. But he didn't raise his eyes. He looked down at the woman between whose legs he stood and there was fury in his face – hatred and fury.

I jerked the gun to my eye and squared the sight on his forehead. I tightened my finger. But I released it again as Felicity bucked up from the bed and slapped Phelps. The sound of skin on skin came through the open window, and he cried out with pain.

She laughed – loud and low – and he pulled back from her, standing, his hand feeling his jaw where she'd hit him. She got to her knees on the bed and crawled toward him, and he embraced her when she came. She wrapped herself around him, and again he turned and lowered himself until he sat on the bed, her legs clenching him.

I sighted the rifle on his spine, my hands shaking – no longer sure what I was doing but unable to stop myself – and, as Felicity bucked backward, lifting her thighs toward Phelps's shoulders, and Phelps plunged deep into her, I pulled the trigger.

The rifle report stung my ears, and I jerked away, ducking behind the woodpile as if it could protect me from myself. When I rose again and peered over the logs with the binoculars, I saw what I had done. Phelps stood over the prostitute, holding a bloody bed sheet against her bleeding leg. He looked frantic, gazing around the bedroom and out the window, apparently unsure what had happened. Still, he stayed with the woman, though he must have known that his own life was in danger.

I could have raised the rifle and shot him in the chest.

I could have finished him and driven to the Phelps mill and shot his father.

But I ducked behind the woodpile, found my shell casing, crawled back into the woods, and ran to my car. I knew I was a coward, but I'd shot the old prostitute in the thigh, and there's just one thing to do when you make a mistake like that. And that's run.

Twenty-Three

Stephen Phelps

My hand on her wound. My hand in her wound.

No, she said.

Yes.

I'm bleeding, baby.

My hand in her wound, bloody, bright – bright as the sun because the yellow of the sun is a lie: if you stand close, the sun is as red as a bloody hand.

Christ, baby, I'm bleeding.

Tears. Mine. Why was *I* crying?

My hand to my cheek. My bloody cheek. Would I ever look in a mirror again?

I'm bleeding.

The tears in my eyes put her in a bubble, in outer space. *My fault.*

Not your fault, baby.

But—

The hospital, baby, the hospital.

Then the roundabout in front of the ER, as if I was supposed to drive around and around until she bled through the front seat. The leather in my Audi as red as the day they stripped the skin from the lamb. As red as the sun.

Leave me here, she said.

I'll carry—

You can't come in. You know that.

219

You'll—

I won't. Her bloody hand on my thigh. As if I was the one with the wound. *I won't die,* she said. *Never. Not till I'm ready.*

I'm coming—

No. She closed the door behind her. She dragged that leg across the sidewalk like a dying animal.

Me in the car. The smell of blood. The salt-and-metal smell of the burning sun. *I'll take care of it,* I said, as if she still sat beside me – because I knew who did it. The idea bloomed like a bursting star. It burned away my nausea, and I felt myself grow hard with unfinished sex. I would take his wife, finish the unfinished.

Felicity was right: not my fault. Johnny Bellefleur's fault. His wife's by extension. I could see his tears. I could taste his salt. He would touch her. He would lift her from the floor, the lawn, the bed, wherever I found her and finished her.

Twenty-Four

Lillian

'Why now?' Tom asked. We sat in my office, the door shut, two students waiting outside for appointments.

'It came out, that's all. I didn't want it to, but it did.' I wouldn't tell him about my obsession with Sheneel Greene and my disastrous trip to Little Marsh Island.

'But why now? He could hurt you. He could hurt *us*.'

The skin on Tom's face was perfect. I'd noticed it the first time we met. It looked as if he'd never bruised or cut it, never had a blemish, never nicked it when shaving. He wore brown loafers, blue cotton pants, a pressed white shirt, and a leather vest. The vest would have looked ridiculous on almost any other man. When I'd first introduced Johnny to him, Johnny had given him the smile he used for men he thought were soft and untried. It was his testosterone smile. I could almost smell it. But that was before he returned from his last tour soft and broken himself.

I gave my version of the smile to Tom. 'You mean he could hurt *you*.'

His face hardened. 'I mean he could hurt *us*. I'm not the one he pulled a knife on. I'm not the one whose bedroom wall he shot holes in.'

'Hole. One in the wall.'

'Come stay with me awhile.'

'At your house?'

'You'll be safe.'

'No.'

'I'll do anything for you.'

That was probably true, but spending even a few nights at his house would involve being with a man who seemed to consist mostly of the first layers of skin, beautiful as that skin was, and lacked the muscle, organs, and blood – ugly, raw, pulsing – that I knew at home. If Johnny would stay – if he would let me stay with him – I would remain with him.

'I can't,' I said.

'You won't.'

'I can't.'

Someone knocked on the door – one of the kids whose appointment times I was ignoring.

'I have to teach in a few minutes,' I said.

'Screw teaching.'

I got Tom out of my office. I screwed nothing. I talked with my students. I taught my classes. We finished the last class with 'The Broken Tower,' which Hart Crane wrote just before killing himself by leaping from a ship and right after he ended an affair with the wife of a close friend. He wrote about how the ideas of good and evil that religion teaches are insufficient. When we love – when our love is full and muscular – no act or thought is evil. It's all good, all heavenly. I wondered if Hart Crane's knowledge that his own extraordinary loves – adulterous and homosexual – broke the stony rules of religion led him to the stern of his ship and pushed him like a wind into the blue-green water of the Caribbean Sea.

I packed my books and papers and left at three-thirty, taking a far hall to avoid passing Tom's office. As part of a campaign to make the campus inviting, the university had installed fountains and planted gardens between the buildings, but the sun remained high and hot. *And so it was I entered the broken world*, Hart Crane wrote. And so it was that *I* did.

As I passed the library, a woman called my name.

She was barefoot and weather-tanned and wore dirty pink shorts and a yellow tourist T-shirt with a picture of a blue manatee. Her brown hair needed washing. I'd never seen her before, but, with her slate-gray eyes, I recognized her. 'Laura Greene?'

She gave me a crooked smile. 'How did you know?'

'I see Sheneel in you.'

Her eyes were bright and hungry. 'Thank you.'

'My husband says he met you yesterday.'

'Interesting man, your husband.'

I nodded. 'He is.'

'But you treat him like dirt?'

'Who says that?'

'In my opinion, he probably deserves it.'

'You know what, let's find some place to sit down.'

Between the library and the Fine Arts Center, there was a garden with four outdoor tables. Students were studying at two of them. I sat across from Laura Greene at another.

She said, 'Guys like your husband, they hold a woman down and keep her down.'

'Who says I treat him like dirt?'

'No one needed to. I could tell.'

'How so?'

'You were sleeping with my daughter.'

'What?'

'Don't look at me like that,' she said.

'Why would I—'

'Alex told me on the phone before I came back.'

'I never—'

'He said Sheneel went on and on about you.'

'I never touched her,' I said. 'I never would.'

She put a hand on my arm. 'Now *that*,' she said, 'is a lie.'

'Why did you come here?'

Her voice dropped and she said, almost as if asking a question, 'I want my daughter and my son back.'

'I know. I wish I could help.'

She squared her eyes on me. 'You could talk to your brother.'

Again I stared at her.

She said, 'He can't bring them back, but he can stop the Phelpses.'

'How do you know so much about me and my family?'

There was sadness in her crooked smile. 'This is a small enough town. If you open your ears, you hear. Besides, I've known Daniel a long time. He goes way back with the Greenes and Phelpses.'

She seemed to sense my hesitation.

She said, 'Did your husband tell you what happened between Stephen Phelps and me? Did he tell you that Stephen is Sheneel's father?'

I nodded.

'When Stephen was done with me, he said I could call the police if I wanted. It didn't matter to him. Well, I didn't want to call them. I didn't want to drag myself through that. But around that time, I'd gotten friendly with a cop who patrolled our neighborhood. Alex was about three years old and loved the lights and noise of the squad car, so we would talk to this cop when we were out in the street. He was a good-looking young guy, new to the police department, and I was single since Alex's daddy left, so that made our conversations interesting. We talked about his job and eventually got around to talking about family

– about Alex's daddy being gone, my connections to the Phelpses, this guy's sister who was smart and spent all her time reading . . . You hearing this?'

'You knew Daniel?'

She said, 'Everyone in the neighborhood did. He was real friendly. A great model for kids like Alex. So, I wasn't going to call the police, but I thought I could talk to my friend, the cop – confide in him, you know, see what advice he could give me. I told him, and he seemed concerned and said he would see what he could do. I guess he went to talk to the Phelpses, though he was just a patrolman. Three days after I told him, I was in the front yard with Alex, and he showed up at my house in his squad car. He had Stephen with him in the front seat. They got out together, and Daniel asked Stephen if he had anything to say to me. Stephen said, *I'm sorry, ma'am*. Like that. He called me *ma'am*, like Daniel had rehearsed it with him. Then Daniel told me I could pursue charges against Stephen, but he was a minor and all that, and so he didn't recommend it. Instead, he said I should take the apology and try to forget what had happened. He asked, was I OK with that? I sure as hell wasn't OK, but I said I was and thank you very much for coming, because I knew then that the Phelpses had bought your brother, just as they bought everyone else they thought was worth buying instead of crushing or killing.'

I wanted to laugh at Laura Greene's story, but I couldn't. I had always trusted Daniel. I knew he had been ignoring evidence and I had heard the rumors about him over the years, but, after growing up and living a life close to him, I depended on him as one depends on a physical force – gravity or inertia or friction. I said, 'It's a pretty ridiculous coincidence that Daniel would be there after you got raped and then would be the detective assigned to Sheneel's death twenty years later.'

She shook her head. 'I thought you would be smarter than that.'

'What?'

'It *wasn't* a coincidence. He gets himself put on anything that relates to the Phelpses. He's their clean-up boy.'

I laughed, but it was an empty laugh. 'Fine,' I said, and I pulled out my cell phone.

I called Daniel's desk at the Sheriff's Office. He wasn't there. I called his cell phone. He didn't answer. I called his home number. His wife Patty said he was at work and I should try him at his desk or on his cell. I called his cell again and left a voicemail message. I said, 'How did you get put on the Sheneel Greene case? Was it just luck, or did you hear that Sheneel was dead and volunteer for the job? Or did someone call your commander and suggest you for the job? Maybe the Phelpses?' I hung up and stared at Laura Greene. 'There. We'll see what he says. But if he's really involved in this, my calling him on it won't make a difference.'

'It won't hurt.'

'Or maybe it will.'

'How hard are you willing to push him?'

I thought about that. I said, 'He's my brother.'

'And he'll hold you down and keep you down too.'

I wondered if her eyes had always looked pained or if they'd become that way only when her children died. She had the same narrow shoulders as Sheneel and the same thin body, though age had widened her hips. Her bare feet were weathered almost brown. 'Do you mind if I ask . . . You were born a Phelps. There's got to be money. But you live like this?'

She gave me the crooked smile. 'I'm one of the poor Phelpses. Sure, there's *some* money, but I've never wanted it. You touch that money, and your fingers come away bloody and hot.'

I drove home.

Traffic was light and the air conditioning created a bubble safe from the outside heat, but my head spun with all Laura Greene had said and insinuated – and also with Tom Corfield's invitation to move in with him *for a while*, as if a few nights would affect my life for less than forever. I wondered if Johnny would be home when I got there. What would I say to him? He would expect me to say something.

And what would I say to Daniel when he returned my call? Laura Green wanted to know how hard I would push him. Had I already pushed too far? My words were easy to say – *How did you get put on the Sheneel Greene case?* – but now that I'd said them, they were no longer easy. They existed in the world and couldn't be unsaid.

My confession to Johnny about Tom couldn't

227

be unsaid either. It existed too, and it would always exist.

I rounded the corner leading to our house, and a crow, perched at the top of a magnolia in front of the corner house, spread its wings and dropped toward the ground, flapped once, and rose toward the sky, its shadow crossing over the windshield. A blue Pontiac was parked on the street, a man sitting in the driver's seat. I stopped before approaching. I knew that Pontiac. It was an unmarked police car. Daniel drove it on most of his shifts and usually took it home for weekends. *Damn*, I said, and I pulled behind his car, got out of mine, and climbed in on his passenger side.

His face looked hard and unfamiliar. 'I'm sorry for the call,' I said.

'You don't know what you're doing,' he said. 'Johnny doesn't either.'

'I don't know what *you're* doing,' I said.

He pushed his thinning hair from his forehead, as if it irritated his skin. 'It's not just me. It's my lieutenant. It's the Sheriff. It's city councilmen.'

I didn't want to push him. He sat in the driver's seat, a big man – almost impossibly big – and I wanted to believe he had acted only in the name of what was right, whether or not I understood what that was. I said, 'They're telling you to cover up Sheneel and Alex Greene's death?'

He shook his head. 'They're telling me that the Phelpses pump money into the city, that the Phelpses contribute to the mayor's election campaigns, that the Phelpses go to their parties and they go to the Phelpses' parties. They don't need to tell me more than that. They know who the Phelpses are and they make sure guys like me know it too.'

'How much have the Phelpses given you?'

'Christ, Lillian.'

'It can't be worth it.'

'It's more complicated than that.'

'No, it isn't. You either do what's right or you don't.'

His face looked hot. 'You're goddamned stupid.' His words were harsh, but his voice gentle. 'You understand nothing.'

'I understand you're in trouble,' I said.

He shook his head.

I asked, 'Why did you come here? To tell me I'm stupid? Because of my call?'

'I was already here when you left your message. I was inside talking with Johnny. I wanted to know where he was this morning.'

I made myself ask, 'What happened this morning?'

His voice softened again. 'Someone shot at Stephen Phelps. Came within a couple of inches of getting him.' He gave me a look that told me more than his words did.

'Not Johnny,' I said, as if saying would make it so.

'I don't know. For a lot of reasons, Stephen Phelps isn't officially reporting the shooting. We won't pursue it, but I think I know what happened.'

I shook my head.

Daniel said, 'Phelps was with a woman. She's in the hospital.'

'Johnny shot her?'

He shrugged.

'Christ. But you confiscated his gun.'

'It wouldn't be hard to get another.'

'No way.' I reached for the car door handle.

'Don't go inside,' Daniel said.

'What?'

'Don't go in your house. I talked with Johnny. He denies he shot the woman, of course. But if you go in, no one can protect you.'

'You think I need to be protected from Johnny? You think he would hurt me?'

Daniel leveled his eyes with mine. 'Yeah, maybe.'

'You know what? You need help as much as he does.' I pushed the car door open and got out. I fumbled with my car keys and they fell to the pavement. I picked them up and dropped them again. I screamed at Daniel's car, 'Get the hell out of here!'

He sat in the driver's seat, the engine silent.

I got in my car, started it, hit the accelerator, and cut around the Pontiac and into the driveway. I sat. I breathed. I tried to think straight. I shifted into reverse, backed out of the driveway, and hit the gas. Daniel stared without expression as I passed.

Twenty minutes later, I pulled into Tom Corfield's driveway. 'I need a place to stay,' I said, when he answered his door. 'For a while.'

Twenty-Five

Johnny

I buried Papa Crowe's .22 in the backyard, wrapping it in a lawn bag, tucking in the box of Remington cartridges and the gun oil, dropping in the spent shell, and sealing the bundle with duct tape – a single tidy package of my latest guilt. But as soon as I finished tamping the dirt with the back of the shovel, Percy started digging the hole again. I dragged him inside and distracted him with a package of sliced ham from the refrigerator.

When Lillian's brother knocked and asked where I'd been when Stephen Phelps's friend got shot – *friend* was Daniel's word – Percy retched and spat up a piece of ham, so I put him back outside, and as we talked in the sunroom, he dug into the ground again. 'I was here,' I said. 'All morning. All day.'

'Alone?'

'After the strippers left.'

'This is serious,' he said.

'Twins. G-strings. Handcuffs. Don't tell Lillian. Not that she would have grounds for objecting.'

'What are you talking about?'

'Strippers.'

Daniel frowned. 'Stephen Phelps could have been killed.'

231

'How badly hurt is the friend?'

'She'll survive. Single shot. Small caliber. Missed the arteries.'

'Are you sure Phelps didn't shoot her?'

Outside, Percy stuck his head into the hole.

'If you did this,' Daniel said, 'you should run. Officially, Phelps is denying he was present when his friend got shot. His friend is denying it too. She's saying the wound was an accident. But Phelps will come after you. He'll—'

I said, 'Are you sure she really wasn't shot in an accident?'

'Someone shot at Phelps. The shot hit his friend. If you call that an accident, fine. I call it attempted murder.'

Percy was pulling the package up to the lip of the hole, tugging at it as if it was a dead animal. 'I hope you catch the person who did it,' I said, and I tried to guide Daniel back into the kitchen.

He didn't move. 'I don't really care if you kill Phelps.' His voice was quiet. 'I don't care if you kill the whole family. I don't care if you die trying. But I care about Lillian. I don't want her to get hurt. I'll do whatever it takes to protect her. That includes hurting *you*.'

'I love her,' I said. 'I wouldn't hurt her.'

'If you think that's true, you have no idea what you've been doing,' he said.

He left. I watched through the front window as he sat in his car at the curbside. He checked his cell phone. He talked on his radio. When he finished talking, he continued to sit. I left him at his post, went to the backyard, and retrieved the rifle. Percy had ripped through the plastic bag

232

and was charging around the yard with the bottle of gun oil in his mouth. I raised the .22 and sighted on him as he ran wide looping figure eights from one end of the yard to the other. 'I would never hurt her,' I said as Percy raced past. 'Never.' I brought the rifle inside and wiped off the dirt with paper towels. I checked the front window. Daniel remained at the curb. I went to the bedroom and took my meds, then carried the rifle into the sunroom, lay on the floor, and did my deep breathing.

When I checked the front window a half-hour later, Daniel was gone and I brought the rifle outside and put it in the trunk of my car. Daniel had said he didn't care if I killed the whole Phelps family. That was an idea, but it would need to wait. I hadn't eaten since early morning, so I drove to my office on Philips Highway and walked the hundred yards to the Sahara Sandwiches Shop. Farouk stood behind the counter, wearing one of the white paper hats that he'd bought by the case from a catalog. He was all smiles. Against the odds, he had developed a steady business over the past couple of months, mostly selling sandwiches to men and women who did drugs, drifted, pimped, or hooked along the highway. As I went in, a man dressed in black jeans and a yellow silk shirt was leaving with a strung-out woman in a dirty plaid skirt and a V-neck that exposed most of her breasts.

I sat at the counter and asked for a falafel sandwich. When Farouk turned to the grill, I considered how to bring up Felicity. But he beat me to it. He poured me a cup of coffee, leaned on the counter, and said, 'You hear what happened to the whore?'

I shook my head and drank.

'A guy picked her up just down from here this morning. Nice car – Lincoln Continental, something like that, they say. He took her to Georgia and shot her.'

'Christ,' I said.

'The fellow that just walked out of here? He says she's dead. His girl says she's alive. An ugly woman like that – who would want to kill her?'

He had a couple of the facts wrong, but Felicity must have gotten a ride to the doublewide somehow, and I doubted she had her own car. 'What did the guy who picked her up look like?'

'Don't know. They say he was a white guy.'

'Young, old? Fat, skinny?'

He gave me a curious look. 'I don't know.'

'Did the car have a color?'

He smiled. 'You're working this, Johnny?'

'I only do skip trace.'

His face fell. 'I don't see you doing no skip trace either. Why do you care what color the car was?'

'Is that falafel ready?'

He looked offended. 'Sure, Johnny.'

He drained the fry basket, cut the pita, and bagged my sandwich. I paid him and left a couple bucks on the counter.

'I don't want your tip, Johnny,' he said.

I shrugged and stuffed the bills into my pocket.

As I left the restaurant, he said, 'Black. They say the car was black.'

'Thanks, Farouk. I'll let you know if I hear anything.'

My office smelled of rubber and mildew, and, after I turned on my computer, I propped open the front door and slid the window wide in the little bathroom. Farouk had told me nothing I could depend on. Still, I was curious why Felicity had hooked up with Stephen Phelps and why she had been hanging out at Tobias Rib when I'd gone there with Papa Crowe.

As I ate my falafel, I Googled *Kingsland Georgia*, which was the town closest to where I shot Felicity. I added *newspaper*, and found an online edition of *The Tribune & Georgian*. If the site updated throughout the day, I expected to find at most a quick mention of an accidental shooting on a local news or crime page. Instead, the homepage opened with a headline that said, *Former Princess of the Night Singer Shot*. The article said a sixty-three-year-old woman named Felicity Metz had been hospitalized with a gunshot wound to her leg after an apparent domestic accident. But the bigger story was that she once had been somebody. At the age of fourteen, Felicity had sung solo at Evans' Rendezvous, the best black nightclub at American Beach, and a guitarist named Arnie Metz had heard her and fallen in love. They'd married on her fifteenth birthday. They'd found a drummer and a trumpet player, and the band had gone on the road as Princess of the Night, she being the princess. The band played black nightclubs in Georgia and Florida and as far west as New Orleans from the mid-1960s until the early 1970s, and had a moment of fame when they traveled to Memphis and recorded a single played by radio stations all around the country.

In the past four decades, the report said, she'd suffered from drug and alcohol abuse and had been arrested for narcotics violations and prostitution. This morning, an unknown driver had brought her to the University Hospital ER. Doctors said she was in stable condition and expected to recover.

I Googled *Felicity Metz* and found a couple of music sites that said she and her band played a mix of blues, rock, and gospel, with Gullah influences that went unrecognized by white listeners at the time but had been noted by archivists in the past ten years. She was born Felicity Thomas, daughter of a St Simons cotton farmer. The Memphis single, called 'Do What You Will,' rose as high as eighth spot on the Rock and Roll charts early in 1967. Her husband, Arnie Metz, credited with inventing a new style of guitar picking, was arrested on narcotics charges in 1973 and died from a drug overdose shortly after release in 1977.

I walked back to the Sahara Sandwiches Shop. Farouk was refilling a Coke cup for a skinny man whose arms were covered with scratches and scabs. I said, 'Did you know she used to be a singer?'

'Of course. Everyone knows that.' Farouk turned to the scabbed man. 'Timmy, tell him what the guy looked like, the one that picked up Felicity.'

236

The man stared at me with narrow, bloodshot eyes. 'A big white dude. That's what they're saying.'

'Who's saying it?' I asked.

'She was hanging out with a couple of girls, and the car pulled up and the dude called her over.'

'Do they say what else he looked like?'

'Nah, just big and white.' He picked at a scab on one of his arms.

'Did she recognize him?'

'Maybe. Funny thing, she got in the backseat, not the front.'

'That's because he was the delivery boy. He was bringing her to someone else.'

Farouk nodded. 'That's good, Johnny.'

I went back to my office, locked up, and drove down Philips to the Barakat Food Store, which sold almost everything a drifter, addict, or hooker might want between destinations, hits, or johns. The store had a sale on Marlboros and Salems, and I bought a carton of each.

Three miles north of downtown, University Hospital was a white cube of a building, about twenty stories high and equally long and wide, connected by an elevated walkway to another cube of the same size and a second walkway to a set of low-rise buildings. Inside the main entrance, a volunteer at the information desk said Felicity Metz was in Room 607. The place was the major trauma hospital in the city. If you arrived at another hospital with a gunshot wound, life-threatening burns, or a bleeding brain, the doctors would stabilize you if they could and then ship you by ambulance or helicopter across town. The neighborhood around the hospital was poor and high-crime, and the hospital rose from among the dilapidated houses and open ditches like a cathedral.

The volunteer pointed me toward the elevator bank, and I rode up with two doctors in scrubs and a halter-topped teenager so pregnant her skin looked as if it would split.

Daniel was stepping out of Room 607 when the elevator door opened. He saw me and said, 'What the hell are you doing here?' I said nothing. As I passed, he grabbed my shoulder. 'What are you doing here?'

'The stripper twins got in an accident,' I said, and shook him free.

He watched as I walked toward the hooker's room. 'You can't go in there,' he said.

I saw no reason why not.

Felicity was lying at a slant in her hospital bed, an IV in her wrist, her bandaged thigh elevated on a pillow, the skin around the bandages gray, her pink hair spread like a halo against a white pillow. She looked perplexed to see me. 'Hey, sugar,' she said, her voice rounded by painkillers.

'Hey,' I said. Afternoon sunlight came through the window. Aside from the intermittent beeping of a monitor, the place was quiet. I checked over my shoulder, expecting Daniel to come after me, but he left me to whatever trouble I made for myself.

'What're you doing here?' Felicity asked.

238

'Everyone's talking about you on Philips. So I brought you a present.' I put the cigarettes on the bed.

She screwed her eyes at me. 'Why would you do that?'

'You're always asking for them.'

'I ain't in no condition for sex.'

'I don't want sex.'

She picked up the carton of Salems and examined it as if looking for tricks. 'You're a peculiar one.'

'But I do want something.'

Her voice became cynical. 'Of course.'

I could tell her it wasn't like that, but again I saw no reason why. 'Who was the man who picked you up on Philips Highway?'

'What do you know about that?'

'Your friends on Philips saw it. They say you got into a car with a big white man. I expect they also told the police.'

'Then I'll tell you the same thing I said to the police when they asked. I don't know what my friends are talking about.'

'How did the police like it when you said that?'

'They seemed happy enough. Less work for them.'

'I'm not happy, though.'

She narrowed her eyes. 'Why do you care?'

'The guy who picked you up is a pale-skinned man. You can see the blue of the veins in his hands and on his forehead. He works for the Phelpses.'

She shook her head. 'I've got enough trouble already. I don't need more.'

'He's a mean man – or maybe just nervous. He sometimes carries a bat, and he'll hit you with it if he gets a chance, though he's big enough to break your back with his empty hands.'

'Sounds like you know him already.'

'Peter Lisman?'

'Does it matter?' she said.

'Where does he live?'

'Will you take back the cigarettes if I don't tell you?'

'No. They're a gift.'

'Then I've got nothing to say.'

'All right,' I said. I stared at her for a long time. She stared back. I asked, 'How are you feeling?'

'Flying high. They say the bullet went in and out. They say I'm lucky. Do I look lucky to you, sugar?'

'I don't know what lucky looks like anymore.'

'Ain't that the truth.'

'When I saw you at Tobias Rib, you said you'd known the Phelpses your whole life – ever since you were fourteen, you said. Did you meet them when you were singing at Evans' Rendezvous?'

She seemed unsurprised that I knew about her singing, the way that once-famous people learn to expect such knowledge, even from strangers.

'Nah, but it was around that time. Mr Phelps hired me to sing at a private party. And afterward, when I went to get my money, I got to know Mr Phelps real good. The bastard never paid me neither. He told me to go back to the swamps where I came from.'

'This was Edward Phelps?'

240

'No, Edward was young – about my own age. This was his daddy.' She gave me a challenging stare. 'Edward came later. Then Stephen.'

'The Phelps men must really like you.'

'*Like* isn't the word.'

'Were you with Stephen Phelps when you got shot?'

She looked suspicious. 'Now, why would you think that?'

'You pretty much said that the man who picked you up on Philips Highway works for the Phelpses, and you just said you've been having sex with Stephen. The Phelpses seem to be involved in just about everything that causes pain around here.'

'True enough.' The suspicion remained.

'What did he threaten to do if you told the police?'

'I don't take to threats. Never did.'

'What did he promise you?'

She smiled a cunning smile, though I saw cracks of uncertainty. 'I still don't understand your game.'

'Simple,' I said. 'I want to bring down the Phelpses.'

The smile spread. '*Simple*, huh? Why do you want to do that?'

Because I had rocked like a baby in the underbelly of a ship instead of taking down another enemy, I thought. Because I hadn't been taken down either. I said, 'To appease myself.'

'It'll never happen.'

'Because?'

'Because you're a little man and they're a big

241

old powerful family. And because no one gets appeased. You can go to church or you can go to a rally, but it's never happened and never will.'

'I don't believe that.'

'Then you're stupid too. The Phelpses will step on you.'

'Like they stepped on you?'

'I never had false hopes, so they couldn't do it.'

I was wasting my time. 'I'm sorry you got shot,' I said.

Again she screwed her eyes at me. 'I do believe you are.'

'Enjoy the cigarettes,' I said, and turned to go.

'Sometimes he sleeps in a room over the garage at Edward Phelps's house.'

'Huh?'

'Peter Lisman. I think he also has a place in downtown Fernandina, over a bookstore.'

'Thanks,' I said.

She shrugged. 'If you bring the Phelpses down, you've got to bring them all the way down. Because if they get back up, they'll step on you. They've done it for a hundred fifty years.'

The Book Loft stood in a row of two-story brick buildings on Centre Street near the Fernandina harbor. The other businesses on the strip sold plastic pirate memorabilia, sea shells, postcards, and starfish-shaped chocolates. I parked outside a few minutes before six, as the restaurants were moving blackboards with happy-hour specials back inside and arranging tables on the sidewalk for dinner. The yellow building that housed the bookstore had only a single door, which led into the business, and so, unless the building had a rear entrance that led to the second story or Peter Lisman entered through the shelves of books, Felicity had made a mistake. Other buildings on the strip had street entrances to their upstairs rooms, though, and I walked up the sidewalk, crossed the street, and walked down the other side, checking the name plates next to the buzzers until I found one, fading with age, that said, *K and P Lisman*. As a man pushed a dolly with a keg of beer into a bar two storefronts away, I tried the knob to the street door. The door was open.

I pushed the buzzer and, instead of waiting for an answer through the intercom, went inside and climbed the stairs. At the second-floor landing, there were two doors, both painted burgundy red, each with a security peephole. I listened for footsteps and heard none. I rattled one of the doorknobs. Locked. I reached for the other knob, but a voice spoke into the intercom from inside the door. 'Yes?' It was a woman's voice, frail and uneasy.

I figured she would check the hall if no one answered from below.

She did.

A lock tumbled and the door swung open. A heavy blond-haired woman sat in a wheelchair. She wore pink sweatpants and a matching sweatshirt and looked about fifty years old. She said, 'Who the hell are you?'

'Is Peter here?' I said.

'Who wants to know?' she said.

'He lives here?'

'Who are you?'

243

I stepped past her into the apartment.

She cried, 'Hey!' and turned after me.

The air in the room smelled like modeling glue. There was a couch, a television, a curio cabinet, and, in the middle of it all, a long folding table covered with parts of porcelain dolls – figurines of pirates, black slaves, little boys in shorts, Confederate soldiers draped in Confederate flags, little girls in dresses, a horse, a dog – and all the miniature clothing or porcelain accoutrements they might need. Some were fully assembled, some already painted and dressed. The woman seemed to have been painting a fat black female doll. She'd set clothing – a polka-dotted house-dress, a head rag, and cotton slippers – and a little black porcelain frying pan next to the wooden rack that held the doll.

'I'm calling the police,' she said, and wheeled toward a telephone on an end table next to the television.

'Are you Peter's mother?'

She picked up the phone and dialed.

One door led from the room into a kitchen, another into a bathroom, and two others into bedrooms. One of the bedrooms had a white canopy bed and shelves lined with porcelain dolls. I went into the other. The window shades were down, the air musty with the smell of sweaty clothes, the bed unmade. There was a red easy chair and, on a wooden desk, a laptop computer. I opened the top desk drawer. Along with assorted pens and pencils, paperclips, and a broken stapler, there were a couple of loose photographs of a sea adventure park employee feeding fish to a killer whale in a large blue pool and a photograph of a tiger in a zoo enclosure – the kind of simple pictures one might find in a desk owned by a ten-year-old boy.

The woman in the other room was on the phone with a police dispatcher. In a town this size, I probably had only a minute or two before officers came up the stairs.

'I'm leaving,' I yelled from the bedroom. I glanced once more around the room and eyed the laptop. I grabbed it and carried it out through the front room and downstairs to the street.

Forty-five minutes later, I let myself back into my office. I searched the computer, and learned that Peter Lisman *really* liked animals. In his photo files, he had hundreds – maybe thousands – of pictures that he'd taken at zoos, at wildlife theme parks, and in nature preserves, as well as in and around Fernandina. A 'Dolphins' file included shots from SeaWorld as well as from a beach. The elephants were from a zoo. Lisman had photographed possums and squirrels in parks and backyards. He'd been to a farm with horses, but most of the horse pictures were of the wild ones that lived on Cumberland Island. The pictures included predator cats, snakes, tropical fish, deer, kangaroos, and alligators. But no birds. He seemed to limit his love to animals of the ground and sea.

His internet search history showed that he spent about equal time looking at pictures of animals and a wide range of porn.

The laptop told me little else about him. He

245

apparently kept no computer records of his finances. If he wrote letters, he wrote them by hand. If he liked music, he listened to it on the radio. If he kept track of the people he smashed on the head with baseball bats, he did so by notching his belt with a pocketknife.

I closed the laptop and checked my cell phone. No messages from Lillian. I locked the office, put the laptop in my trunk, and drove home. Maybe Lillian would be there waiting for me. What would she say? What would I say?

Her car wasn't in the driveway, and the house was dark and quiet. The sun was lowering, reddening into a western haze. Usually, she would have been home a couple of hours ago.

Should I call her?

Yes.

Would I?

I needed her to call me.

What would I do if she didn't call?

Disintegrate.

I left the .22 and the laptop in the trunk and went inside. The air conditioning chilled the sweat on my arms, and when I flipped on the front hall light, the house looked empty and sad. I felt like turning around and driving far away to a place where the people I encountered would look past me as insignificant to their lives. I felt like unlocking the car trunk, retrieving the .22, and going to a farther-away place.

I needed my meds. I went to the bedroom, swallowed a Xanax, and lay on the bed in the dark. After a while, my blood calmed and my breathing slowed. I got up, checked my cell phone again, though I knew it hadn't rung, and walked to the kitchen. Usually, when Lillian and I came home, Percy barked until we let him in from the backyard. This evening he was quiet. A lamp shined through the kitchen door from the sunroom.

'Lillian?' I said.

I stepped into the sunroom.

The plate glass on one of the doors to the outside was shattered. A man sat on the sofa. He was enormous and pale, with blue veins visible in his hands and forehead.

He had stretched a white T-shirt over his big body and blue jeans around his big legs. He wore brown cowboy boots on his enormous feet. He'd taken our butcher knife from the kitchen and held it in his big hands. Percy lay at his feet, calm.

As I entered the room, Lisman stood up. His eyes were dull and flat. If he had any opinion about me, he kept it to himself. He moved toward me with the knife.

I wanted to run, but my muscles failed me.

I wanted to speak, but words failed me.

Twenty-Six

Lillian

Tom poured me a vodka tonic, heavy on the vodka, and I stood in the kitchen, watching him cook. He knew I was watching. I could feel him feeling it. He wore green cargo shorts, sandals, and a bleach-white T-shirt. He was tall and tightly muscled. He talked about a kayak trip he was planning with a guy I didn't know in the Chemistry Department – easy, gentle conversation that filled the silence and meant I could avoid speaking or even thinking. I was grateful to him. But I didn't want him. Not tonight.

He opened a bottle of wine with dinner, but I asked for another vodka tonic. As I ate, he got up and put on music – the Gene Harris Quartet, soft jazz, but not pathetic. Then he sat across from me and asked, 'How are you doing now?'

I said, 'No sex.'

'What?'

'No sex tonight. I can't.'

'I wasn't going to suggest it.'

I put my hand on his.

He did everything right. After dinner, he poured me a third drink. When Gene Harris ended, he let the house fall quiet. He looked at me as if he wanted to kiss me but he didn't do it. He gave me his bed and took the couch.

I lay in bed, looking at his ceiling, the room turning with a gentle alcohol spin, his sheets smelling of his body, but his body lying a room away. I didn't telephone Johnny. But I put my cell on the bed beside me as if it could keep me close to him. I closed my eyes, and the alcohol spin got faster, so I opened my eyes and gripped the bed sheets and tried to slow the world before it broke into pieces.

Eventually, I slept.

When I woke again, Tom was in bed with me, close against my body.

Vodka and sleep fogged my mind. 'No,' I said.

'I can't sleep. I want to. But with you here . . .' He sounded sorry, pained and sorry. He stayed with me, pressed against me.

'No,' I said.

He put a hand on my belly.

I pulled away.

For several minutes, we were quiet and still, and then he put his hand on me again.

I untangled myself from the covers.

'Come back,' he said.

My pants and shirt were on the floor. I pulled them on in the dark.

He turned on the light. 'Don't go,' he said.

I put on my shoes.

'You belong here.' His chest was hairless, filmed with perspiration.

I found my car keys on the dresser. The clock on the bedside table said the time was twelve thirty-one. Was I too drunk to drive? Definitely. Was I too drunk to stay? Definitely.

I left the room, and Tom scrambled out of bed and followed me. 'Where will you go?'

I said nothing.

When I reached the front door, he said, 'We're *right*, Lillian. We are. *This* is. You shouldn't walk away from it.' I let myself out and closed the door. As I climbed into my car, he opened the door again and shouted, 'Where will you go?'

I drove home. I wanted to see Johnny, to be with him. What would I say? What would I do?

Nothing, nothing. I would just be with him. If he hurt me – if he hurt himself – I would stay with him anyway.

I opened the car windows. The air smelled of the sweet chemical fumes from the paper mills. The moon hung in a thin haze. Cars passed and a truck played loud hip hop on its sound system. I gripped the steering wheel, slowed and stopped for a stoplight, counted to three when the light turned green, and accelerated.

Ten minutes later, I rounded the corner to our house and my headlights shined on the front yard. The driveway was empty, the house dark.

I unlocked the front door, flipped on the hall light, and called Johnny's name, though I knew he was gone. In the bedroom, the bed looked as it had when I left in the morning. Johnny's vial of Xanax was on the bathroom counter – a good sign that he was staying on the right side of sanity. I shook the vial and pills rattled – a good sign that he had kept himself from pouring them all down his throat. I went into the kitchen and switched on the light. There was dirt on the counter. I heard a growling from the sunroom – Percy growling a warning.

I felt suddenly as if I'd been lured into the house and into a danger I hadn't anticipated, my senses and logic softened by vodka and fatigue.

I called Percy. He growled, and from the darkened sunroom a breeze blew into the kitchen. I backed toward the kitchen door. Percy's growl became a soft whine.

'Percy.'

Nothing.

I wanted to run.

In one of the kitchen drawers, we kept a small tool kit, a ball of twine, an extension cord, and a flashlight. I got the flashlight, inched close to the sunroom without going in, and shined the light.

Percy lay on the floor on his belly, his eyes gleaming yellow in the dark. The black fur under his jaws looked wet. A small, white, fleshy object, streaked with blood, lay between his front paws. As I stepped closer, he growled and took the object in his mouth. The breeze, with its sickening chemical smell, breathed into the kitchen. I raised the beam of the flashlight. Broken glass lay on the sunroom floor. The window on one of the doors to the backyard was shattered.

What had Johnny done?

As Percy growled, I switched on another lamp. The sunroom floor was a mess of glass, blood, and dog fur. The object in Percy's mouth was flesh – but from where? Johnny's leg? His arm?

A tooth – long, bloody, one of Percy's – lay near the broken door. A shred of bloody denim lay next to it. The sofa had been pulled away from the wall.

What had Johnny done?

I sat on the floor in the doorway from the kitchen and spoke to Percy, 'C'mere, baby.'

He looked uncertain who I was.

I reached my hand toward him.

He growled.

'It's OK. C'mon . . .'

He stopped growling.

I slid a couple of inches across the floor toward him.

He rose on his haunches.

Would he come after me as he had gone after Johnny? What had Johnny done to make him tear into him?

I slid closer.

Percy sprang to his feet and disappeared through the broken door into the dark backyard, the bloody flesh in his mouth.

The energy went out of me, but I got to my feet, went to the kitchen, found the phone, and dialed Daniel's home number. It rang four times, and Daniel answered.

I said, 'Johnny's gone off.'

'Gone off?'

'I don't know what he's done—'

'Calm down,' he said. 'Tell me what happened.'

I told him what I'd found when I came in.

'Slow down,' he said.

I told him again.

He said, 'Get out of the house.'

'What?'

'Now. Get out. If Johnny comes back, you don't want to be there. Do you understand?'

I felt exhausted. 'I do.'

'Are you all right?'

'I don't know.'

'Get out now. You can come here.'

'OK.'

'Now,' he said again.

'I'm leaving.'

I hung up and stared at the kitchen walls. The ceiling lamp cast an icy green light. I stared into the sunroom at the broken glass door. Percy was racing through the dark with a chunk of skin and muscle. 'Percy!' I called, but he also had gone off, crazed by the taste of human blood. I wandered into the front hall. The hallway light was icy too, illuminating a world without human or animal warmth. The night outside the front door would take me back to the living. A twenty-minute drive to Daniel's house would restore me to his voice and his wife's.

But I went into the bedroom. I stripped off my clothes and climbed into our bed. I pulled the covers around my body. I was neither hot nor cold. I felt half-dead. I pulled Johnny's pillow to my face and breathed in, sucking his smell deep into my lungs. If life remained possible, this was where I must find it: in the dense layerings, the nearly suffocating air that had passed through our bodies and bones. The upper atmosphere might sustain people who are light and able to float on the thin currents. But I knew that, like a deep-sea creature that would disintegrate in a fisherman's net when brought to a higher depth, I depended on the heavy weight of submersion.

Twenty-Seven

Johnny

I drove across the St Johns River on the Hart Bridge, the headlights gleaming on the skeletal steel. Peter Lisman sat in the passenger seat, the knife on his lap, blood soaking the remains of his jeans around his right calf and running down his leg into a cowboy boot. His pale, heavy face was blank. He kept his pain to himself.

When I had stepped into the sunroom, he had stood and raised the knife.

Percy, who had lain at his feet a moment earlier, lunged at him. With the knife in the air, Percy seemed to anticipate the harm the big man meant to do me. He sank his teeth into Lisman's leg and held.

Lisman could have killed Percy with the knife. He could have planted the blade between his raging eyes or reached under Percy's head and sliced his neck. Instead, he grabbed Percy by the collar and pulled him away. Percy tore skin and something more from the big man's leg, yelping as his teeth caught in the muscle or ligament. Lisman could have flung him into the backyard through the broken plate-glass door. Instead, he set him on the floor and stood over him with a look as old as the glowering that must have tamed the first wolves. He splayed his fingers in front of Percy's face and said, 'Stay.' Percy lay at his feet and stayed.

Lisman spoke to me in the same tone, 'Let's go.'

'Where?'

He led me through the house and out to the driveway, staying close enough to reach me with the knife if I disobeyed. Now, I steered on to the S curve that dropped from the Hart Bridge into the city, passed empty office buildings and churches, and cut south on to the streets that hugged the river down to Ortega.

'I met your mother,' I said.

'I know.'

'I get the sense she doesn't know what you do for the Phelpses.'

'You took my laptop.' His voice was pinched.

'I did.'

He shook his head as if I'd disappointed him.

'What's wrong with your voice?'

He said nothing.

'Sounds like you're castrated.'

'When I was little, my dad was beating my mom. I tried to stop him. He hit me in the throat. This is what I sound like.'

'Oh.'

He shrugged. 'He's dead now.'

'It happens,' I said.

'It happens,' he repeated, pinched.

'How long have you been doing dirty work for the Phelpses?'

'Turn left up there,' he said.

I turned on to a dark winding drive, the sides planted with trees and flowerbeds.

'I know you killed Alex Greene,' I said. 'How about Sheneel? Was that you too?'

He said nothing.

'You look like Sheneel,' I said. 'Same pale skin. But bigger, of course. Any relation?'

'Pull to the side by the garage.'

The driveway ended in a cul-de-sac with a large carriage-house garage on one side and a long brick house on the other. Flood lamps, set in a front garden, cast a golden light up the walls and into the branches of nearby oaks. From the hazy sky, the moon shined through the trees.

I pulled on to an apron of black pavement and turned off the car. 'You can't be her brother or father,' I said. 'What's the relation?'

'Mr Phelps is waiting,' he said, and got out. But when I got out too, he said, 'I want my laptop back.'

I was hoping he would say that. 'No problem.' I went to the trunk and opened it. I gave him his laptop.

As he was looking it over, I reached into the trunk again, brought out Papa Crowe's .22, and shoved the barrel against his belly. 'Give me the knife,' I said. He considered me awhile before giving it to me. I dropped it into the trunk and nodded toward the front door of the house. 'Move.'

He lumbered up the steps. When he'd hit me on the head at Alex Greene's house, he'd moved fast, but if he wanted to go slow now, I was happy to go slow. He let us into the house without knocking. I kept the gun barrel on his back as he led me through a high-ceilinged front hall into a formal living room, through a room full of family portraits, and into a room with a wide-screen TV. Edward Phelps, wearing khakis, loafers, and a pink polo shirt, stood when we came in.

He looked at Lisman, at me, at the gun, and said, 'You can put that away. It won't do you any good.'

I pressed the barrel into Lisman's back.

Phelps said, 'Peter, will you pour me a drink? I have the feeling this gentleman is going to try my patience.'

256

Lisman tried to step around me, but I said, 'No.'

He stepped past me anyway.

I aimed at his back. 'Stop.'

He kept going.

I shifted the gun a couple of degrees and pulled the trigger. The slug splintered the wooden molding on the doorframe.

Lisman didn't flinch.

I chambered another bullet, but he disappeared into the next room.

'Make that a double,' Edward Phelps called after him. I was merely a joke. He said to me, 'Do you realize how much woodwork costs? Carpenters see this neighborhood and this house and they triple the price before walking in the door.'

I pointed the rifle at him. 'You've got that man well trained.'

'He's spectacular, isn't he? But you're mistaken. No one is capable of training Peter. He makes his own choices. Do you know where I found him? He was working at one of our timber sites. He'd been incarcerated for twenty years, since he was twelve years old – first on a work farm for juvenile offenders and then in jail. On the work farm, they taught him forestry and some animal husbandry. We hire a lot of felons to cut timber. They're used to a hard life, and, contrary to popular belief, they're mostly an honest group of men.

'I saw Peter on one of our work crews, and he stood out. At the time, my family was doing some heavy work on our Cumberland Island vacation house, so I brought him over to help lifting beams and coquina. One afternoon, I was watching the progress when a wild horse, a pregnant mare, stumbled on to the property acting crazy, crashing through the low branches on the trees. She was having trouble birthing a foal.

'No one would go near her. She looked like she meant to kick a man or two in the head. Well, Peter put down his load and walked over, talking steady and soft if you can imagine that. The mare didn't respond. She went crashing through more branches. But Peter went after her, calm and steady. And when the mare ran out of energy and collapsed, Peter reached up inside her – right into the birth canal – and pulled out the foal. Still birth. I thought that was remarkable. I thought, this is a man who can handle difficult situations.'

Lisman came back with a cocktail glass.

'I've been singing your praises, Peter,' Phelps said as he took the glass. Then he turned again to me. 'I see *you* as a difficult situation.'

I gestured at Lisman. 'Why was he in jail?'

Phelps said, 'He killed his father. Isn't that right, Peter?'

'Yes, sir.'

Phelps said to me, 'As I see it, you've been working against us. Is there nothing I can do to change that? You understand, I was never in the armed services myself, but I have great respect for those who have served. I would like to be able to demonstrate that respect, if you will let me.'

'I think you already own enough people in this city.'

He smiled. 'What's enough?' He sipped from his drink and looked pleased with himself. 'Is there nothing you want? Nothing you need? I have a lot to offer.'

'What did Sheneel Greene want? Or her brother?'

'That's beyond your understanding.'

'Try me.'

He sipped again from his glass. 'I think not.'

'Well, that's what I want from you. I want to know what happened to them.'

'That's a stupid wish.' He narrowed his eyes. 'I'm offering you a way out.'

'I don't want it,' I said, 'at least not from you.'

Phelps sighed and spoke to Lisman. 'Take his gun, Peter.'

Lisman stepped toward me, and I aimed the rifle at his chest and said, 'Don't.'

Phelps said, 'You'd better knock him down with your first shot, because if he's still standing, he'll turn you inside out.'

I pointed the gun at Phelps. 'I'll shoot you first.'

His face colored. 'Take it, Peter.'

But a woman's voice spoke from the doorway behind me. 'What in God's name is going on?'

Lisman stopped and Phelps frowned. The monstrous woman I last had glimpsed in the backseat of a black town car outside of Papa Crowe's house stepped into the room. Last time, Papa Crowe had drawn a muddy cross on her forehead with an unction he stored in a mustard pot. Now, Cecilia Phelps wore a long white cotton bathrobe, and the glassy skin on her face was bare.

She stared at me with one moving eye, the other eye fixed under an overgrown eyelid. She asked, 'Did you shoot that gun in here?'

Her husband said, 'Cecilia, go upstairs.'

She didn't seem to hear him, but the glaring eye softened, and she came to me and placed a knotted hand on my cheek. 'You poor man,' she said. 'You poor, poor man. You've seen it too, haven't you?'

'What are you talking about?' I said.

Phelps said, 'My wife is—'

'I am *not*,' she said. 'I know what I've seen, and this man has seen it too.'

'My wife is troubled,' Phelps said.

She moved close. 'You've seen it.'

'Cecilia, go upstairs.' For the first time, Edward Phelps sounded angry.

His wife only gazed at me gently and touched my wrist with her disfigured hand.

I yanked away and swung the gun barrel from her to her husband to Lisman. 'You're all insane,' I said.

She smiled from one side of her mouth. 'Don't believe that. Edward will—'

Her husband said to Lisman, 'Take his gun.'

I pulled the trigger and shot a slug into the ceiling. Cecilia Phelps said, 'Don't do that!' Her husband and Lisman froze.

I chambered another bullet. 'What happened to Sheneel and Alex Greene?'

'Is that all?' the scarred woman said. 'Tell him, Edward.' Her husband said nothing, so she continued, 'It's the salt. Edward says it depends on moisture. If it's dry-salted, it will last for a

260

hundred years. If it's wet, it will eat away in two or three months.'

Edward Phelps stepped toward her and hit her in the face. She stumbled back and balanced herself on the arm of the couch. She stared with rage at her husband, Lisman, me. A vein-like blue line showed through the surface of her glassy skin as if something inside had broken.

Then she laughed.

Her laughter was more terrible than tears or howls. She touched her cheek as if afraid that her fingers would penetrate the fire-scarred skin. She said to me, 'Use just enough fire and you'll preserve a body for hundreds of years. Like sand turned into glass. It will never grow old.'

Her husband said to Lisman, 'Get her out of here.'

Lisman extended a gentle hand. 'Come on, Mrs Phelps. I'll take you upstairs.'

She reached for him, as if he were offering to pull her from a deep liquid pool, and she went with him.

For nearly a minute, Phelps and I listened as Lisman coaxed her through the house and upstairs. Then Phelps drank the last of his cocktail, and I said, 'Tell me about Little Marsh Island.'

'You've got to be kidding.'

'Why would I be?'

'Would you put that damn gun down?'

I held it level.

He looked from my eyes to the gun and back. 'We're building a facility there, that's all. In Cecilia's diseased mind, the place has assumed greater significance since Sheneel's death.'

'It's just a coincidence that her body was on land that you were looking to develop?'

'I didn't call it a coincidence. Sheneel was part of our family. When she killed herself, she chose a place that was meaningful to us.'

'I'm tired of people saying she killed herself.'

'I'm tired of people implying it was more.'

'So, why Little Marsh Island? Of all the places your family owns and controls, why there?'

'Why not?' He shrugged. 'It's a pretty spot to die.'

'And she knew you were going to buy it?'

'A friend owned the land before us, and my family has used it for years. My grandfather shared a hunting lodge there. After that fell down, we still hunted for deer and wild pigs.'

I wanted to pull the trigger. 'What was your wife saying about salt?'

His laugh was bitter. 'She says a great deal that escapes my understanding.'

'That's why you hit her?'

He quieted. 'I hit her because thirty years have passed since her accident, and there are times when only violence can cut through her delusion.'

'It seems to be your preferred response.'

'No,' he said. 'It's a last choice, but I don't hesitate to make it when necessary.'

'That's why you had Lisman bring me here – so you could make a last choice?'

He shook his head. 'I had him bring you here so that *you* could make the choice for me. Now you've made it, and we'll deal with the consequences.'

I hugged the stock of the .22 to my ribs and leveled the barrel on his chest. 'You seem to think you're the only one who can use violence.'

Again he shook his head. 'I know that's not the case. You reminded my son of it this morning.' He walked across the room and picked up a telephone from a table between two leather easy chairs. 'I also know, though, that you missed. I've seen your training and service records. I know the kind of marksmanship you're capable of. With your abilities, it's a shame that the Navy put you into a non-combat job. You certainly had the physical skills for action. Your officers must have suspected character weakness. To commit deadly violence against another man requires a certain integrity of commitment.' He looked at the phone and touched three buttons – the one high and two lower notes of nine-one-one.

I tightened my finger on the trigger. I *needed* to shoot him.

'You missed Stephen by only an inch. But how far away were you standing? You surely—' He interrupted himself when the police dispatcher answered. 'Yes,' he said, 'there's a man outside our house with a gun.' He listened to the dispatcher's response, added a few *Yes ma'ams* and *No ma'ams*, listened again, and said, 'He looks like someone who has been bothering our family. His name is Johnny Bellefleur.'

I could shoot him and end his telephone call mid-sentence. I could be done with him.

He took the phone from his ear and pressed the mouthpiece against his shirt. He said, 'You can leave if you want or you can wait for the police.'

I needed to pull the trigger.

He turned his back to me, listened to the phone, and said, 'Yes, ma'am. He's trying to get inside.'

Still aiming the gun at him, I picked up the two bullet shells that the .22 had expelled. The slugs would stay until the police pried them out with a chisel and tweezers.

'Please hurry,' Phelps said to the dispatcher.

A quarter-ounce more pressure and the trigger would snap and the hammer would fall.

I lowered the gun. 'I'll be back,' I said.

Phelps pressed the telephone against his shirt. 'I'm sure you will.'

I ran through the rooms and into the front hall, then out into the night. My car stood where I'd left it. The moon hung in the hazy sky. The warm air smelled of jasmine and roses. A woman, barefoot and robed in white, stepped across the dark lawn toward me, her footfalls delicate and slow as if she feared crushing the grass. Cecilia Phelps. She looked up at the moon or maybe at the second floor of the house where lights shined from the bedroom windows. She seemed not to see me at all as I ran to my car. But as I opened the driver's door, she said, 'You should have children.'

I stopped. 'What?'

'You and your wife,' she said. 'Children. Even if they turn out to be little bastards. They'll complete you.'

A loud crack sounded from one of the upstairs windows. I felt the sound as a physical jolt, and I looked at the house. A man sat at the window

264

directly over the room closest to my car. He held a rifle, as small as the .22 that I carried – a squirrel-hunting rifle, a gun to teach a child to shoot.

A pain started in my side, above my left hip.

I paid no attention to it. I focused on the man. He was big, but his features, backlit from the room behind him, were unclear. I thought he must be Lisman.

The pain spread and I felt a damp heat in my belly.

No, the man wasn't Lisman. But I recognized him. 'Daniel?' I said.

The man held still and said nothing.

'Daniel?' I said again.

My legs weakened under my body, and, as my mind made its slow computations and the pain webbed outward from my belly, I realized that I had been shot. The realization sucked air and energy from my lungs and took me down to the black driveway. Cecilia Phelps stood near me, dressed in her white bathrobe. She reached to me as if she would help me to my feet. I reached for her too. But she turned away and walked into the big house.

PART THREE

Twenty-Eight

Lillian

They didn't let me see Johnny in the hospital, but I visited him when they released him to jail. They'd charged him with criminal trespass, malicious destruction of property, and unlawful discharge of a firearm, though the State Attorney's office decided against attempted murder. Everyone seemed to agree: as a vet, Johnny needed help if he could get it, not long-term incarceration. They said he drove to Edward Phelps's house and yelled insane threats. They said he shot three bullets into the outside wall of the house before Phelps leaned from his wife's bedroom window and sank a single shot into the left side of his belly. Phelps owned big guns – for hunting, pleasure shooting, and self-defense – and the police were praising him for his restraint in using a small-caliber rifle.

The doctors at the hospital said that, for a luckless man, Johnny got lucky. The bullet entered his abdomen above his left hip but missed his pancreas and threaded past his intestines. It passed above the hipbone and below the bottom rib. It tore through muscle and ligament. Except for the risk of infection, the doctors could have released him after twenty-four hours. They kept him for seventy-two, an IV dripping antibiotics into his wrist, a shackle locking his ankle to the bed frame, a full-time police guard standing at his door. Then they dressed him in orange coveralls, the jailhouse equivalent of a hospital gown, and transported him in a locked van to the county jail.

Johnny's lawyer, with some help from a letter signed by a hospital psychologist, convinced the police to allow Johnny and me to meet in a private conference room, though Johnny's lawyer warned me to say nothing that Johnny wouldn't want heard in court because the police might record our conversations. The room had a long wooden table surrounded by ten chairs, four bare walls, no windows, and fluorescent lighting embedded behind clear-plastic ceiling panels. When a uniformed woman let me in, Johnny sat with his hands cuffed, his fingers folded on top of the table as if he might pray.

'No touching,' the woman said, and closed the door on us.

Johnny hadn't shaved since getting shot, and his eyes looked strangely brilliant.

'How are you feeling?' I asked.

He tipped his head, noncommittal.

'Much pain?'

'Not bad.'

'Are they giving you your meds?'

Another noncommittal nod.

'You've got to take them.'

'I'm done with all that,' he said.

'Johnny—'

'I'm sorry,' he said, and his eyes moistened.

I stared at him and felt something breaking in me. 'No, *I'm* sorry,' I said.

270

He leaned across the table and whispered, 'Daniel shot me.'

'Shh,' I said. I looked around the room for a microphone. I spotted none, but that meant little.

'I saw him. He shot me from the window.' His eyes were brilliant, frantic.

Screw the lawyer. 'No. Edward Phelps did.'

'Phelps was downstairs. I talked to him and his wife in their media room.'

'You were outside. You shot at the house.'

Tears filled his eyes.

I said, 'I talked to Daniel only an hour or so before you got shot. He was at home. He wasn't there.'

'He was there.'

I shook my head. 'The police found three bullets and three shells outside. Saying that you were inside will make this worse.'

He leveled his voice. 'I shot the gun twice inside. Once into a doorframe. Once into the ceiling. Edward Phelps is lying.'

'Why? To make things easier for you?'

'Nothing's easy for me.'

I stared at him. 'I love you, but you—'

'You saw the blood in the sunroom. You saw Percy. You saw the mess.'

'I saw the mess.'

'And the blood.'

'I don't know whose blood.'

'Peter Lisman's.'

'I cleaned it up. It's gone.'

'You saw what Percy did to him. That was skin from his leg. Get it checked out.'

I stared at him.

'What?' he said.

'It's gone.'

'What do you mean, *gone*?'

'Percy. He ate it.'

'Jesus Christ.'

'He's a dog. It's what dogs do.'

He laughed. It was an unpleasant laugh. He said, 'You've got to believe me.'

'I don't know what to believe.'

He stared at me, his eyes moist.

I said, 'I'm going to try to get you out of here.'

He sighed. 'Good.'

'The lawyer says they'll set the bail high. I'll need to put up the house.'

'Do it.'

'You'll have restrictions. Probably an ankle monitor. You'll need to agree to take your meds.'

'I'll tell them whatever they want to hear.'

I breathed deep. 'Will you go after the Phelpses?'

'What do you want me to say?'

'Johnny—'

'No,' he said, 'I won't go after the Phelpses.'

We sat together awhile, quiet. I wanted to reach across the table and touch his hands, his face, his skin. Would the guard know? I said, 'With Tom Corfield and me, there's nothing. Nothing that matters. There never has been.'

He stared at me.

I said, 'You need to believe me.'

'*You* need me to believe you. We have that problem, don't we? You believing me, me believing you.'

Not with a Club the Heart is broken, Nor with a Stone, I thought. I said, 'Let's work on it.'

* * *

272

The judge refused to set bail. Johnny's lawyer said that, considering the charges, he had no basis for keeping Johnny in jail, and he filed an appeal. A week passed, then two. The lawyer re-filed the appeal. No one would explain the delay.

Outside, the yellow and white jasmine blossoms turned brown on the vines. The magnolia trees forced enormous white flowers from their branches, and then the flowers turned brown too. *How odd the Girl's life looks – Behind this soft Eclipse.* When Tom Corfield asked me to move in with him, I said, *No. Not yet,* and I wondered why I couldn't say, *Never.* As spring pushed into summer, late-afternoon storms broke the heat with sudden dark downpours and brilliant bolts of lightning. I walked Percy in the mornings, read in the backyard in the early afternoons, and visited Johnny when they let me. I slept on his side of the bed at night, though the sensation of closeness that at first came from that had faded.

One afternoon, when I thought Edward Phelps must be at work, I drove to his house and knocked on the front door. A maid opened and I asked to see Mrs Phelps.

'She's sleeping,' the maid said.

'I'll wait.'

The maid narrowed her eyes. 'Sometimes she sleeps through dinner.'

'I'll still wait.' Then footsteps approached through the front hallway.

'Who is it, Sharon?' Cecilia Phelps's voice.

The maid tried to close the door. 'Mr Edward told me—'

'Am I a child?' Cecilia Phelps asked.

'No, ma'am,' the maid said.

Cecilia Phelps opened the door. 'Oh,' she said when she saw me. She wore green cotton exercise pants, a matching long-sleeve shirt, and bright white tennis shoes. She had pulled her stringy black hair tight behind her head and knotted it. She had drawn red lipstick on to her burnt, crooked lips. 'You can't be here,' she said. 'Edward will be upset.'

'Are you a child?' I asked.

She seemed to consider the question. 'Come in.' As I stepped into the front hall, she said to the maid, 'Tea, Sharon.'

'I don't need any,' I said.

The maid hesitated.

'Tea,' Cecilia Phelps said again, and then to me, 'What can I do for you?' She spoke with the stiff, formal politeness that you might program into a machine.

'When my husband came here, what happened?'

'You don't know?'

I heard no irony. 'What led to the shooting? Who shot him?'

'He came to our house with a gun.' Her good eye held me calmly, warmly. Her frozen eye was opaque. Sunlight shined through the windows above the front door. A vase of tulips stood on a credenza positioned against one wall in the front hall. Cecilia Phelps looked at me helpfully, expectantly.

'I'm sorry for this,' I said, and I walked past her into the living room and through the portrait-lined sitting room that Edward Phelps had showed me as he guided me through the house when I first came here. Cecilia Phelps followed me as I stepped into the media room.

The room looked exactly as I remembered it. The ceiling showed no sign of having been damaged by a gunshot. The doorframe ran flush and intact around the length of the doorway. I looked for evidence of new paint or new wood. Cecilia Phelps watched me looking. The whole room was clean, untouched, unused. 'I'm sorry,' I said again.

She smiled from the side of her mouth. 'The men in my life exhaust me too.' She walked back into the sitting room, saying, 'Come.'

The maid set a table for tea on the patio facing the backyard pool and the river. The teacups, saucers, and teapot were white with blue abstract designs on them, the starched and pressed cotton napkins white with blue prints of shepherd boys, girls, and lambs. The maid poured tea and set a silver platter of cookies between us.

Cecilia Phelps nibbled the edge of a cookie on the working side of her mouth and said, 'I married into this family. I'm not, properly speaking, one of them. From time to time, Edward reminds me of this. He says the difference between a Phelps and everyone else is that, when the fires start, everyone else gets burned.'

'What a nice man.'

'I never cared much for nice men. I suspect you understand the feeling.'

'Johnny is nothing like your husband.'

'Give him time,' she said. 'When we first married, Edward treated me as if I were as fragile as spun sugar.'

A breeze blew from the river, and the leaves on the live oak trees shined like silver spangles. Soon, that breeze would bring thunderclouds and an afternoon storm.

I said, 'Johnny swears that he came here with Peter Lisman. He says he talked with you and your husband inside your house. He says he shot his gun twice inside. He says he was leaving when he was wounded.'

Cecilia Phelps fixed me with her good eye. 'Does it matter? Either way, he landed in the hospital and now jail.'

'Are you saying that he *was* inside?'

'The police have a recording of Edward reporting a man outside our house. They have an affidavit in which Edward admits shooting your husband. They have physical evidence. So that is what happened. Some stories are more compelling than others – ours being more compelling than your husband's.'

'Is Johnny telling the truth?'

'Why would you want to challenge our story?'

'Johnny's in jail.'

'The situation could be worse. Anyway, he'll be out soon.'

'They won't even give him bail.'

'Be patient.'

'Everyone thinks he's out of his head.'

'That reputation might keep him safe.'

I said, 'Did my brother shoot Johnny?'

She sipped from her cup, a drop of tea rolling down her chin from the stiff side of her mouth. 'Don't try to change the story,' she said.

The maid came with another pot of tea and, as

she refilled our cups, I asked Cecilia Phelps, 'So what do you recommend I do?'

'Whatever you wish to do,' she said, 'but stay away from my family. Stay away from here. Stay away from Little Marsh Island and my husband's mills and Sheneel and Alex Greene's old house. This family has always fed on its own misery. You don't want to be consumed by this.'

A week later, the State Attorney dropped all charges against Johnny. Daniel called to tell me, and an hour later Johnny's lawyer called too, as perplexed by the decision as he was by the judge's unwillingness to grant bail.

I cleaned the house, put my books on the shelves, and, on the night that Johnny came home, sat on the bed as he came out of the shower, a towel wrapped around his waist. The bullet wound had mostly healed. The last of the bruising tinged the skin over his ribs. The scabbing had flaked away. The pock over his left hip looked like another navel, as if he had experienced a second birth. He had lost weight in jail.

Would he want me after all he'd been through?

Did I want him?

He stood in the bathroom doorway, and I thought he must be wondering the same thing. Outside, a rainstorm had cooled the hot afternoon. The bedroom windows were open and the sweet smell of humidity and of the mix of living and decaying vegetation combined with the steam from the bathroom shower. Water dripped from Johnny's hair on to his shoulders. He stared at me as if uncertain whether pain or pleasure would follow.

Then he came to me, and we had uncomfortable sex, facing each other, looking into each other's eyes, gripping each other's half-familiar skin, unsure, bony, awkward, as if we were rediscovering ourselves in each other, rebirthing uncertainly, uncertainly reconnecting.

When Johnny lay on his back afterward, I watched him for a long while and wondered whether our lovemaking had been more than an illusion and whether we were now together or apart. I asked, 'What are you thinking?'

For a while, he said nothing.

'What are you thinking about?' I asked again.

'Chromium-six,' he said.

Twenty-Nine

Johnny

'Chromium-six,' Papa Crowe said when he visited me in jail.

'What?' I said.

'Anything that got a number in it ain't a real name. Real name is jimson weed or cockleburs or alligator root or dogwood.'

'What are you talking about?'

We sat in a room with three other prisoners and their visitors, the prisoners lined on one side of a long partitioned table, the visitors on the other.

'I'm talking about chromium-six. It what

Sheneel find in Georgia where my family use to live. It what she worry about on Little Marsh Island.'

'I still have no idea—'

'It come from the mills. It get in the water. Too much, it give people the cancer. Pulp mill owners, they got to regulate it. The Phelpses don't even regulate how much they piss on each other leg.'

'Where did you find out about this?'

'These eyes old but they can read. Phelpses is in the Georgia papers yesterday. They make a settlement with the government – pay a fine and quit dumping waste where it run into the water supply.'

'Sheneel found chromium-six on your family's old land in Georgia?'

'She put water in a bottle and dirt in a box, and she send it in like a raffle ticket, and now a judge tell the Phelpses to quit poisoning the water. Don't you see? That why the Phelpses kill her. They got so many folk and so much money in they pocket, they no room for the keys, but Sheneel cut a hole in the pocket.'

'So they killed her, and I went after them, and now I'm here.'

'Where you think they going to dump the chromium now?'

'Little Marsh Island?'

He nodded. 'They put up some big walls and dig a hole in the middle. They right on the salt marsh, and the tide wash out what don't sink into the ground. That neighborhood on the other side of the road, they drink well water. I wouldn't drink it after the Phelpses move in, no.'

279

'Tell it to the people who live on the other side of the road.'

'Maybe I do that. I knock on the doors and tell the people about the Phelpses, and then the Phelpses maybe pick me up like they pick you up and maybe they shoot a bullet in my head instead of my belly. Or maybe they call the police and the police put me in the cell next to yours. Then we can talk about the Phelpses all day and all night.'

'So why did you come to see me?'

'To tell you the news. And to tell you, you owe me a new rifle.'

'It's at the top of my list when I get out of here.'

'I bet.' He pulled a plastic baggie from a pocket and laid it on the table. 'Also, I bring a present.'

Inside were three dark berries, dried and flat. 'What are they?'

'You eat one these and you go away awhile. You come back in a couple day and you think you been on vacation.'

'Put them away. I've got enough trouble already.'

'OK, if you like it here so much.'

Few sounds are more despairing than metal closing against metal, and few sounds more hopeful than metal pulling free as a door swings open after the electronic locks slip their bolts. Though the wind that blows into the cell through the open door has blown from other closed and locked corridors, it feels as full of promise as the ozone breeze that follows a summer rain. The voice that says, *C'mon, let's go – you're out*, tickles your ears like a sexual tongue.

Sex at home afterward was a comparative disappointment. The pain in my belly kept me from letting go. As I touched her skin – as she touched mine – I couldn't forget that it all comes to pain and disintegration sooner or later. Everything else was a distraction, a denial, including sex – especially sex. But I went through the motions because she expected me to, and if I didn't, I might as well be still locked up.

In the morning, Lillian cooked eggs, and we ate outside on the patio. She had repaired the sunroom window and cleaned the house of blood and broken glass. Percy, lying in the shade of the live oak, showed no sign of having eaten a chunk of a man's leg. The world turned as if my collision with Peter Lisman and the Phelpses had never occurred. But the air smelled of the paper mills, and the sun glared in the haze.

'What next?' Lillian asked.

I drank my coffee. 'I figure we have two choices. We get out, or we go in deeper.'

'Why would you want to go in deeper?'

'It's not a question of what I *want*.'

'Then what is it?'

I shrugged. How could I explain, without sounding as crazy as everyone seemed to think I was, my need to go down through the skin that clothed my life and the lives of everyone I knew – my need to blast through the barriers that the men whose torn bodies I'd processed had blasted through?

281

Lillian said, 'This doesn't fix you. You don't get back what you've lost.'

I said, 'I just want to do *something*.'

'Even if it kills you?'

I felt a dull pain in my stomach and I tried to hide it. 'Especially if it kills me.'

'I don't understand.'

'I'm glad. You wouldn't want to be where I am.'

She gave me the funniest smile. 'But I do. I want to be where you are.'

I liked the smile. 'I need to run an errand this morning,' I said.

'I'll go with you.'

I considered that. 'I need to do this on my own.'

'I want to—'

But I left her and Percy in the backyard and drove north on the Interstate, then east into Fernandina. I needed another gun and hoped Papa Crowe might have one.

A log truck carrying slash pines dropped bark and wood splinters on the road in front of me, and I accelerated around it and fell in behind another log truck. A police car stood in the driveway of a white clapboard Baptist Church. A dark-skinned woman holding an umbrella against the sun pushed a stroller on the sidewalk. When I reached Papa Crowe's house, a long black town car was parked in front – a car I'd last seen when Papa Crowe leaned through its window and pasted a muddy cross on Cecilia Phelps's forehead. Now, all four windows were open, and Peter Lisman sat in the driver's seat, as placid as a sleeping man.

I drove past, turned around, pulled beyond the house again, and parked at the edge of the Bosquebello Cemetery. I walked back on the road shoulder, trying to stay out of sight, but when I came to Papa Crowe's yard, Lisman was standing outside his car waiting for me. A pair of dark sunglasses hid his eyes and made his pale face look all the more like death.

There was no avoiding him, so I crossed the yard and said, 'How's the leg?'

His shrug was hardly a shrug. 'How's the belly?'

'Real good,' I said, and turned to the house.

'I wouldn't go in there,' he said in his pinched voice.

I stepped on to the porch, knocked, and, when Papa Crowe didn't answer, let myself inside through the screen door.

The front room was dark. Two corked Coke bottles – one full of a yellow liquid, the other with the remains of something black and syrupy – stood on the wooden table. I glanced into the kitchen. A fly was buzzing above the sink. The refrigerator hummed.

A second, mostly closed door led from the front room. On my earlier visits, I'd guessed it went into Papa Crowe's bedroom. I started to knock but heard a murmuring voice and I pushed the door open. Sun fell into the room through mostly closed slat blinds, and the air smelled of sour sweat. The floor was pinewood and the walls gray with age. A single steamer trunk stood in the center of the room, open and stuffed with clothing, the only furniture other than a metal-legged sleeping cot.

Cecilia Phelps lay on the cot, her yellow cotton dress peeled down to her waist. Her breasts seemed shaped of melted, glistening plastic. Her belly was a mix of blisters and jagged scars.

Papa Crowe kneeled by her side, wearing only blue jeans, his shoulders taut but mottled by age. He held his hands over her naked skin, touching or almost touching her, lightly caressing her breasts and belly, her blisters and scars, as if his healing fingers could draw the fire and pain from her body.

She lay still, her eyes closed, and he murmured words in a language that I didn't understand, then lowered his hands until his fingers kneaded her skin. She made a sound, a moan of pleasure or pain. Her skin blushed. He lowered his head over her body as if he would pray for her, and he opened his mouth as if he would speak more strange words, but he said no prayer, said nothing. He parted his lips and kissed the burnt skin of her breasts, kissed as he had touched and caressed them, and her hands rose from the cot and lowered between her own legs.

'Jesus Christ,' I said.

My voice drew them out of their intimate trance. She turned and her stare accused me. For a moment in the half-light, I mistook the damp on Papa Crowe's lips for blood. He said, 'What the hell you do in my house?'

All I could say was, 'I need another weapon.'

Cecilia Phelps stayed on the cot, her dress at her waist, her disfigured face fierce, as Papa Crowe pushed me through the door into the front room. His voice low, he said, 'I give you my gun already.'

284

'I—'

He waved at the front door. 'Get out.'

'I need a weapon.'

'You a man that lose things. I got nothing for you.'

'Give me what you have.'

'You don't listen. You humming your own music and don't hear nobody else.'

'I'm sorry for walking in on you.'

'Damn right. Too many men walk through my door without knocking. Then you sit in my chair and you say this house is yours, not mine, and it time for me to be gone.'

'I'm sorry.'

'Not sorry enough,' he said.

'I need a weapon.'

'You need something, that for sure.' But his anger was easing. 'You a hard-headed man.' He walked back to the bedroom. 'Wait in the kitchen.'

When he rejoined me, he placed a balled flannel shirt on the kitchen counter. He ran his fingers through his gray hair and said, 'When I take you to Cumberland, I tell you about the Confederate general that owned the island till his son shoot his own boy and himself too.'

'Right,' I said.

He unwrapped the flannel shirt, exposing an old steel revolver with a dark wooden grip. Next to it was a little cardboard box. Unlike the dusty rifle that he'd loaned me, the revolver shined with oil and polish. 'My granddaddy give me this gun. It one of the first double-action. He say it did the general's son his business.'

I picked it up. 'It isn't much of a gun.'

'It kill a man just the same.'

'How did your grandfather get it?'

'He there when the general's son do it. He carry it away.' Papa Crowe picked up the cardboard box and removed four handcrafted bullets. 'This gun old. Closest ammunition you can buy is thirty caliber, but I wouldn't do it if you like your fingers and hand.' He offered the bullets to me. 'You shoot these and you find more yourself.'

I sprang the cylinder and loaded the bullets. 'Thank you,' I said.

Papa Crowe held me with his eyes. 'You lose that gun and you lose a part of me.'

'I understand.'

'It shoot no good from far away but it do the job up close,' he said as I stuck the barrel into my waistband. 'You go after Edward and Stephen?' He kept his voice low. Cecilia Phelps wouldn't hear from the bedroom.

'Not this time,' I said.

'You going to tell me?'

'No.'

He stared at me, then shrugged. 'Get moving, then.'

I nodded toward the bedroom. 'You hate her husband and son. You hate her family—'

He said, 'The Phelps men give her as much grief as they give me. More maybe.'

'You're a good man,' I said. 'Strange, but good.'

When I stepped from the front porch into the sand-and-oyster-shell yard, Lisman was sitting in the town car again, the windows open, his pale skin glistening with sweat. I went to the car and

286

leaned in at the driver's door. 'How many years has it been since Edward Phelps pulled you off the timber crew and brought you into his house?'

He looked at me through his dark sunglasses. 'Enough to know when to mind my own business.'

'But they've got you minding *their* business – and the worst of it too. They've put you in their septic tank with a brush and told you to scrub. That doesn't bother you?'

'Nope,' he said.

I brought the old revolver up from my belt and pointed it at his vein-marbled forehead. 'Well, if that business ever takes you back to my house, I'll kill you. I've learned the danger of hesitating.'

He looked unworried. So I stepped from the window, and, using the tip of the revolver barrel, I scratched an almost complete circle on the car hood. Lisman watched through the windshield as I added an open-mouthed, diamond-shaped head to one end of the circle, completing a rough picture of a snake biting its tail. 'I've decided I know what this means,' I said. 'You think you're moving on. You think you've taken care of Sheneel and Alex Greene. You might think you've taken care of me. But you've only gone in circles. You've gone nowhere. It comes back to get you.'

I drove back through Fernandina, then south on the highway into Jacksonville. The woman at the phone desk at the Sheriff's Office said Daniel was off duty, and when I asked when he would come in, she connected me with the Homicide

Room where a man said his shift started at two p.m.

Daniel and his wife lived in a ranch house with a dock that backed into Black Creek outside the southern end of the city. Patty spent most of her time in the front garden when she wasn't working as a pediatric nurse. When Daniel wasn't on duty, he spent most of his time fishing from the dock.

I checked my watch. Ten-fifteen. I knew where to find him.

Patty had trained a purple-blossomed bougainvillea up a trellised arch that covered the first part of a brick walkway from the street to the front door. She'd used railroad ties to raise three small flowerbeds above the front lawn. Patty's car was gone, but Daniel's stood on the driveway.

I tucked Papa Crowe's revolver into the back of my waistband and knocked on the door. Loud seventies music played inside – REO Speedwagon singing 'Keep on Loving You.' The air on the front porch smelled of flowers and freshly turned soil. I knocked again.

Nothing.

But as I stepped off the porch to go around to the back of the house, the door opened. Daniel, his hair wet and feet bare, wore a black bathrobe. He hadn't shaved in a couple of days.

He eyed me, then smiled. 'Johnny.' If he'd noticed the revolver, he didn't show it.

'Hey, can we talk?'

He glanced at the yard, looked across the street. 'Of course. C'mon.'

He held the door so I could pass, but I waved

him ahead and followed him into the front hall. He was a big man – wide-hipped, wide-shouldered.

'Patty home?' I asked.

'She went to work early. And I was out late last night, so I slept in.'

As we came to the kitchen, I reached for the revolver, but at the same moment he spun and threw a punch at me. His face had pinked as if he'd been straining or holding his breath, and as he lunged his robe pulled open, exposing his chest and belly.

I dropped back, and his punch missed, but I fell against the hallway wall. I tried to get the gun out of my belt. He regained his balance and charged at me, a man whose size and violence could crush me, but my fingers touched the wooden revolver grip, and the gun came into my hand and up until I aimed it at his chest.

He stopped.

He stood and stared at me, his naked body exposed by the open robe. He laughed. 'What the hell kind of gun is that?'

'The kind that will shoot you.'

He stopped laughing. 'I don't think so.' But he stayed where he was.

'Close your robe.'

Keeping his eyes on me, he did. 'What's this about?'

'Why did you try to punch me?'

'I saw the gun in your pants when I opened the door. A man like you should never have a gun. When he does, only bad can come.' His face was red.

'Why did you shoot me at the Phelpses' house?'

He stared at me a moment as if he might answer, but turned and walked toward the back door.

I pointed the gun at his back. 'Stop.'

'Go to hell. I need some air.'

The cylinder held four bullets. One would be enough.

He went out through the back door. I followed him as he walked down the lawn to the dock. When he built it, around the time I started seeing Lillian, he'd painted the pressure-treated wood white, constructed a bench at the end to sit on while fishing, and bracketed a length of PVC pipe to the back of the bench to hold a flag on the Fourth of July and Memorial Day. Now the bench and pipe were gone, and gray wood showed where wind and rain had stripped the paint.

Daniel walked to the end of the dock and stared at the water. An anhinga, its black wings stretched to dry in the sun, perched on the exposed branch of a fallen tree that had snagged near the close bank of the creek.

Daniel breathed heavily. His neck was sweaty. If I shot a bullet in his back, it would push him into the water and he would float with the lazy current to where the creek emptied into the St Johns River and, if no one pulled him out with a net or a hook, down the St Johns into the Atlantic Ocean.

He said, 'It's real bad with the Phelpses and it's getting worse.'

'You got yourself into it,' I said.

'That makes it better?'

'Why did you shoot me?'

'You know, I could have shot you in the head,' he said. 'Then we wouldn't be standing here. I told the Phelpses it would be better that way. But Edward wanted you to live if possible. For what that's worth.'

'I should be grateful to him?'

Daniel shook his head. 'Who wants to be responsible for killing a vet?'

'But shooting me in the stomach is OK?'

'If you come to his house, crazy with a rifle, yeah. Extra points if it turns out you're not hurt too bad.'

'You know it didn't happen that way.'

'I know how it goes down on paper. That's all that matters to the Phelpses.'

'You do everything they ask you to do?'

'More or less.' He sounded resigned.

From up the creek, a small aluminum motorboat approached, driven by a man who looked to be in his early twenties. He wore camouflage cargo pants, a blue sleeveless T-shirt, and a yellow baseball cap. Three fishing rods hung over the stern. He waved at Daniel, and Daniel waved back. As the boat passed, I tucked the revolver behind me.

I said, 'Did you help kill Sheneel and Alex Greene.'

He waited for the boat to disappear down creek. 'No.'

'Who killed them, then? Did Peter Lisman do them both?' I pointed the gun at him again.

'If you want the truth, I don't know.'

'The truth?'

'Such as it is.'

291

'You've got to stop the Phelpses,' I said. 'It's all you can do. It's your only chance.'

At first, he said nothing. Then, 'This dock is my favorite place. I sometimes wish I could cut the pilings and float into the middle of the creek and stay there.'

'Your last chance.'

'Are you going to shoot me?' he asked.

Before I could answer, a voice spoke from the base of the dock behind us. 'You bastard.'

It was Lillian.

I was holding a gun to her brother's back. But she wasn't looking at me. She was looking at Daniel. 'You goddamned bastard.' She must have arrived at the house, knocked, and known – as I'd known – that if her brother didn't answer, she would find him on the dock.

She came to us, and, for the first time since I'd known him, Daniel looked distressed. He tried to speak but failed. He was big and pathetic in his bathrobe.

Lillian reached for my gun. 'Give it to me.'

I gave it to her.

She pointed it at Daniel. 'You lied to me, and you' – a look of incredulity crossed her face – 'shot Johnny?'

Again, he opened his mouth to speak.

But Lillian said, 'No. If you say a word, I swear to God I'll kill you.'

He said, 'Lillian—'

She pulled the trigger. The gun blast seemed to shock the air. The anhinga lifted from its perch and disappeared into the trees on the other side of the creek.

Daniel froze, amazed. He looked at his hands, his legs, his torso. They were bloodless. Lillian had drawn the barrel up as she'd pulled the trigger.

'I don't ever want to hear another word from you,' she said to Daniel, and she turned and walked back up the dock. I stared at the fear and surprise in Daniel's eyes. I wanted to remember that look. Then I followed Lillian across the back-yard, through the fence gate, and to the street.

Thirty

Lillian

My Life had stood – a Loaded Gun.

Johnny and I agreed to meet at home. I drove with the revolver on the passenger seat. It was a strange object, and I'd almost killed my brother with it, my rage at his betrayal seeming to stream through the gun barrel like pressurized air, like sexual release, like . . . Christ, I'd almost killed my brother.

On the roadside, kudzu and wild grapevines draped the low-standing trees. Other cars and trucks drove like a slowly advancing wash, but the sun warmed me through the windshield.

I knew exactly where I was going and I felt lost.

About thirty seconds after I arrived, Johnny pulled into our driveway. When we went inside, he mumbled something about feeling sick and went to our bedroom. A minute later, the shower started running. I made coffee, then sat on the floor with Percy. I fumbled with the gun until the cylinder sprang open and I saw three bullets and three dark holes. I went into the sunroom and watched a cardinal hopping on the lawn. When Johnny came into the kitchen a half-hour later, he had changed clothes, and I was sitting at the table with the gun in front of me.

He looked at it and at me and said, 'You could have killed Daniel.'

'Yeah.' When he said nothing, I asked, 'Were *you* going to?'

'I don't know.' He poured himself a cup of coffee, then asked, 'Are you sorry you didn't?'

'I don't know.'

He drank from the cup. 'How did you know I would be at his house?'

'I didn't. I went to talk to him.'

'About?'

'I thought you'd gone off again.'

'Off?'

'Off.'

'I hadn't.'

I said nothing.

'Or I had, but for a good reason.'

'I know.'

He stared at me, at the gun, at me. He asked, 'Do you want to go in deeper?'

'Yeah,' I said, 'I do.'

We drove across the Hart Bridge with Percy in the back seat, the sun shining on the slow, flat water, then hooked into the Interstate and cut back toward the river on Heckscher Drive.

Johnny said, 'On the night that Daniel shot me, when I asked what happened to Sheneel and Alex Greene, Cecilia Phelps started talking about salt. She was going on about how salt preserves when it's dry but eats away at things when it's wet. It sounded like nonsense, but Edward hit her to stop her from talking. Little Marsh Island is on a salt marsh. Why are the Phelpses building their waste-processing plant there? What happens when you mix salt water with pulp waste? What does salt water do to chromium-six? Do you know anyone at the college who could tell us?'

I hated to say it. 'Tom might know someone.'

Johnny shrugged. 'Call him.'

I did, and he gave me the number of his kayaking friend in Chemistry. 'He does environmental studies, so he might know,' Tom said. When he added, 'We need to talk,' I hung up.

Tom's friend laughed nervously when I phoned him. He said Tom had told him about me. I asked about salt and chromium, and he said, 'They bond and that slows biosorption.'

'Slows what?'

'Biosorption is when plants and animals absorb heavy metals. Like chromium. If a human absorbs a lot of heavy metal, that's bad, and so, if you use salt to bond with chromium and keep it out of the food and water supply, that's good. But, of course, if you add too much heavy metal to any body of salt water, that's bad.'

'Let's say the body of salt water is next to a neighborhood that uses freshwater wells,' I said.

Again he laughed. 'Why take a chance? I would put up a *For Sale* sign.'

We arrived at Little Marsh Island a little after one p.m. and parked by the chained service road. Johnny tucked the revolver into his pants and fastened the leash to Percy's collar. Then we walked back to the fence gate with the sign for Phelps Paper Company. Johnny drew Percy close to him on the leash and we went in.

Since I last trespassed on the construction site, a crew had laid a wide foundation into the cleared and filled marsh. Fingers of steel rebar jutted from the concrete. A pile of long, thick pipes stood on one side. A pile of iron I-beams stood by the pipes. A tractor crane stuck its yellow arm into the sky. The two white construction trailers, their windows dark, stood off to the side.

We walked to the foundation, Percy straining on the leash. The concrete and metal – the uncertain architecture of a factory or plant – meant nothing to my eyes. We crossed the concrete slab toward the construction trailers. The first of the afternoon thunderclouds hung in the sky to the west. Percy saw a blue heron in the grass by one of the trailers and tugged to get free.

'Let him run,' I said.

Johnny said, 'Last time I let him go here, he brought me Sheneel Greene's arm.'

'I don't think that's a danger anymore.'

He unclipped the leash, and Percy shot after the heron, which lifted into the air on awkward wings and flew toward the outer marsh.

The door on the first trailer was locked.

'Try the other one?' I said.

But Johnny kicked the door. It was made of metal. He kicked it again, and again, and the frame bent inward. He kicked it again. He held the door handle and pulled it with his weight. The metal whined, but the door remained standing. He kicked it, pulled it again. Metal snapped and the door sprang open. He went inside and found a light switch, and I followed him in.

A wall-unit air conditioner was off, but the musty air was cool. Someone had been here recently. I wanted to go back through the door and run through the construction site and up the dirt road to our car, but Johnny walked through the trailer, inspecting it as if he was thinking of buying it.

He found blueprints, construction diagrams, and a binder of permits on a metal desk at the back. The blueprints showed a two-story building with a double smokestack at one end and a half-dozen pipes reaching out into the marsh. Three windows, all in a second-story office, would face inland. There were two doorways and a triple ramp into a bay that would accommodate large trucks. The diagrams showed machines and boilers, labeling their dimensions but not their functions.

'Do you understand?' I asked.

'No.'

Johnny rolled the diagrams into the blueprints and carried them out the door.

The second trailer also was locked, but a window on the side was open, so I pulled out the screen and Johnny boosted me through.

The inside of the trailer was partitioned into three rooms. It appeared clean but smelled like gasoline and rotting meat. A worn couch stood in the middle of the main room. A small sink was attached to the back wall next to a little stove and a miniature refrigerator covered with Bible verses written on magnets. A computer stood on a table nearby, with a black-ink sticker on the monitor that said, *I will lift up my eyes to the hills*.

Johnny called from outside: 'Hey.'

I unlocked the door and let him in.

He let his eyes adjust and said, 'What's that smell?'

'Garbage?'

'A month ago.'

Johnny went to one end of the trailer and looked behind the partition. I went to the other end. The smell seemed to be coming from there. When I looked, I choked on my breath and whispered, 'Johnny!'

An old black woman wearing only underpants and a bra was sleeping on a small bed. Her hair was dyed henna and pink. One of her legs was swollen and had an open and infected lesion, slathered with ointment. The other leg looked as if it belonged to a much younger woman – muscled and curving toward an ankle around which hung a thin silver chain with a silver medallion. Flies hovered over her.

The old woman opened her dark eyes and fixed me with a terrible stare.

Johnny came and peered around the partition. 'Felicity?' he said.

The woman said, 'Hey, sugar.'

He said, 'What are you doing here?'

'Who is she?' I asked.

The woman answered, 'I watch this place at night. Sleep in the day unless someone knocks on my door.'

Johnny said, 'She's a hooker.'

That made no sense. 'Yours?'

He gave me a look. 'She works the strip on Philips Highway near my office.'

'What's she doing here?'

The woman said, 'He gives me cigarettes and I give him—'

'She gives me nothing,' Johnny said.

'He came to me in the hospital and brought me a carton.'

'I brought you two.'

The woman looked at me for confirmation. 'I *told* you he's my sugar. Two cartons of cigarettes. He wants *something*.'

'You're hurt,' I said to her.

Johnny said, 'Your leg is rotting.'

'My leg is fine,' she said. 'I've got medicine.'

I said, 'You should be in a hospital.'

'Do I look like I can afford a hospital?'

'You'll die here,' Johnny said.

She laughed. 'I'll never die, sugar.' She lifted herself to her feet, took a black metal cane from a corner, and stepped into the main room. She took a jar of clear liquid from the top of the mini-fridge, went to the table, and sat. She unscrewed the cap on the can and poured something that smelled like turpentine over her wound.

'Jesus, save me,' she said as it boiled on her leg.

'You're out of your mind,' Johnny said.

When her eyes cleared, she said, 'I've been told that before.'

'Did Papa Crowe give that to you?' Johnny asked.

She nodded. 'He gave me a poultice and sent me to the hardware store. I feel better already.'

'You look like death,' I said.

'Is this your wife, sugar?' she asked.

'Yeah.'

She peered at me. 'You don't look so hot yourself.'

Johnny said, 'The Phelpses hired you as a security guard?'

'A girl's got to make a living. I'm not so good on my back right now, and I never did like taking it from behind.'

He said, 'They're building a waste-processing plant here?'

She glanced out the window. 'Not this afternoon, they ain't. Most days they've got trucks rolling and men shouting. Makes it hard to sleep.'

'What have they told you about the plant?' he asked.

'They don't tell me nothing. But I listen. Edward says they're going to process pulp waste. Everyone else says, *Yes, sir* or *No, sir*.'

'How are they going to process it?'

'When was it they gave me the engineering degree?'

'All right.' He glanced around the trailer. 'What are you supposed to do if someone breaks into the site at night?'

'I've got a telephone. I call Peter, and then I call nine-one-one.'

I asked, 'Peter Lisman?'

'Yeah. He's another good-looking one, ain't he?' She smiled. 'But he's part of the family, so they ain't going to kick him out of the nest.'

Johnny asked, 'What do you mean, *part of the family*?'

'Where's the confusion?' she said.

Johnny shook his head. 'Edward told me about taking him in from a prison work crew.'

'That's true, Edward did. But he's still part of the family.'

'What part?' I asked.

She shook her head. 'You have to talk to Miss Cecilia about that. Even when everything is your business, there's still some things that are none of it. I've lived a hard life,' she said, 'but she's lived harder. She's got the houses and gardens, but I wouldn't want to live in her head. No silver coins can buy her way out, and no brooms can sweep out the evil.'

Thirty-One

Stephen Phelps

A hole in the one, as good as a hole in the other. When Daniel Turner, crouching like a sniper at Mom's bedroom window, shot Johnny Bellefleur in the ribs, I sighed. That was all. Sighed. Like an extra rib that was lodged in my chest melted and I could breathe. I could breathe at midnight when the trellised jasmine blossoms made the night sweet as if the stars would pollinate them, or the moon. I could breathe at noon when heat rippled from the sun and sky.

I tore a strand of jasmine from the front porch. White sap sticky on my hands. Perfume in the night air. Stinking the inside of the car as I drove to the hospital.

But Felicity had checked out. No forwarding address.

I needed none. I drove to Philips Highway, talked to the other girls.

They said, *In the hospital.*

They said, *A bastard shot her* – eyes like I might be the bastard.

They said, *Felicity who?*

I bought one of them, abused her for an hour, paid her forty bucks, and tucked the jasmine in her hair. *Get out*, I said.

She did.

But with each breath, the pain in my chest grew.

I found Felicity and put her in the construction trailer where I could get her when I wanted her.

Not enough.

I forced Kathryn in the garage while Samantha slept in her car seat.

Not enough.

I parked by Johnny Bellefleur's house and watched his wife's comings and goings. The way she stood on the driveway and smoothed her blouse over her breasts when she got out of her car. The way she fumbled with the keys every time she unlocked the front door. The way she left the door open as she turned on the inside lights – to escape if someone was hiding inside? To let me shove into the house from outside?

Not enough.

I climbed over the fence into the backyard. Screwdriver in my belt. To stop the dog? To jimmy the lock on the sliding glass door? To hold against her throat as I smelled her fear.

I stepped on to the back porch and watched through the window as she and Johnny Bellefleur struggled in bed. Her fumbling hands on him. His on her. I rested the screwdriver against the windowpane. I pressed the tip against the glass and dragged it across the invisible grit. It left a thin white scar. What couldn't I do to him with it? What couldn't I do to her?

But he rolled off and she sat on the bed. Did she stare at the window? Did she see me watching?

I drew back from the house, slipped across the dark lawn, and went out over the fence.

Coward, I called myself as I drove back to Fernandina. And I hated cowards.

Thirty-Two

Johnny

'Why not believe in fictions? If they make life livable, why not? Yes, we're all dying. Yes, everything we've built will fall down. Yes, in the end,

303

it comes to nothing. But why beat yourself up over it? Why not believe it's all a gift?' The Baptist Hospital psychologist drum-rolled his fingers on the table. The putting-green-colored carpet in his office banked against the floor-to-ceiling window. In the distance, beyond the St Johns River, white clouds hung in the sky, as soft as fictions.

Why not believe in them?

The previous afternoon, as we'd left the construction site trailer, I'd said to Felicity, 'You didn't see us here, OK?'

She'd answered, 'They don't pay me to see during the day. Only at night.'

Why not blind myself to the daylight? And the darkness too, if that helped?

I said to the psychologist, 'I know a woman with a leg wound. It's infected. It's so bad you can hardly bear to be in the same room with her. She *believes* she's getting better. But she's dying – you can see it.'

'There's a difference between stupidity and believing in fictions,' he said. No drum roll.

After my appointment, Lillian picked me up in front of the hospital. As we drove up the entrance ramp to the highway, she asked, 'How are you feeling?'

I said, 'I believe I'm doing better.'

She glanced at me. 'Are you being sarcastic?'

I said, 'I don't know.'

She'd arranged for us to meet with a man named Jerry Fernin who taught engineering at her college so we could show him the Phelps blueprints and diagrams. When we got there, we spread the

304

blueprints on a conference table, and Fernin inspected them, spending a long time on the sheet that showed the pipes extending into the marsh. He wore jeans, flip-flops, and a white T-shirt, and, except for the gray in his ponytail, I would've thought he was a student. Lillian said he consulted around the country on environmental engineering problems.

He looked concerned. 'Where'd you get these?'

Lillian said, 'Is there something wrong?'

He looked again at the pipes. 'No, it's nice work. Better than nice.'

Lillian gave me a look, and I asked him, 'What do you mean, *nice*?'

'I was at a convention in Atlanta last month, and a couple of designers introduced something like this. They thought it could actually be built three to five years from now at the earliest.' He went to the other end of the table, brought back one of the machine diagrams, and laid it over the blueprint. 'They call this zero-impact filtration. It brings in outside water, which cleans the waste and then goes back out with its natural organisms and bacteria intact. Even the water temperature stays the same.'

'That makes no sense,' I said.

He tapped the diagram. 'This is the future. Clean processing, or very close to clean.'

I looked at him. He wiped a bead of sweat from his nose with a finger. 'How much did they pay you?' I asked.

'Huh?'

'What did they give you to say the plans are good?'

Lillian shook her head. 'No, Johnny—'

The man looked vaguely amused.

I gathered the blueprints and diagrams from the table, folding them, rolling them, balling them together. 'Nothing these people touch is good. Nothing. It's filth, and so is anyone they get their hands on.'

Lillian said, 'Johnny!'

The man smiled. 'It's cool,' he said. 'I've seen you in the newspapers and on TV. You've got problems. I understand. But your problems aren't mine. These designs are great, the best I've seen. If you don't like me telling you that, ask someone else. You'll hear the same thing.'

As we drove from the college, I said, 'It makes no sense.'

Lillian said nothing.

I said, 'Your friend is full of shit.'

'You can't accuse everyone,' she said.

'Even if everyone's guilty?'

She looked hard at me. 'Everyone? *You're* guilty? *I* am?'

'Us especially.'

She shook her head like I might be too far gone for saving.

We ate lunch at a Thai restaurant, and when we came out, the little white clouds that I'd seen from the psychologist's office had darkened and thickened. A stiff breeze blew the blossoms from the crape myrtle trees planted at the edge of the parking lot. So much for believing in fictions.

But the lemon-grass chicken seemed to have

lifted Lillian's mood, so I said, 'It still makes no sense.'

'Or maybe it does,' she said. 'The Phelpses build a perfect plant like this, and no one worries about them anymore. No one inspects them very closely. They could get away with a lot. What else are they doing on Little Marsh Island?'

'Other than finding Sheneel Greene's body? Nothing.'

'And hiring the strangest watchman I've ever seen.'

'They know her,' I said. 'Edward and Stephen Phelps do, and it sounds like Cecilia also might. They do their business close to the family.'

'It's easier to keep secrets that way.'

'But Felicity has no loyalty to them.'

'You think?'

'I know it,' I said. 'They've abused her since she was a girl.'

'And yet there she is, sleeping on their bed, in their trailer, on their land.'

'Fine. What would she be guarding? What else are they doing?'

She looked nervous. 'Let's find out.'

So we drove toward Edward and Cecilia Phelps's house. As we crossed the river, rain started to fall, pocking and misting the water below the bridge. By the time I turned off the engine in front of the Phelpses', the sky was slate and rain smeared the windshield. We ran from the car, rang the bell, and Cecilia Phelps opened the door.

'Oh dear,' she said when she saw us in the rain. 'Two of you.'

We followed her into the house, and the sound of the pounding rain fell to a hum. She took us to the living room and sat on a long white couch. 'I would offer you tea, but . . .' She let the sentence die.

A painting behind the couch showed a luxuriant green swamp shadowed by thick oak branches, Spanish moss, and red-flowering vines. The sky above the swamp hung low with storm clouds. The heads of two alligators rose from the brown water. One held a large fish in its jaws. A smoke-like vapor came from the nostrils of the other.

When Cecilia Phelps saw me staring at it, she said, 'It's based on an eighteenth-century drawing by William Bartram. He came from Philadelphia and was ill-equipped for the climate and people here. He expected strawberry fields but found this instead.'

'His mistake,' I said.

'He persisted,' she said. 'He paddled upriver and he never was eaten. He survived. Most men aren't so lucky.'

Lillian said, 'Who is Peter Lisman?'

Cecilia Phelps turned her one-eyed gaze to her. 'What a strange question and from such a strange woman.' Her tone remained polite. 'I could as easily ask, Who is Tom Corfield?' Lillian looked stung. 'I know about your little life and dramas, more than I care to know. Edward finds out about these things. He knows everything. You should understand that.'

I said, 'What is Peter Lisman to you?'

She smiled on the good side of her mouth. 'Nothing.'

'Who was his father?' Lillian asked.

She considered me. 'His name was Aaron Lisman. A bad man, if you must know.'

'And his mother?' I asked.

'I believe you've met her. I've heard that you stole Peter's computer from their apartment.'

'I was thinking about her,' I said. 'She looked about fifty years old. And Peter is, what, about forty? So she was ten when he was born? Seems unlikely.'

'It's time for you to leave,' she said.

Lillian said, 'He looks so much like Sheneel. We noticed that the first time we saw him. Others must have noticed it too.'

Cecilia Phelps called into the house, 'Kathryn!'

I said, 'If Sheneel was still alive and we stood them side by side, I'll bet we'd swear—'

'Kathryn!'

Stephen Phelps's wife stepped into the room from the hallway. She held her daughter in her arms. She gave me an uncertain smile.

Cecilia Phelps recovered her calm and said, 'Kathryn, will you show my guests out?'

Thirty-Three

Lillian

The periodicals librarian at the Main Branch brought out two large leather-bound volumes on a metal cart, and Johnny and I lifted them on to the reading table. They included copies of the *Times-Union* from thirty years ago, when Papa Crowe said the stove exploded in the Phelpses' house, burning Cecilia Phelps and killing her younger son. A family with the Phelpses' money and power should have gotten front-page coverage, but I found the story, along with black-and-white photographs of the burning mansion, in the Metro section of the October-sixth paper.

The paper said that a kitchen fire at the Phelpses' Ortega house erupted the previous afternoon, causing severe damage, one death, and several injuries. Dead was a one-year-old infant, Darren Phelps. At Wolfson Children's Hospital, suffering from smoke inhalation, was three-year-old Stephen Phelps. Transported by helicopter to the Shands Hospital Burn Center was their mother, Cecilia Phelps, with life-threatening injuries. Also at Shands, in critical condition with smoke inhalation, was Avis Greene. Treated and released from Baptist Hospital was Jacob Alexander Crowe. Two engine companies fought the blaze. Fire damage was limited to the kitchen and the rooms above it, but smoke and water damage were extensive.

Edward Phelps had said that the family used to call Papa Crowe Jacob, so his full name must have been Jacob Alexander Crowe.

But who was Avis Greene?

The October-eighth paper gave more details and more pictures. Fire department investigators were trying to determine whether a gas-line leak or mechanical failure caused the stove to explode. They had no reason to suspect arson, a spokesman said, but the explosion was enormous, blowing out windows and knocking down part of a side wall, which meant that gas had collected in the kitchen. Why no one smelled it, the investigators couldn't say. Avis Greene, who was married to Jacob Alexander Crowe, died of her injuries the previous afternoon. Cecilia Phelps had been transferred from Shands to Johns Hopkins Hospital in Baltimore, where investigators were unable to talk to her. Doctors said they would release three-year-old Stephen into the care of his father later in the week.

When Papa Crowe told Johnny about the fire, he'd said that Cecilia Phelps carried Stephen to safety, then returned for her other son, and that the burning ceiling collapsed on her. The newspaper told a different story. It credited household gardener Jacob Alexander Crowe – Papa Crowe himself – with saving both Cecilia and Stephen, who were unconscious in the kitchen when he found them.

The story included a picture of Jacob Alexander, a black man in his forties.

I showed it to Johnny. 'Recognize him?'

Johnny smiled. 'Papa Crowe.'

'He was married,' I said. 'His wife was there too. She died after the fire.'

We paged through the newspapers, looking for follow-up reports. Three articles from the end of October discussed the ongoing fire investigation. The investigators ruled out a gas-line leak or a problem with the stove. They also determined that the windows in the kitchen were shut, though, on the cool, early-October afternoon of the fire, other windows throughout the house had been open. They said the swinging door to the kitchen was latched shut. The concentration of gas in the room would have asphyxiated anyone in it if the gas hadn't first exploded. Cecilia Phelps and her baby boy were in the kitchen at the time of the explosion. Three-year-old Stephen was in the next room with the Phelpses' maid, Avis Greene. Jacob Alexander Crowe was out in the side yard.

The last paper, at the end of October, said that Cecilia Phelps remained in the Johns Hopkins burn unit, and doctors were continuing to turn away investigators and reporters.

Without ever saying so explicitly, the articles implied that Cecilia had caused the gas explosion, probably in a suicide attempt.

'Damn,' Johnny said.

'Uh huh.'

After October, the coverage stopped. Cecilia Phelps was probably still refusing to talk, and the Phelpses' insurance company probably had decided that paying off the family would be easier than fighting them in court, or else the Phelpses had withdrawn any claim they might have made.

Johnny said, 'They bought them off too.'

'Maybe.'

When we returned the bound volumes, I asked for recent copies of any South Georgia papers the library subscribed to, and the librarian brought a stack of the Kingsland *Tribune & Georgian*. Johnny found what we were looking for in the Saturday paper – a story that followed up on the information Papa Crowe gave him when he visited him in jail. The story detailed the court settlement between Phelps Paper and the State of Georgia. Phelps Paper had agreed to pay a fine of just over a million dollars and to hire an outside firm to remove and dispose of the topsoil over a thirty-acre site, a job that would cost another two to three million dollars. A spokesman for the Georgia Department of Environmental Protection praised Edward and Stephen Phelps for addressing problems that occurred during an era of laxer environmental standards.

'Now they're cub scouts,' Johnny said.

We wanted to know more about Peter Lisman's past, but the librarian said the collection included no birth records. We could have searched newspapers for stories about him killing his father, but if he was a juvenile at the time, the papers might not have named him and, without more details about the crime, our search would likely come to nothing.

'We could call Daniel and ask,' Johnny said.

'Hah.'

'Then let's talk to Papa Crowe.'

We drove back up the highway, the windows open, the warm, humid breeze buffeting us. A west wind had pushed the storm clouds out over the ocean, and the air smelled of the swamps and salt marshes. Semi-trailer trucks, their cabs closed tight, barreled past, heading north from Miami. Turkey vultures circling over a clearing on the highwayside seemed to know where they were going better than the rest of us. I watched Johnny, a man who had packed the carrion of soldiers into bags and shipped it home from a faraway sea and had returned home half transformed to carrion himself.

'What?' he said when he saw me watching.

'I love you,' I said.

He turned his eyes back to the road.

When we stopped in front of the half-painted wooden house where Papa Crowe lived, Johnny got out, put Papa Crowe's revolver into his waistband, and stepped on to the porch.

On the other side of the screen, through a gap between the front door and the jamb, the room was dark. An odor of rotting plants and medicine drifted out.

Johnny knocked and then knocked harder.

No answer.

Johnny knocked again and yelled, 'Papa Crowe?'

I said, 'Let's go in.'

'I've made that mistake before.' But he went to the other end of the porch, peered through a dirty window, and said, 'Damn.'

We went inside.

The front room was a mess of broken bottles, crushed metal canisters, overturned cabinets, and wooden shelves that had been ripped from the walls. Strange-colored liquids pooled on the floor. Various powders and sprigs of dried plants lay in the pools and among the shards of glass.

Johnny yelled, 'Papa Crowe?'

No answer.

I stepped into the kitchen. Broken plates and more broken glass covered the counter and floor. A toaster lay on its side in the sink. The refrigerator stood open, emptied of its contents

– carrots, a carton of milk, a stick of butter, and a chunk of ham strewn among the wreckage.

Johnny went into the bedroom and I followed. A metal cot had been twisted and broken, the thin mattress tossed against a wall. A large trunk lay upended, clothes and a worn Bible scattered around it on the floor. On the wall, someone had painted a large blood-red snake biting its own tail, the picture still glistening and wet.

'Christ,' I said.

Johnny touched the snake.

'Don't,' I said.

He moved close and breathed in the snake's smell. 'It's not blood.'

'How do you know?'

'I know what blood smells like.'

'What is it, then?'

He gestured at the front room. 'Maybe something from one of the bottles. It's sweet.'

'Let's leave,' I said.

He kicked through the clothes. He picked up the Bible. It was old, the pages yellow under the black leather cover. Three bookmarks – made from the small striped feathers of a blue jay – stuck from the top. Johnny opened to one of them. He read, '*I will lift up my eyes to the hills. From whence shall my help come?*' He looked at me.

'Where does it say help comes from?'

'It used to say, *from the Lord*, but that's scratched out, and Papa Crowe wrote his own answer.'

'Which is?'

Johnny raised his eyes to mine. '*No help nowhere.*'

315

Thirty-Four

Johnny

That night, I grilled salmon steaks on the patio. Lillian drank white wine until she was drunk, and I downed two more beers than I should have, even without meds. As the sun dropped and the city darkened, a crescent moon rose and, with it, off its lower blade, Venus or Mars or one of the planets that shines brighter than the stars in the night sky. Lillian moved her chair close, and if I held her hand in mine and focused my eyes on the moon so that the rest of the sky disappeared, I could forget everything that had happened since I shipped out to the Arabian Sea.

I said, 'I don't need to believe in fictions if they believe in me.'

'What does that mean?' Lillian asked.

'It means I need another beer.'

We stayed on the patio until nearly midnight, blotting out thoughts of Sheneel Greene, her brother and mother, Papa Crowe, the Phelpses, Peter Lisman – everyone but us.

Then, in the dark, by the fence at the back of the yard, Percy began whining.

'Did he catch something?' Lillian said.

I got up and found him curled against the fence, panting hard, his stomach distended. 'Hey,' I said, but when I reached for him, he tried to bite me.

I made calming sounds and moved toward him, and now he let me. I carried him to the patio and inside to the kitchen, then set him on the cool tile floor.

Lillian got towels from the hall closet. As she wrapped them around him, I walked back outside with a flashlight.

A few feet from where he had been lying, I found the rotten, half-eaten remains of a blackbird. I got a shovel from the shed, dug a hole deep into the sandy soil, and scooped the bird into it. Once before, I had buried a sparrow that had bounced off the glass of the sunroom door, and Percy had dug it up again. I'd buried it a second time, eighteen inches or more below the surface, but he'd dug at it like an old scab until we'd put a potted Satsuma orange tree on top of it, and even then Percy had paused by the tree as if he could smell the old stink of death.

Now, I went to the patio, pried out a concrete paver, carried it to where I'd buried the blackbird, and dropped it on the ground.

When I went back into the kitchen, Lillian was lying on the tile, cradling Percy. Percy had fallen into a heavy-breathing sleep, but Lillian's eyes were wide and watchful. I said, 'I'll get you a blanket if you want to stay here.'

She pulled herself from the dog. 'I want to stay with you.'

Later, as we slept, I fell hard into a dark, dreamless space, deeper than exhaustion. When I had muttered about fictions believing in me, I should have said that I had always needed Lillian to believe me, or at least needed to believe that she

317

believed me. Tonight I believed that. She held me, cradled me, sick dog that I also was, and I fell into the tunnel of sleep. I fell, knowing that Lillian was holding me. If I crashed, we would crash together.

Hours later, when a dim light fell on my face and pulled me toward consciousness, I smiled under the sheet without opening my eyes. This was the first time in weeks that the morning sun had shined me awake. I felt the warmth of Lillian beside me and wished for this kind of peace always.

But when I pulled back the cover and opened my eyes, no sunlight met them. Instead, a man stood at the foot of our bed, aiming a flashlight at me. I listened. Lillian still slept. The silence of the house except for the man's thin breathing terrified me. Behind the flashlight beam, he was a shadow.

I said, 'Who is that?'

'It me,' Papa Crowe said.

His voice should have relieved me but didn't. 'What are you doing here?'

'Don't feel so good for another man to walk into your house without you asking, do it?'

'What are you doing?' I asked again, and reached to turn on the bedside lamp.

'Don't move,' he said.

'Don't be ridiculous—'

A gun blasted at the foot of the bed, and wallboard dust rained into my face and my eyes like flecks of night. I yelled into the roar.

Lillian woke and got to the lamp on her side.

The room lighted up. Papa Crowe stood in front of us in jeans and a red T-shirt. He held his revolver in one hand – I'd left it on the dresser when Lillian and I had gone to bed – and a yellow flashlight in the other.

Lillian said, 'What the hell?'

Papa Crowe fixed his eyes on hers. 'I see the two of you leave my land this afternoon. You wreck my house—'

'You saw *what*?' I asked.

'I come across the marsh behind my house in my johnboat, and you step off the porch, go through the yard, get in your car, and drive away. When I tie my boat and go in, I see what you do. I swear to God I don't understand.'

'We didn't do that,' Lillian said, her voice hushed.

'Like hell you didn't.' He pointed the gun at her.

When he had loaned me the gun, he'd given me four bullets. He'd shot one, and Lillian had shot another on Daniel's dock. Unless he'd brought more ammunition, that left him one each for Lillian and me. 'Why would we do that to you?' I asked.

'That what I don't understand.'

'We went to your house because we wanted to talk to you.'

'And you walk in and tear it apart.'

'The door was open. I saw the damage through a window. We thought you might be inside and hurt.'

He didn't believe it. 'So you come in to help me?'

319

'That's right.'

'No,' he said. He pointed the barrel of the revolver at the wall and pulled the trigger again. Lillian screamed, and dust rained down on us. He tossed the revolver on to the bed sheet between my legs. 'The last one is for you to put a hole in your own head.'

He moved toward the door, but I said, 'Why did you lie about the kitchen fire?'

He turned and stared at me with hard eyes.

'Your wife, Avis, died,' I said. 'You pulled Cecilia and Stephen Phelps out of the fire.'

'Yeah.' His voice was small.

'What was Cecilia Phelps to you? Who did you try to save first? Her or your wife?'

That stung him. 'You way off, boy.'

'Is this why you won't get rid of Edward and Stephen yourself? Would she keep coming to see you if you put down her husband and boy?'

'I don't know what you doing, but you way off. I tell you before, she take more evil from Edward and Stephen than the rest of us together. I give her the touch of my hands, that all.'

Lillian sat up against the headboard and pulled her knees against her chest. She eyed him as if she was trying to see inside. 'Who is Peter Lisman?'

Papa Crowe looked at her and screwed his lips. He seemed to be trying to square our questions with his belief that we'd torn apart his house. 'You know who he is. He work for the—'

'Yeah, he works for them,' she said. 'But who is he?'

'I don't know,' Papa Crowe said.

She said, 'We can find out in public records. They'll say where he came from. They'll explain why he killed his father.'

'He was juvenile. The records is sealed.'

'We would rather hear from you,' she said.

He ran a hand along his face. 'His daddy, Aaron, he one of Edward Phelps's cousins.'

'And?'

He hesitated again. 'And he a bad man. He make Edward and Stephen look like gentlefolk. He beat Peter till Peter kill him.'

'Who's his mother?' Lillian said.

'Peter's? She live in an apartment in Fernandina,' he said.

I said, 'That's not his mother.'

Again, his hand rubbed his face. For a long while, he said nothing. When he spoke, he spoke quietly. 'Miss Cecilia only fourteen when Aaron Lisman take her. I know her then myself. She live with her family on Ash Street. She a beautiful girl, and Aaron, he a strong man and one of the Phelps clan, and what she going to do? When she have the baby, her daddy give it to Aaron and tell him this his bastard, he bring it up and feed it. Aaron could've killed Cecilia's daddy right then – he done it for less – but he take the baby home with him and start beating it before it cut its first teeth.'

I said, 'Why didn't you tell me this before?'

'What's it matter?' he said. 'That woman, she been beat enough. She mine to worry about.'

Lillian said, 'Cecilia knows who Peter is?'

'Sure. You look at that white face.'

'And Edward knows?' she asked.

'The Phelpses and Greenes have the sickness of some kind. It in the blood – and the soul too, I think. It show in about one out of a hundred – make a body white like Sheneel and Peter. Sometimes it make them stupid. Sometime it make them mean.'

'Peter knows that Cecilia is his mother?' Lillian said.

'Sure.'

I said, 'Why are you protecting her?'

'Why you wreck my house?'

'We didn't,' I said.

'Who, then?'

I said, 'What would someone be searching for in your house?'

'That no search. That pissing in my well. That telling me to be gone.'

Lillian asked, 'What do you mean, *No help nowhere*?'

'You break in *and* you been reading my book too?'

I said, 'What do you mean by it – *No help nowhere*?'

'I mean what it say. No help come to you. You make it happen or it don't happen. You wait on the Lord to do your work, the Lord knock you down and call you the lazy-for-nothing that you is. You wait on your neighbor, the bus never come. You ain't helpless. What you asking others for?'

I said, 'What's really between you and Cecilia Phelps?'

His voice was small again. 'We both lose somebody.'

Lillian said, 'You lost your wife. She lost her baby.'

'The baby? Yeah, she lose the baby. So I lay my hands on her. I hold her.'

'And she holds you?' Lillian said.

He shook his head. 'No. I never let that woman touch me.'

I thought about the comfort that Lillian had given me as we'd fallen asleep a few hours earlier. 'You help her, then,' I said. 'You bring it to her.'

He shook his head. 'I ain't helping her. She past help. I help myself mostly. Cecilia start the fire that kill my wife. Now every time I lay hands on her, I take my fingers up and down her throat. I use to think someday I break her neck, but I never do it. It better to hold her life in my hands like that. It better to watch her suffer and to have her coming to me for something and for me to choose if I want to pity her and give it to her. Her family take so much from me for so many years, I never give this up.'

Thirty-Five

Stephen Phelps

Four seagulls turned with the wind above the construction lot – a hundred yards inland, the way they do when a storm is coming. But no storm was coming. Sunny morning – me sitting on the stoop of the trailer with a shotgun, Felicity inside cooking something that smelled like burnt electric wires. I spotted each gull in the sight. But no one eats seagull, not even a dog.

Baby, it's ready. Felicity. Inside.

When a woman cooks a meal that smells like burnt electric wires, best to stay outside.

Baby, it's—

Blackbird. On the roof of the backhoe. Dropping down to the sandy dirt. Looking for what? No food here.

But I was on my feet, charging like a goddamned soldier after the goddamned bird. Squeezing off one shot. Two. Three – and a spray of black feathers.

It wanted to fly. But with one wing gone? It spun into the air and crashed on the ground. I got to it, picked it up. It weighed almost nothing. Pecked my palm. I broke its neck.

Its little breastbone and ribcage – like a box. What little gifts, what diamond rings and ancient coins wouldn't fit in such a box? A knife slice, and three Paxil tablets from Kathryn's medicine cabinet melted into the blood and organs. Bitter meat but meat nonetheless.

Poor blackbird. Shot and *then* poisoned. Never fly again – unless launched in the night over the fence behind Johnny Bellefleur's yard.

What dog could refuse?

Not theirs.

A whine and a yip. Poor dog.

One down, two to go.

After the words and whispers, the shovel scraping the dirt, and more whispers – silence. Light off in the kitchen. Light off in the bedroom.

324

Over the fence I tumbled. Following the blackbird.

I sat in the yard, waited. I wanted them asleep – so deep that they would hear no sound as I approached their bed, so far away that their dreams would change the first touch of the screwdriver on their necks into a cold pendant necklace, a sexual fingernail.

Waited.

Midnight.

One o'clock.

Two o'clock.

Time to give her a cold pendant, him a fingernail.

I stood, stretched. Jogged in place. Breathed deep in, out, in. Started across the lawn – almost whistling I was so happy.

Stopped.

Like a hand held my shoulder. Like Dad slapped me.

No hand. No slap. But a pair of eyes by the fence gate. A man – skinny, dark – watching me. Nightmare eyes. Arresting eyes.

My imagination? My creeping cowardice?

I started across again.

The man said, 'Get you home, boy.'

I knew the voice. Hated it. But in the night, screwdriver in my hand?

'Get you gone,' the man said.

I ran at him. Thinking about the soft spot under the breastbone.

Bastard stood where he was. The night was his own. The yard, his own. Me, his own.

I stopped. Eye to eye with Papa Crowe. I said, 'I could kill you.'

He said, 'But won't.' He unlatched the gate. 'Go on! Get!' Like I was a dog.

'What are you going to do to them?'

'I take care of it. This no place for you.'

'I need to do this.'

'It ain't yours. It been mine since before you born.' He stepped toward me. I could stab him or I could run. 'Get on home,' he said.

I went through the gate. I stood in the front yard. Waited.

Heard one gunshot. Two.

I grinned, laughed, whistled.

Was I sorry Papa Crowe did the job I'd come to do? A little. No shame in that.

Thirty-Six

Lillian

Papa Crowe drifted out of our house around four-thirty. Johnny's eyes were wide, his face pale. We sat in bed, silent, the lamps on for a half-hour. Then I got up and checked Percy. He was sleeping where I'd left him, but the towels had fallen from his body, and a puddle of vomit was drying on the tile by the oven. I sat by him on the floor and petted him as he slept.

Johnny came from the bedroom, wearing jeans and a white T-shirt. He looked at me, looked at the puddle of vomit, then went to the refrigerator, poured a glass of orange juice, and sat at the kitchen table. He watched me pet Percy and asked, 'Is he still breathing?'

Johnny finished the juice, closed his eyes, and crossed his arms over his chest as if he would sleep sitting in the chair. The sun rose, graying the sky outside the kitchen window. Maybe traffic was filling on the roads throughout the city and in our yard birds were singing, but in the kitchen the only sound was the hum of the refrigerator and, now and then, a clicking of the plumbing in the walls.

When Johnny abruptly opened his eyes, as if frightened by the quiet, I asked, 'What?'

'Get dressed,' he said.

As the sun came higher into the sky, we drove back to Little Marsh Island. Egrets flew across the road from swamp to swamp, their stark white feathers flashing against trees and grasses, or stood sentinel-still in the shallows, watching for fingerling fish.

The chain was down on the sandy service road to the construction site, and, as we approached, three dump trucks pulled on to it, the empty metal dumping-beds thundering against the under-carriages. A red sedan stood on the shoulder of the road as the trucks entered.

A half-mile past the entrance, we pulled to the side and hiked back. Johnny carried the revolver in his waistband, his T-shirt hanging over it. When we were a couple of hundred yards from the service road, Johnny walked through the long grass on the shoulder and on to an overgrown path that angled through the trees. We ducked

327

under a tangle of branches and vines and continued over sandy soil covered with pine needles and rotting leaves. When Johnny saw a small pool of brown water, he left the path, dipped a finger in it, and brought it to his mouth.

'What's it like?' I asked.

'Terrible.'

Then the path turned to the left and opened into a sandy clearing. 'This is where Peter Lisman says he found Sheneel,' Johnny said. A gray tarp, stretching over two tent poles, hung near the center. Two blue duffel bags weighed down the edges. A pair of jeans, a bra, and a pair of underpants were draped on the side that the sun was shining on. Laura Greene sat on a long log in front of a little campfire. She wore dusty pink shorts and a grimy yellow T-shirt with a logo for the Atomic Cantina. She was smoking a cigarette and talking to herself.

She looked startled when she saw us and said, 'What do you want?'

Johnny and I glanced at each other. He asked her, 'Where does the water turn salty?'

She looked confused and asked, 'Why do you have a gun?'

Johnny touched the revolver. 'It's Papa Crowe's. He loaned it to me.'

'Who are you going to shoot with it?'

I asked, 'Why are *you* here?'

She looked at me as if I didn't belong. 'I need to see them do it.'

'What?'

She got up and walked into the woods. Barefoot, she stepped through the bramble and scrub. We followed as she pushed through the branches for a hundred yards or so until she reached the chain-link fence that surrounded the construction site. I stopped. On the work site, a crew was starting to frame the processing plant. The large crane swung an iron I-beam across the concrete slab, and a group of men in orange vests and white hardhats looked at a large diagram that they had spread across the hood of a pickup truck. Toward the marsh, a backhoe dug a trench. At the trailer where Johnny and I had talked with the prostitute, a man, tucking his shirt into his pants, stepped on to the makeshift wooden stairs from inside. The prostitute's head stuck out of the door and she looked across the site where the men were working as if she was searching for someone in particular. When she faced me, over the space of rough sand and weed, she hesitated – and I felt that she saw me – before disappearing into the trailer and closing the door.

I hurried away along the fence until I saw Johnny standing with Laura Greene. In front of them, outside a section of fence that had been removed, a square-sided pit that could have seated a building the size of a one-car garage had been cut cleanly into the marsh. Except for a swill of brackish water and white froth and foam at the bottom, it might have served as a grave for an enormous animal.

Johnny pulled the revolver from his waistband, handed it to me, and, before I could stop him, lowered himself into the pit, stumbling in the ankle-deep muck. When he got his balance, he looked up through the glaring sunlight and smiled, as if this was the place he had longed to be. He dipped his hand in the water and brought a finger to his mouth again.

'Salt?' I said.

'Of course.'

Laura Greene said, 'This is why Sheneel died. And Alex too. Sheneel found out what the Phelpses had done in Georgia at the Garden House. They're digging there now too. I've been to see it.'

I said, 'The government ordered the Phelpses to clear the topsoil.'

'That's scraping and cleaning, not digging. Yesterday morning, they went in with shovels. I watched them pulling them out.'

Johnny scrambled up the sandy side of the pit. His shoes and pants were wet and filthy, and when he wiped sweat from his forehead, he left a mark like a bruise. He cleaned his hands on the sides of his pants, and I gave him the revolver.

Laura Greene stepped close to him, gestured at the revolver, and said, 'You have the plantation gun. I went to Papa Crowe's house looking for it after I saw what the Phelpses were doing in Georgia. But the gun wasn't there. You had it. You do it.'

'I'll do what I need to do,' Johnny said.

She gave him the smile of a lover who shared a secret. 'I think you will.'

'Wait,' I said, and asked her, 'When did you look for the gun at Papa Crowe's house?'

She kept her eyes on Johnny. 'I told you. After I saw the Phelpses digging at the Garden House. Yesterday morning.'

330

'Did you wreck his home?'

'I might have, a little.'

'Why?'

'When I couldn't find the gun, I knew Papa Crowe wouldn't face what's real. He would never use the gun himself. He's been sleeping for more than thirty years. I wanted to wake him up and make him angry.'

'I think you succeeded,' I said.

She said to Johnny, 'If you don't want to use the gun, give it to me.'

Johnny looked at the revolver. Its wooden grip fit neatly in his hand. Its cylinder held a single bullet. He looked back at Laura Greene. 'I'll do it.'

She smiled, closed-lipped. 'All right.' She started back along the fence.

I called after her, 'Why did you draw the snake on Papa Crowe's wall?'

But she was gone.

I looked at the pit, looked at Johnny. 'What did you just agree to do?'

He said nothing, but stuck the revolver into his waistband.

A half-hour later, we drove across the Georgia border, exited on to a strip lined with gas stations, an auto body shop, a tire shop, and a Hardee's, and drove into an area of old lumber roads lined with timber and pulp pines. We drove until we reached a trail where heavy machinery had recently broadened the road shoulder and cleared the trees at the edge of the forest.

We parked and walked a quarter-mile or so,

following tire and tractor tread marks down through a thick grove and up an incline. A woodpecker hammered against the upper trunk of a tree, went silent as we passed, and started hammering again.

At the top of the incline, we found the charred remains of a house. The ashes were fresh. The first wind would blow them through the woods.

'That was the Garden House,' Johnny said.

Fifteen yards away, the blackened corrugated-metal roof of a carport rested on the burnt remains of a car.

Down a long slope from the second fire, there was another newly dug pit, larger and rougher than the one outside the Phelps construction site. The machinery that had dug it had piled the dirt at the edge of a narrow creek, forcing the water out of the creek bed and through the surrounding vegetation.

We stepped into the pit. The sandy loam was dry, and broken tree roots twisted into the open air like mangled fingers. The air just three feet below the surrounding land felt cool and smelled of old earth. On a hot night, one could lie in the dark under the lace of branches and breathe a deep and familiar comfort.

Johnny reached into the soil between two roots and pulled out a broken piece of an old green-glass Coke bottle. I kicked the loam under my feet. Fragments of shell were mixed with the dirt and sand. I pulled out a rusted can lid.

We prodded the sides of the pit without finding anything more. But as I climbed out, Johnny picked up a white object: bone – a circular chunk,

332

a couple of inches long, sawed clean on either end, a hole straight through where there once was marrow.

'Let me see,' I said.

He gave it to me like a fragile thing.

I turned it over in my hands. 'Beef bone,' I said.

'No.'

'It's too big for a person. This came from a butcher.' I threw it back into the pit. 'Let's go.'

He remained where he was, scuffed the dirt with the toes of his shoes.

'Let's go,' I said again.

But he bent and pulled another thing from the dirt, something small, which he held in his palm, spat on, and wiped clean on his shirt.

'What is it?'

He put it in my hand. It was a golden ring for a man's finger – cut, twisted, and shaped like a little coiled rope. I wiped it on my shirt too. It was old but it came away polished brilliant.

He took it back from me and slid it on to his middle finger.

'We go tonight?' I asked.

He gazed at the ring. 'Yeah.'

Thirty-Seven

Johnny

Papa Crowe stood with me on his front porch. When I knocked, he looked broken and small as

333

he swept the glass from the floor of his front room. Now, holding the broom as if it could prop him up, he glanced into the sky, then down to my car where Lillian waited in the front seat. 'What she do there?'

'She doesn't trust you after you broke into our house.'

'I know how she feel.'

He had swept the debris into piles and rescued various dried leaves and powders, sorting them into little mounds on the wooden table on the porch, but the syrups and oils that he'd kept lidded in jars and stoppered in soda bottles had soaked into the flooring.

I decided to let Laura Greene tell him that she did the ransacking. I showed him the gold-rope ring. 'Do you recognize this?'

He looked stunned. 'Where you get that?'

'Whose is it?'

'That my uncle's.'

'The one who disappeared from Garden House with his family?'

'He don't disappear. He walk off. I see them go.'

'Where did they walk off to?'

He said, 'Where you get it?'

'Where did they go?'

'It was a night the Phelpses send their men to clear the property, which they lie and say they own, though we be living there a hundred years. Bunch of security men in blue jackets, they come with baseball bats and axe handles and a can of gasoline. My uncle get my aunt and my cousins and the children together, the twelve of them, and

334

he say they leaving, they going where no one can kick them around or burn their house – my daddy say they go across the ocean even if it only Atlanta – and they walk through the woods and out to the road, and that it for them, they gone.'

'What did the Phelps men do?'

'Nothing. My daddy and me and the others, we not ready to go. We leave the next week, except my cousin Mary and her boy stay till they get the cancer and die. The Phelpses only come to scare us this time. They do the business later. These men follow my uncle through the woods to the road. They shoot their guns in the air. They don't want no blood or mud on their pretty jackets, not this time.'

'They followed your uncle to the road?'

'That the last we see of the Phelpses for about three days.'

'I found the ring down by the creek at Garden House.'

'I don't think that likely,' he said. 'My aunt give my uncle that ring, and there ain't nothing he love more except his children and her and maybe the house where they grow up.'

The ring felt warm and heavy on my finger, clean of the sand and dirt that I'd dug it out of. 'Did you ever dump trash by the creek?'

'Why would we do that? We drink that water. Man don't defecate in his own kitchen sink.'

'The Phelpses have been back on the land in the last couple of days. They burned Garden House and the carport. They dug a big hole by the creek. We found old garbage in it, and I found the ring.'

'How big a hole?'

'Big. You could put this house in it, or almost.'

'Deep?'

'Not so deep. Three feet. In some places, four.'

He thought about that and his forehead moistened with sweat. He asked quietly, 'What else you find?'

'Bottle glass. A can lid. A beef bone.'

He thought. 'Horse.'

'Huh?'

'Horse bone, not cow.'

'How do you know?'

'Metal, glass, bone. Horse bone – bone that carry a man's weight. Heavy things. Hard things. You bury them with your dead. Things that don't disappear back into the earth over-quick.'

'I don't get it.'

'Mary and her boy must've buried those things in their last days.' His voice was quiet and sad. 'The rest of us already run off – to Fernandina or Savannah or Jacksonville.'

'Did the Phelps security men catch up with your uncle and the others on the road?'

'Must've done.'

'Mary didn't report it when the Phelpses brought them back?'

'Maybe she did. Maybe no one believe her. Maybe she and her boy sick and dying, and she think it all the same anyway. They soon be where the others go.' He began sweeping the porch, though it was already clean. Sometimes if you don't put your hands to work, they'll start shaking. He asked, his eyes elsewhere, 'They burn Garden House now, do they?'

336

'It's just ash.'

He stopped sweeping and looked hard at me.

I stepped off the porch.

He dropped the broom on to the planking and came after me. 'Give the ring to me.'

I balled my fist.

'It don't belong to you,' he said.

I stared at him.

'Goddamn it, give it to me.' Then his voice softened. 'It all I have.'

I twisted the ring from my finger as if I was uncoiling the golden rope, and I laid it in his hand.

At noon, Lillian and I pulled up to the security booth at the Phelps Paper Company headquarters. The white factory buildings and silos stood bright and still in the sun. The single smoke stack pumped sweet white chemical smoke into the sky. I wondered how many decades the factory would need to be gone before the stink washed into the soil and streams.

The Hispanic woman in the security booth wore a white open-collared blouse under her blue blazer, and I wondered too how long she stood in the shower at night to get rid of the smell, and whether, when she climbed into bed with a lover after she cleaned herself, she brought the poisonous odor with her.

I had last seen the security guard months earlier, but she seemed to recognize me. I told her that Lillian and I were there to see Edward and Stephen Phelps. In case the Phelpses wanted to turn us away, as they almost certainly would, I added, 'Tell them we've come about the hole at the Garden House.'

'The what?'

'They'll know what it is.'

Ten minutes later, Bob Peterson, head of security, met us outside the main building. He had rolled up the sleeves on his shirt so his muscles showed. I'd tucked Papa Crowe's revolver under the front seat of the car so I looked like no threat at all. He led us through the maze of hallways, past Stephen Phelps's office, to a suite where a blond ponytailed secretary sat across a large room from a long light-stained pinewood conference table that must have been meant to remind everyone of the origins of the paper and pulp processing business. The secretary smiled blandly as Peterson led us through to Edward Phelps's office and left us there. Inside, Edward Phelps sat at a pinewood desk. Stephen Phelps, looking pale and nervous, sat across the room on a brown leather couch. If Lillian and I faced either father or son, the other would have our backs. That was week-one Navy armed-strategy training. I crossed the room to a floor-to-ceiling window, which neatly framed the end of a factory building and the smokestack behind it, and made the Phelpses turn to look at me. Lillian repositioned one of the chairs at Edward Phelps's desk so that she faced me. The Phelpses couldn't look at both of us either.

Edward Phelps smiled at that.

I said, 'If I had a really dirty secret, the kind that could bring me down and make my sons and daughters and grandkids want to change their names, I would bury it deep in the Georgia woods.'

Edward Phelps dropped the smile.

Lillian said, 'It would seem safe there. For a while. You could even draw a toxic metal circle around it. Who would dare to go near it? But you would worry. If the secret was so bad that it could make your kids and grandkids want to change their names, you might think it would take on a life of its own, no matter how deep you buried it.'

'It could tear a man's family apart,' I said. 'It might lead his wife to try to kill herself. Being around a lot of death, if that's what the secret involved, can make a person want to die – even if the person isn't responsible.'

Edward Phelps said, 'You don't know what you're talking about.'

'I think we do,' I said.

Stephen said, 'Dad—'

Edward spun on him. 'Shut up.'

I said, 'This morning, we drove up to the land where Papa Crowe and his family used to live. Looks like you wanted to do some clean-up before the court-ordered work. Your people did a pretty good job, but they missed a few things. Thirty-one years is a long time, but not in good dry, sandy soil. Glass or metal or bone could probably last hundreds of years before crumbling.'

Stephen Phelps said to his father, 'If you won't, I will.'

Edward Phelps looked at Lillian. 'Your husband came home from his last tour in bad shape. Broken. What wouldn't you do to help him? And what wouldn't he do for you? You know what happened on his ship. You know what his job was. But, still, here you are with him, and I'll bet you still kiss those hands that crammed the dead soldiers into bags. And your husband knows about your friend Tom Corfield – I made sure he found out – but, still, here he is with you.'

'Stop it,' she said.

He said, 'Some of us are less perfect than others. But I'll tell you something that's true. What happened to those people in Georgia happened because of fear and love, not meanness.'

'What happened?' Lillian asked.

Stephen Phelps stood up and said, 'Enough.' He held a black pistol in his hand.

Edward Phelps put his fingers on his lips and looked resigned.

'Enough and enough,' Stephen said.

Lillian said, 'Too much.'

He glared at her. 'We gave you every chance. All you had to do was walk away.'

'And what will you do now?' I said. 'Shoot us in your dad's office?'

He glared at me too, then fished in his pocket for a cell phone, dialed, and said, 'We're ready.'

Lillian and I exchanged a look. If we rushed Stephen Phelps, we might surprise him into shooting wildly or doing nothing at all. But we stayed where we were, and, seconds later, Bob Peterson entered the office with a pistol that matched Stephen Phelps's.

340

Peterson looked at Edward Phelps for a cue, but the old man gazed down at his desk. Peterson turned to Stephen Phelps, who simply nodded.

Peterson pointed his gun at me and then at Lillian. 'Let's go.'

We went back through the maze of hallways, and when we stepped outside of the building, he told us to get in our car, me in the driver's seat, Lillian behind me. He climbed in beside me, his gun pointing at my head. 'Go,' he said.

'Where?'

He said nothing, so I started the engine.

We drove out the company road. The sun glinted on the hood of the car, and I felt light-headed.

As we approached the security booth, Peterson set his pistol on his lap and waved at the Hispanic guard. She smiled big and waved back. I glanced at Lillian in the rearview mirror. Her eyes met mine, and she ducked below the seat. Her hand rummaged in the space under me, and, as I accelerated hard, she came up with Papa Crowe's revolver. Peterson, realizing in a moment that he'd lost control, jerked his pistol up and pressed the barrel against my ribs. Lillian brought the revolver to an inch from his ear.

He remained steady. 'Put it down or I shoot him,' he said.

I looked over my shoulder, and Lillian and I locked eyes again.

She said to Peterson, 'He's been trying to kill himself for months. You'll be doing him a favor.'

Peterson almost laughed. 'And *you*? You want me to kill him?'

'You know about me and Tom. If you pull the trigger and then I kill you, I'm free.'

'Yeah, right.' But he was losing his nerve.

'Go ahead and do it,' Lillian said.

Peterson's eyes wavered between us.

Lillian shouted, 'Shoot him!'

Peterson lowered the pistol to the center console.

I grabbed it and pointed it at him. Sweat broke on my back. I said to Lillian, 'You overplayed that last bit.' But she was breathing hard.

I drove another mile before finding a private road that crossed a long embankment with wetland marsh on either side. No one had driven this way for a long time, and gravel and sand crunched under the tires. When we were far from the cars and logging trucks on the main road, I pulled to the side and turned off the engine. 'Get out,' I said to Peterson.

He sat, defiant.

I held the pistol close to his head. 'I have nothing to lose.'

He opened the door and got out. The hot midday air washed into the car.

'What now?' Lillian said.

I got out too, and she followed me.

Peterson stood at the edge of the marsh, the sun reflecting off the car and the brackish water. Dragonflies hovered and darted above the sawgrass and cattails. A blue heron stood in a shallow pool. A hawk circled off toward a stand of live oak trees. You could buy this kind of picture at weekend art markets around the Southeast, except that Peterson looked as if he

342

was having a heart attack as Lillian and I held guns to his head.

'How long have you worked for the Phelpses?' I asked.

Peterson's eyes looked down a tunnel of fear. 'A long time.'

'How long? Five years? Ten? Twenty? More?'

'More than thirty.'

Lillian said, 'Were you in Georgia with the Phelpses on the night those people got killed?'

He said nothing.

I pressed the pistol barrel against his soft skin. 'Were you?'

'Yes.'

'You must have been young,' Lillian said.

'Twenty-three.'

'Just a child,' she said.

He said nothing.

She said, 'You weren't responsible.'

'Go to hell,' he said.

I asked, 'Who told you to kill them?'

He said nothing.

'Edward Phelps?'

'No.'

'Who?'

'It wasn't like that.'

'What was it like?'

'I told you to go to hell.'

'What was it like?' I asked again.

'An accident. A goddamned accident.'

'An accident? And all those people got killed? I don't think so.'

'You asked. I told you.'

'You told me a lie.'

343

'Go to hell.'

I looked at Lillian. She seemed to shrug with her eyes.

I said to Peterson, 'Give me your cell phone.'

'Are you going to kill me?'

'Give me the phone.'

'No.'

I held the gun to his head. 'Don't be an idiot.'

He reached into his pocket and gave it to me. I threw it far into the marsh. It disappeared without a splash or a sound.

I pointed down the private road, away from the direction we'd come. 'Walk.'

He glanced nervously at me and then at Lillian, seemingly unsure whether we would shoot him in his back.

'Go on,' I said.

He did.

Lillian climbed into the car. I looked at Peterson's pistol. It might be useful later. But I threw it into the marsh after the phone.

We drove back to the main road, kicking dust with our tires, the windows open to air out the smell of sweat and fear.

Thirty-Eight

Lillian

None stir the second time – On whom I lay a Yellow Eye – Or an emphatic Thumb.

As night fell and the first stars shined in the sky over the highway, we drove back to the Phelps construction site. We had finished talking. More words might have broken our resolve.

The Interstate north of Jacksonville reached up through the Mid-Atlantic to the cold granite of Maine, but, on our stretch, sabal palms lined the embankments, truck drivers drove in T-shirts, and, now and then at night, headlights exposed the carcass of an armadillo or a possum on the road shoulder.

When we left the highway, and the lights of the interchange service stations dimmed behind us, we entered a quiet space. Palmettos and coontie flashed in the headlights and disappeared. Two enormous cylindrical power-plant cooling towers stood against the dark – dull red beacons flashing from their tops to warn away airplane pilots.

We passed the line of fuel storage tanks at a BP depot. We drove into the marshland. We crossed narrow bridges where, during the day, fishermen pressed against the steel railings to stay clear of cars and pickup trucks, and now we bumped on to the inclines, and the pavement slid under us before we returned to the solider road.

When we reached Little Marsh Island, the road into the construction site was chained, and we drove past to the spot where we'd left the car when we hiked to the clearing where Laura Greene set up her camp and where Peter Lisman found Sheneel's body. We assembled our supplies in the dark – a flashlight for each of us, bottles

345

of water in case we needed to wait, and Papa Crowe's revolver.

'You OK?' Johnny asked.

'I'm good.'

We got out of the car, and Johnny turned the revolver in his hands, sprang the cylinder, snapped it shut, and weighed the heft of the gun in his palm before sticking it into his waistband.

We walked in, our flashlights shining on the green and black plants. Frogs, insects, and night birds dropped into silence as we stepped near.

In the clearing, Laura Greene's campsite was gone, all but the gray tent tarp, which had been ripped and thrown into the tree branches, and a bra that lay by the fire pit. Johnny kicked the charred wood. He stooped and felt the ashes for heat. 'Nothing,' he said.

We pushed through the branches, found the chain-link fence, and turned off our flashlights. Beyond the fence, a bright light showed in the trailer where the prostitute would sleep when she wasn't watching the construction site for trespassers. A pickup truck and two cars stood in the shadows near the trailer. Farther along the fence, near the spot where Laura Greene had showed us the large hole, floodlights glowed in the brush and trees. An engine – from a truck or a big machine – purred, shifted gears to a low roar, and shifted back to a purr.

As we moved along the fence, the headlights on the pickup by the trailer flashed on, the engine raced, and the truck shot across the dirt and sand toward us. We froze. The truck bounced over the uneven ground, its lights flicking against insects in the night air. I sank toward the vegetation by the fence, but Johnny put a hand on my shoulder and held me still. For a moment, as the truck neared, the headlights shined in our eyes, but it veered and charged toward the gate to the service road. Seconds later, it went through the gate and disappeared.

A little laugh came from Johnny's mouth.

'Breathe,' I said to myself.

Johnny said, 'OK.'

A hundred feet farther along the fence, the floodlights grew bright and the machine engine loud. We slowed, lowering each footstep without making a sound. The floodlights, strung above the hole on wooden posts and running on the power of a generator that sat in the bed of a pickup, glared against the foliage and humid air. A white backhoe tilted to the side on tractor treads. In the open-sided cab, Peter Lisman held two of the four joysticks in his hands. Edward Phelps stood on one side of the hole next to Bob Peterson. On the other side, Daniel, holding a rifle, stood next to Stephen Phelps. The men watched Peter Lisman as he maneuvered the arm of the backhoe to a dump truck, lowered it, dropped its bucket into the dumping-bed, and raised it again. When the backhoe arm swung over the hole and the bucket tilted, a mix of sandy soil and broken pieces of yellowed and blackened bone fell out.

'Christ,' I said, too loud, but the engine on the backhoe keened as Peter Lisman raised the arm and swung it toward the dump truck.

As the bucket dipped low and scooped another

load of dirt and bone, Edward Phelps reached into a shirt pocket, removed a pack of Newports, and shook out a cigarette. Stephen Phelps stood with his hands deep in his pants pockets. Daniel held his gun across his chest. Then the backhoe arm swung, the bucket tipped, and more bones tumbled into the hole.

The backhoe arm returned to the dump truck and scooped again. As it swung away, a skull fell from the bucket and bounced over the dirt. Bob Peterson picked it up, regarded it, and threw it into the hole. He turned, laughing, and said something to Edward Phelps. Phelps didn't find the joke funny. He raised his cigarette to his lips and inhaled hard.

Johnny stepped out from our cover into the floodlight. He held the revolver in his hand. Peter Lisman was too busy swinging the backhoe toward the dump truck to notice him, but Daniel pivoted and aimed his rifle at him, and Bob Peterson stepped toward him but stopped when he saw the revolver. Stephen Phelps froze and stared. Edward Phelps let his cigarette hang in his hand a few inches from his mouth. Then Peterson yelled at Lisman to cut the engine, and, when Lisman saw Johnny, he did, and the night was silent except for the hum of the generator that powered the floodlights.

I stepped out from the cover and stood next to Johnny.

'Oh, shit,' Daniel said.

'Shoot them,' Stephen Phelps said.

Daniel pointed the rifle at Johnny. But he looked at me.

348

I felt nothing – no anger, no sadness, no fear, no regret.

Daniel turned his eyes to Johnny. Johnny pointed the revolver at him.

'Shoot them!' Stephen Phelps shouted at Daniel.

Daniel eyed me again.

Edward Phelps asked in a soft voice, 'What now?'

Johnny said, 'Now we're done.'

'What does that mean?' Bob Peterson said angrily.

Johnny pointed the revolver at him. 'This is over. It's done. No more killing. No more burying.'

'Shoot them!' Stephen Phelps yelled.

Daniel stared at me, and in his eyes I saw none of the secrets we'd shared as children, none of the love and anger we shared as adults. But he lowered the rifle.

Stephen Phelps yelled, 'Goddamn it!' and tried to take the gun from him. Daniel threw a punch at his face and missed, and Stephen Phelps kneed Daniel in the ribs. The rifle fell to the ground. Daniel was bent – hurt – and Stephen Phelps leaned for the gun, but then Daniel straightened and kicked him in the face. There was a crack – maybe the jawbone, maybe the neck – and Stephen Phelps landed in the dirt and didn't move. Daniel stared at the rifle on the ground. The other men stared at it.

Then a gunshot blasted from outside the circle.

Johnny fell backward and dropped the revolver – a patch of blood sheening on his shoulder. Cecilia Phelps stood by the open door of the

349

pickup truck with the generator. She wore a white cotton dress. A white headscarf covered the burns on her forehead. She held a black pistol.

She shuffled toward us as if uncertain that the ground would hold her, aiming the pistol at me. She glanced around the circle of men, but she went to her son where he lay face down in the dirt. She prodded him with her toes. He made a sound, tried to push himself on to his hands and knees, thought better of it, and lay down. When she saw that her son was alive, she said to Daniel, 'You're very fortunate.' She turned to me with a gentle smile. 'I'll protect myself and my family.'

She went to Johnny and stared down at him. Blood leaked from his shoulder and stained his arm. She said, 'I did my best for you. But you kept coming.' She gazed at his bloody shoulder. 'You insisted on this.'

Papa Crowe's revolver lay on the ground between Johnny's feet and me.

Cecilia Phelps spun toward me. 'And *you*. What in God's name do you think *you're* doing?'

I gestured at the bones in the pit. 'What happened to these people? Did your husband kill them?'

She smiled gently.

Johnny pushed himself backward along the ground, inching away. Cecilia Phelps turned and watched him, fascinated, stepped toward him, and, as he slid backward, stepped forward in a touchless dance. The revolver lay on the ground behind her.

She said to Johnny, 'Edward made me go with him. He said it would be fun. The boys were little – Darren was only a baby – and we seldom got out. Fun. I could use a little fun. I was so young myself. We drove into the woods, following the other cars. The roads were dirt back then.' She glanced at me over her shoulder. 'So much has changed in thirty years.' Then, to Johnny, 'And so much has stayed the same. When we got to the place where those people were living, Edward told me to stay in the car. He would go in with his men and put some scare into the trespassers – those were his words. He promised, no one would get hurt. He said he only wanted them off the land. But it wasn't *really* about the land. It was jealousy and fear. They had something, and he wanted it. He needed it. You understand that kind of desire, don't you?'

Edward Phelps dropped his cigarette and moved toward her. 'Cecilia—'

She turned the gun on him. 'Be quiet, Edward.' She turned again to Johnny and said, 'I begged him to stay with me or let me go with him, but he took a gun from the glove compartment and set it on my lap. He said, "You'll be fine." His words. He kissed me and got out of the car.'

Johnny had reached the edge of the circle of light. If he slid further, he would disappear into the brush.

'I heard the shouts,' Cecilia Phelps said. 'I heard the dogs barking. The skies were blacker in those days. A man came from the woods about fifty feet from the car. Others followed. Dark shapes. Women. Children. More men. They moved on to the road and walked toward me.'

351

'Cecilia!' Edward Phelps's voice was pained and gruff.

She seemed not to hear him. 'What could I do? I told them to stop. But they kept coming and coming. The children and the man who led them – they scared me most. If they had all been women, I might have let them pass. But I felt they had come to do me harm. I felt they wanted me.'

Johnny stopped sliding backward, and Cecilia Phelps stood in front of him.

'I had Edward's gun,' she said. 'It didn't seem like an extraordinary thing. I knew how to shoot it. Edward had taught me. More of his fun. I got out of the car and pointed the gun at the dark shapes of those people. I only wanted them to stop – only wanted them to go back into the woods. They must have seen me – the man who was leading them did. I saw his eyes. I swear they were the eyes of a man who already was dead. He could have turned around, but he kept coming for me.'

Johnny said, 'You shot him.'

She said, 'I shot him and I shot the girl by his side. I didn't want to, but they were coming.'

Johnny said, 'They only wanted to pass. They wanted to get to the main road.'

But she was lost in her own mind. 'Edward's men came from the woods. They rounded up the others. We couldn't let them go. They'd seen what had happened. You can't blame us.'

'We don't need to,' Johnny said. 'Edward probably said it wasn't your fault. The other men who were there that night probably agreed. But you knew better.'

She shook her head. 'I don't blame myself. The blame is gone. It's about who survives.' She stepped closer to Johnny and pointed the pistol at his head. 'If Sheneel had survived, *we* wouldn't have. If Alex had survived, *we* wouldn't have. If you survive, *we* don't. If you don't, *we* do.'

'You killed Sheneel and Alex?' he asked.

She looked calm. 'Did I have a choice? She would have told.'

'And Peter cleaned up for you afterward?'

'No choice.'

I went for the revolver.

Edward Phelps could have alerted his wife to the danger.

Daniel could have.

Peter Lisman or Bob Peterson – one of them – yelled, but too late.

As Cecilia Phelps spun and aimed the pistol at me, I lifted the revolver from the dirt and pulled the trigger.

Blood appeared on her chest like a magic corsage. She stepped back, off balance. She seemed to lose interest in the gun in her hand. Her eyes fixed on no one – not her husband, not her son Stephen, not Peter Lisman. She seemed to look inward. Then, as if, in her inward gaze, she saw no bone, no spine, nothing that would hold her vertical in the world, her legs melted and she collapsed.

Everyone started to move. Daniel went for the dropped rifle, swung it to his shoulder, and aimed at me. Stephen Phelps pushed himself to his hands and knees, his chin hanging crooked where Daniel had broken bone. Bob Peterson ripped the revolver from my hands, raised it as if to crush me with the butt – then, seeing Daniel with the rifle, lowered it. Peter Lisman scrambled from the backhoe and ran to Cecilia. He lifted her in his arms – the mother he had lost when he was an infant and she was only a teenaged child – and he looked frantically around the pit, but she was dead and there was no place to take her. Only Edward Phelps stood still and he made a sound that was more animal than human.

Daniel stared at me, a pleading in his eyes, as if I could answer a life-or-death question. I stared back. I had no answers for him. Bob Peterson spoke to me – words that I couldn't understand, couldn't hear – and Daniel and I held each other with our eyes. Then Daniel seemed to find his own answer. He turned the rifle away from me and aimed at Edward Phelps.

Bob Peterson spoke again, and I heard him over Edward Phelps's keening. He said, 'No.'

Daniel shot Edward Phelps in the belly. He watched the old man as if he wondered whether a single bullet would be enough. Then he shot him in the head.

No one moved. Even Phelps seemed to hang in the air as his cry carried through the woods and over the marsh. When he fell to the ground, Stephen Phelps tried to speak, but his broken jaw mangled his voice.

Daniel swung the rifle so he aimed it at Bob Peterson, paused, then turned again until he found Stephen Phelps. As Peterson watched, Daniel shot Stephen Phelps too.

Thirty-Nine

Johnny

When Edward Phelps finally went silent and the trees and the marsh absorbed the sound of the gunshot that killed his son, when Peter Lisman carried his dead mother in his arms, like a groom at a threshold with his bride, away from the hole, through the gap in the fence, and across the construction site, Bob Peterson lifted the revolver from his side, pointed it at Lillian, and pulled the trigger.

The hammer slammed into the empty cylinder.

As if he couldn't understand the sound, he turned the gun on me, drew the hammer, and pulled the trigger.

Daniel said, 'It's over, Bob. It's done.' Daniel pointed the rifle at him.

Peterson turned, aimed at him, and pulled the trigger.

Nothing.

He stepped toward him, stepped again, pulled the trigger.

Nothing.

He seemed in no hurry as he moved toward Daniel and pulled the trigger once more.

When Peterson was close enough, Daniel threw the butt of the rifle into his forehead. A bright line of blood creased Peterson's brow and he fell.

Daniel went to him and held the rifle barrel against Peterson's head. Peterson stared at him, and Daniel looked into his eyes as if he was looking for a reason to let him live. Then he shot him dead.

Daniel set the rifle on the ground, which seemed as much as stripping himself naked. Then his body started shaking.

Lillian came to me and touched me. My shoulder burned where Cecilia Phelps had shot me, and the arm below it was numb and weak, but I knew that the bullet had only skipped through skin and muscle. I looked up. The night above looked black and thick. The generator on the pickup stuttered, then hummed. Lillian asked, 'Can you walk?'

'I don't know.' I pushed to my feet. My shoulder burned.

'Lillian?' Daniel said. He wanted reassurance.

'Get Papa Crowe's gun,' I said to her.

She found the revolver at Peterson's feet.

'Lillian!' Daniel said. He needed her, but she came to me.

'Can you do it?' she asked.

'I don't know.' I stepped and stepped again until we reached the fence. We skirted the construction site, stumbled through the grass and brush. Orange light glowed on the dirt and sand lot on the other side of the fence. When we found the rough trail back to the clearing, we shoved through the branches like animals breaking from a predator. We crossed the clearing and then we were running, our flashlights strobing against the leaves, long grasses, and tree trunks. The burn in my shoulder died away as I found my muscles and I breathed the warm night deep into my lungs.

Lillian drove us home and bathed my shoulder in the kitchen sink. The towel came away soaked in blood, then pink, and soon almost clear, though the wound bled until she wrapped it. 'You need a doctor,' she said.

'No.'

'What do you need?'

I pulled her to me.

That night I knew that the disintegration of bodies is nothing to fear, that stars shine brightest as they collapse, the gas and flame changing into pure energy. This knowledge wouldn't lessen the pain of disintegration – my own, that of the soldiers whose bodies the distant minefields obliterated, that of a Gullah family whose bones the salt and sand would chew away on Little Marsh Island – but it made me believe that I could live on the crumbling earth while my life lasted. Morning might shake that belief, but first I would hold Lillian close to me, not with fear but with love. That was all we had left, and it might be enough.